# mums

## the

# word

## STACI HART

Cover by Quirky Bird
Editor: Jovana Shirley, Unforeseen Editing

# mum's

## the

# word

To those of you
Who've never followed your heart:

There is magic in that place
And it's waiting for you.

## AUTHOR'S NOTE

Many of us can claim our love for Jane Austen, but only a few of us are foolish enough to retell her stories.

I have taken some liberties with *Pride and Prejudice*, and I hope you'll allow me to imagine the Bennet sisters as unruly men (less our Lizzie) and Longbourne as a flower shop in Manhattan. And I hope beyond hope that you enjoy my nod to the Bennets, who we love so well.

# Thunder and Lightning

## MARCUS

**A** peal of thunder split the sky open.

Rain fell in a sheet of fat drops, the deluge too sudden for a single person on Fifth Avenue to even reach for their umbrella, never mind open one. With a swear, I held my briefcase over my head in a useless attempt to protect my suit from the torrent.

The foot traffic scattered like ants in a scrambling, tumbling blitzkrieg for cover after the mound had been kicked. But I trucked on, winding my way through the erratic crowd, which required all of my attention to navigate. Scanning the sidewalk ahead of me, I calculated the fastest path to the subway station, the trajectory of the flow of people laid out before me like a map. The lady with the stroller running obliquely for a coffee shop up ahead. A businessman still on his phone, squinting through the rain as he beelined for a newspaper stand. A pack of kids playing hooky, trotting and laughing and horsing around, the rain just another thing to note on a day of freedom.

I was so busy looking in front of me, I didn't have a chance to dodge the small body before we collided.

We spun from the impact, a whirl of arms and hands. My briefcase hit the ground, abandoned so I could grab her. At the same moment, her newspaper, which she'd been using for an umbrella, flew into the air and opened like a soggy bird with a broken wing before spiraling to the sidewalk.

They said it was adrenaline that sped up your brain in moments like these, a rapid firing of neurons to catalog every detail. And as the moment stretched on in slow motion, I noted each one.

She was soft and small, the sound of her surprise striking a chord of recognition in me. I felt every flex and release of her arms beneath my palms, felt the curves of her body locked against me, felt the shift of her legs in perfect time with mine, like we were caught in the tango and not in a matter of physics. But it was the scent of her that slipped over me like that incessant rain— delicate, velvety gardenia so perfectly feminine, I found myself momentarily lost in the luxury of it.

I stopped us with a well-placed bracing of my foot that once again mimicked the tango, her body flush with mine and my hands—now somehow around her waist—holding her to me, holding her still.

But when she looked up, a thunderbolt split my ribs open.

It wasn't just the bottomless brown of her eyes or the button of her nose, dashed with almost imperceptible freckles. It wasn't the gentle bow of her lips, full and pink and parted in wonder. It wasn't the shape of her small face or the curve of her cheek that I somehow knew would fit exactly in my palm. It wasn't her fair hair, made darker by the rain, curling and clinging to the gentle line of her jaw.

It was all of her.

Every cell, every molecule, the whole of her was so utterly right. Had we been in a room full of people or packed in a subway car, I had no doubt I would have seen her just as I did now.

With all of me.

I didn't know how many breaths had passed that we stood motionless in the rain before she smiled, and lightning struck again.

Figuratively and literally.

She jolted in my arms, face turning up to the sky in shock. Instinctively, I held her closer.

"Are you all right?" I asked over the rumbling rain, leaning back to inspect her for injury.

"Yes, I-I think so. Just wet and embarrassed. Did I hurt you? Oh! Your briefcase!"

I glanced in the direction of her eyeline to see said briefcase—which was Italian and leather and more expensive than I'd ever admit aloud—as someone tripped over it, leaving a filthy boot print on its previously pristine surface.

With an infinite sense of loss as we separated, I righted us and let her go. "It's not important. Come on. Let me get you out of the rain."

She stood there uncertainly as I swept up my briefcase and swiped the side with my palm. I didn't wait for her answer. Instead, I snagged her hand and towed her toward a coffee shop a few doors down.

As we trotted our way there, I arched over her with my briefcase to shelter her from the rain. The Bennets were a large breed where its men were concerned, and I towered over her by nearly a foot. A useful trait in many instances and, in this one, convenient.

I wanted to be as close to her as I could, for as long as I could.

It was strange and foreign, this feeling, an unlikely meeting with an improbable outcome. The rarity of such things happening to me was undefinable. My brothers would be the ones to stumble into a girl they immediately wanted to know. But I found most people tedious, and with my mother parading me around her garden club, its members salivating at the thought of yoking their single daughters to me, I generally questioned every woman in my acquaintance.

Some called it cynicism. I called it self-preservation. I knew no other way, having never been given a reason to consider an alternative. No woman had ever affected me. No one had ever stood out.

Not until a moment ago when I'd collided with the girl tucked into my side.

And I aimed to find out the why and the how of it. I wanted answers. I wanted logic and reason, an explanation as to why I felt like I'd woken from a long and deep sleep the moment I looked into her eyes.

I wondered if kissing her would give me the answer I was looking for.

My shock at the thought left me too curious to even consider caution.

We ducked into the crowded coffee shop, panting and shaking off the rain.

She laughed, self-consciously running a hand over her hair. "I must look like a cat that crawled out of the East River."

"Not at all," I answered a little too quietly, covering it with a smile. "I've never met a human cannon before. I think you might have dislocated one of my ribs." I patted said ribs, which felt nothing more than the ghost of her body against me.

Her face softened. "Oh, I'm so sorry. Are you sure you're all right?"

"I'm fine, just wet."

A shiver racked her, and my smile slid into a frown.

"Let's get coffee. Warm you up."

Her brow furrowed, and she checked her watch. "I'm going to be late for a meeting."

"You and me both. But running in, soaked and freezing, won't help anyone. What do you say? Let me get you a cup of coffee as an apology."

"For what?"

"For not seeing you coming."

Again, she laughed, and again, I felt that fundamental familiarity. "No one ever does."

"No, I don't suspect they do."

Her cheeks flushed, lips still smiling as we stepped into line. "It's just that I'm so short," she clarified without changing my mind. "I really am so sorry. Your poor briefcase."

"This old thing?" I held it out to inspect it. "I was due for a new one anyway."

"The newspaper might have done more harm than good—all I could see was my feet. I'm afraid the years I've been gone erased what I thought was concrete knowledge of Manhattan and how to navigate it, especially in the rain during rush hour."

"Where were you?" I asked as we shuffled forward a step.

"England. Yorkshire, with my aunt. My mother sent me with the intent to teach me some sort of lesson, but luckily for me, my aunt doesn't like to listen to her any more than I do. Mostly, I spent a couple years in the countryside, picking flowers," she said on a laugh that died too quickly. "But I knew I'd have to come back."

"I, for one, am glad. Otherwise, who would I play human pinball with in the rain?"

"I'm sure you have no trouble finding girls to bang balls with."

A laugh shot out of me, and her cheeks flushed.

"I didn't mean …" She sighed. "Actually, I did, but I don't know why I said it out loud. God, why am I so nervous? I think I've talked to more sheep than people in the last couple of years."

"I've heard terrible things about sheep. Deplorable table manners."

"And filthy minds." She watched me for a breath. "I feel as if I know you. Is that strange?"

My heart lurched. "Not at all."

An impatient voice from in front of us snapped, "Next, please."

We stepped up to the counter and ordered our coffees, receiving them too quickly to speak again. But when we were out of the way and face to face once more, the exit looming, we watched each other, searching for some reason, some logic to whatever lightning had struck us out there in the rain.

"What's your name?" I asked.

"Maisie," she answered. "Are you sure we've never met before?"

"There's no way I'd forget meeting you." I paused, overcome with sudden boldness. "When can I plan on catching you in the rain again?"

She drew a shallow breath, and a blush smudged her cheeks. "Oh, I ..."

My hope sank, the answer obvious. "You have a boyfriend. Of course you do."

"No. No, it's not that. I want to say yes, but—"

"Then say yes."

I waited, watched her, holding my breath through a handful of heartbeats as indecision flickered across her face. But like dawn on the horizon, she smiled.

"All right. Do you have a pen in that soggy briefcase?"

"Better yet, I have one right here." I slipped a hand into my suit coat to retrieve the pen and slips of paper I always kept there. The one that had been closest to my heart was still dry.

Our fingers brushed when she took it and jotted down her name and phone number, the letters and numbers half connected, soft and slanting.

I took the paper, sliding it into my pocket with the reverence I'd give a treasure map. "Can I call you a cab?"

She glanced outside to the drizzling rain. "I think you've done enough. You stopped me from skinning my knee or spraining my ankle, *and* you bought me a coffee. Maybe I should call you one instead."

"I'll take the subway, thanks. Next time you need a coffee, let me know."

"I think I just might," she said over her shoulder as she walked to the door. But before we reached it, she stopped so suddenly, I almost tripped over her again. "Wait, you haven't told me your name."

My smile tilted as I reached around her to open the door. "Marcus."

Her brows quirked, face cocked like a bird for a beat before she seemed to shake whatever thought she'd had away. "Well, I hope you don't wait too long to call, considering I get hungry every night around seven."

"Are you asking me out, Maisie?" I said with an arch smile, one she answered with the prettiest flush of her cheeks.

"Maybe I am, Marcus."

We stepped out, facing each other under the awning. I didn't want to go. I didn't want her to go. Because I had the feeling that the second we parted ways, whatever this was would disappear with nothing left to show for but fairy dust.

"Tell me when, and I'm there," I said, eager to dispel the thought, to prove the notion was crazy and as quickly as possible.

"Is tonight too soon?"

"Absolutely not." My heart chugged in my rib cage. "I'll text you when I'm free, and we can firm it up."

I stepped to the curb to hail a cab, filled with hope and promise. When I opened the door and she slid inside, I held her there for a brief moment with my gaze, trying to shake the feeling that I shouldn't let her go.

"It was nice running into you, Marcus."

"Let's do it again."

"Tonight."

"Tonight," I said, that immovable smile on my lips. I didn't think I'd smiled so much in years.

And I shut the cab door and waited in the rain until she was gone.

I didn't feel the chilly drizzle, didn't notice my soggy jacket or my socks slipping in my oxfords. I didn't feel the spring chill or mind my pruny hand in my pocket. Didn't think twice about my scuffed-up briefcase or the meeting I was about to walk into, which would be brutal and pivotal and something I should have been preparing for.

The only thing on my mind was Maisie.

Twenty minutes later, I was mostly dry and trotting out of the station. Every train stop had brought me closer to today's problems by increment, leaving Maisie and our encounter sadly behind me.

*Tonight. You'll see her tonight.*

I'd have already texted her if I'd had service, and now that I was off the train, I had to get to the meeting as quickly as possible. There was only time to answer one text, and that was to let our attorney know I was close.

Ben was an old friend from college and the first person I'd called when our family business was sued by our rivals. And as grateful as I was for his help, I wished I hadn't had to call on it.

I pushed into the building, the sweeping foyer bustling and echoing with noise and movement as people came in and out. Ben shot off the bench by the door like it'd caught fire when he saw me.

"I'm sorry," I said as our paths merged on our track to the elevators. "I was held up by the rain." *And my dream girl*, I thought with a flurry in my chest.

His brows furrowed with worry. "Well, Bower Bouquets is already upstairs, and they're not happy to have been kept waiting."

"I couldn't give a goddamn about what Evelyn Bower wants," I snarled as we stepped into the elevator with a stream of people.

The story was long and winding and began and ended with

my mother. Mrs. Bennet was known for many things, but being a savvy businesswoman wasn't one of them. When our family's flower shop, Longbourne, had fallen into decline, she'd taken on a contract with Bower Bouquets, selling wholesale flowers from our greenhouse to make ends meet.

The second I realized the shop was in trouble, I bought the flower shop and called my siblings home to help me turn things around. And I took on the financial burden, including contracts she'd signed.

All except one.

My mother kept the contract with Bower from us. Until we breached it, I'd had no idea. And when we had been served with a lawsuit, we'd all been unprepared.

Longbourne had been engaged in silent warfare with Bower for generations, but where our business had waned, Bower had flourished. Evelyn loved to make a fool of my mother—I had a feeling it was Evelyn's part-time job to embarrass her—and this contract was just a new, cruel way for her to do it.

That, and potentially put us out of business for good.

Ben and I didn't speak as we rode the packed elevator to the eighty-fourth floor, and by the time the doors opened, I was prepared for battle. Bower might have pulled one over on my mother with this ridiculous contract, but those days were done.

I'd be damned if she made a fool of me.

We marched past the lawyer's receptionist and into the boardroom where we'd been directed. Hellfire licked my heels and roared thunder at my back, though I knew I looked calm and unaffected. That impassive mask was always in place, the cool demeanor my armor. My family was reactionary, wearing every emotion not only on their sleeve, but on their faces and lips, and I was the steady one. The sensible one. The logic and reason to anchor their abundance of feeling. But that mask also kept everyone out, led them to assume I was dispassionate when I was just as excitable as the rest of them.

Let Evelyn Bower think I was unmoved. Let her think me passionless. Because my control and restraint would be her undoing.

The door handle was cool in my hand, the battle before me plain and clear, my focus singular, my resolve unwavering.

Until I opened that door.

Because sitting next to a snidely smiling Evelyn Bower was Maisie.

My thoughts slid and clicked like pins in a lock as Maisie and I stared, dumbfounded, across the room. I heard the words from Evelyn's mouth as if from some great distance, one sticking, then repeating on a loop as it dawned on me exactly who the girl at her elbow was.

Maisie, the human pinball. Maisie, the sheep whisperer. Maisie, the thunderbolt.

My Maisie was Margaret Bower.

The daughter of my enemy.

# Knock On Wood

## MAISIE

**E**verything went on around us, but Marcus and I were caught in a moment, just like we had been in each other's arms in the rain. Only this time, there was no magic. No shimmering possibility, no blossom of warmth. Just cold, hard realization.

The man I'd just stumbled into in the rain was Marcus *Bennet*. The son of my mother's sworn enemy.

The reason for the feud was a mystery to us all. Beyond some long-standing dispute between our grandmothers, there was no reason for my mother's dogged tenacity to ruin Longbourne and the Bennets. It wasn't as if they were competition—their shop had been in decline for a decade or more, run aground by a drought orchestrated by my mother. On her way to build an empire, she had set out to raze the Bennets to the roots.

And she'd succeeded. Stealing accounts. Tarnishing their name. She'd sink to any depths to make the Bennets feel small.

Of course, this lawsuit business was low, even for her. That she'd taken out a contract to buy flowers from Longbourne was its own curiosity. But recently, the Bennets' shop had started making money again, and Mother tugged on the chain she'd used to bind Longbourne, with the intent to heel them.

Heel and geld, if she could manage it.

My stomach turned over as Marcus and I stared at each other across the chasm that was the boardroom table between us. Of all the men in all the world, the sliver of hope I'd found in the drudgery of my life was a Bennet.

"Your hair is a mess," Mother said under her breath as everyone sat down. "You could have put in a little effort, Margaret."

"I can't control the weather, Mother," I answered, barely able to think with Marcus sitting across from me, his face cold and closed, flat but for the slightest crease between his brows.

It was then that I realized the door to him—the one I'd only just opened—was firmly shut. And locked. And that he'd thrown the key into the Hudson.

Our lawyer began to talk, but I didn't hear a word he said over the thundering of my heart. This room was hell on a good day, but today, it was so deeply unbearable, I fought the urge to get up and walk out just to put a block between my mother and me.

If Bower Bouquets was our religion, my mother sat on a throne in the clouds, frowning down at all of us, with her blonde hair coiffed into a flawless French twist and cool eyes unforgiving as she cast her judgments and delivered the consequences.

And I was her favorite subject to exact her power on.

I had been a disappointment to her for all of my living memory. As a child, I was too messy and loud. As an adult, I was naive and unambitious. My hair was too short, my appearance never to scratch. A little lipstick wouldn't hurt, I'd been told. Heels would make me taller, more elegant, I'd heard.

I was under no illusions—I would never please her, and I'd stopped trying. I would have wondered why I was here if I hadn't known it had nothing to do with support and everything to do with control. The thing my mother wanted most in the world was to fashion me after herself. Once upon a time, I'd done as I was told. But thanks to my father, I was nothing like her, which served only to intensify her determination to restrain me. To force me into the box she'd built for me before I was even born.

And she'd use every tool in her arsenal to make her dream a reality.

The failure of her life was that I'd rather work in the charity division of Bower than the executive suites, a point that had prompted her to send me to England and subsequently lure me back to New York, where all the things I didn't want awaited me.

Little had I known there would be someone else waiting too. One I wanted badly and without question couldn't have.

Marcus sat silently across the long table, his eyes locked on Mother's lawyer and mine locked on his.

I should have known who he was when I saw him. I'd thought the familiarity I felt was magic, a chance meeting, a fated beginning. It had been too perfect for words. After a solitary, lonely life, something had flipped on, illuminating me. It was a glimpse of another world, one brighter and happier than the one I inhabited.

And I'd floated away from him with the hope that maybe New York wouldn't kill me after all.

And then he'd walked into this room and shut off all the lights in my heart.

Fate had intervened all right. Just not in the way I'd hoped.

I tucked my hair behind my ear, the locks wavy from the rain. Mother wasn't wrong—I looked a mess. The second I'd walked in, her jaw had come unhinged, but there hadn't been enough time for a true dressing down. I'd get one—of that, I had no doubt—but I didn't care. I didn't care what she thought or about this stupid meeting. I didn't care about the frivolous lawsuit or her absurd vendetta with Longbourne. All I really cared about in that moment was what the man across the table thought of me.

Half an hour ago, he'd held me in his arms in the rain, the topography of his lean, rugged body leaving an impression against mine that I could still feel. I'd lost myself in the blue of his eyes, in the damp locks of his hair, black as a raven. He was majestic, his features touched with aristocratic grace. But those elegant lines were strong and square, proud and striking, the only incongruence his nose—the bridge flat near the top and shape that of a Spartan general, a Greek archer, a lean, battle-worn ancient. And he was just as mysterious, carrying a quiet air of command, of certainty and confidence that hadn't only struck me then, but clung to me like the ghost of a scent.

There in those arms, I'd felt inexplicably safe. Sheltered by his body as we ran for cover in the rain, I'd somehow known he wouldn't let anything hurt me. It was such a rare thing, to feel protected. Perhaps nothing more than a testament to the power he emitted even now as he sat both feet away and a world apart.

Even now, he drew the authority of the room without having to speak or even move. His eyes were stony, his jaw set in a determined line. Something in the way he sat in that chair, as if it were his throne and he were king of us all.

That he could even come close to dominating a room with my mother was a feat of its own. And the fact that he hadn't said a single word was a testament to that authority

My mother, however, had barely stopped talking. My guess was that she felt that shift toward him and was grappling to get it back on her.

"I think we can all agree that this lawsuit is frivolous and unconscionable, Mrs. Bower," the Bennet lawyer said. "You took advantage of Rosemary Bennet when Longbourne was in disrepair with a deal that you knew would sink them. In exchange for Bower's monthly wholesale flower purchase, you snuck in a clause that bound them to a noncompete no judge will back up. A noncompete, which is only binding on the loosest of terms. Are you saying you're going to put your money and weight behind something so trivial?"

"I'm saying that nothing has changed," she said before her lawyer could, her back straight and nose in the air. "*You* called this meeting, but if you really believed you could convince me to change my mind, you've wasted your time. Longbourne is under contract with me. You breached that contract and thus damaged my business."

"Longbourne is not a threat to you, and it hasn't been in a decade." Marcus's voice was calm, controlled, commanding. "This lawsuit will do nothing but cost you money."

Mother's eyes narrowed. "It will do a great deal more than that."

"Is that a threat?" Marcus asked, and his tone sent a chill down my spine.

But she smiled that smile reserved for the cameras or the cover of her magazine. "You Bennets have always had a flair for the dramatic."

Something in him tightened. "You're suing us for a pittance in the hopes that it'll sink us. I wouldn't say we're the ones being dramatic." His gaze slid from my mother to her lawyer.

To the dismay of her lawyer, Mother answered again, "Longbourne was promised five thousand dollars per month in exchange for flowers from your greenhouse. But you were not to compete with Bower. Your little flower shop grossed two hundred thousand in one quarter, which is expressly forbidden by the contract *your* mother signed. You've kept your business running illegally—"

"Not illegally," I said over her, "because this contract is unethical—"

"And so you will pay me the overage or the agreed upon two million dollars for breaking the contract ahead of schedule. We are prepared to take this all the way to the end, Mr. Bennet. So think long and hard about what you're willing to sacrifice for your honor."

"I'll do that," he said flatly as he stood, prompting us all to stand.

Fruitlessly, I willed him to look at me. To make some kind of contact, anything to give me a glimpse into his thoughts. But there was a blank space where I should have been.

No one moved to shake hands. Mother stood straight and proud, a cruel smile on her lips as she watched them leave.

It wasn't until the door closed that Mother and her lawyer sat. I, however, stood numbly at their side, caught in indecision. Because my only chance to talk to him slipped away with every second.

"Well, that went well," Mother said cheerily before she and her lawyer launched into their strategy to take down the Bennets.

"Excuse me," I muttered, adrenaline zipping through me, the decision made.

"Where are you going?" Mother asked, her cheer instantly gone.

"To the restroom," I lied. "To … clean myself up a little."

"Too late for that, dear," she said with snide superiority. But she turned to the lawyer again, dismissing me.

My heart climbed up my esophagus and into my throat as I hurried around the table.

I didn't have a plan, didn't know what I'd say as I rushed through the bullpen of cubicles. The open space afforded me a view all the way to the front desk, but I didn't see him. Panic overwhelmed me. I had to catch him. He would never text me—of that, I was certain. I wouldn't see him again until we had another meeting. This was it, and I couldn't seem to stomach letting him go.

I hurried toward the elevator without a thought, wondering over the likelihood of finding him. And I was too consumed by my thoughts to see the large, long hand reach out from a conference room and grab me by the arm.

He pulled me into the darkness and closed the door behind us. If I hadn't known it was Marcus the second he touched me, I'd have picked it up when met with the scent of him—clean soap, a hint of spice, the smell of rain. For a string of heartbeats, we stood there in the dark, his hands still on my arms and mine resting on his chest without knowing how they'd gotten there.

"Did you know?" he finally said, his voice both tight with suspicion and tinged with hope.

"I didn't. I had no idea. Please, believe me."

A quiet sigh and a softening of his grip. "I do. I don't know why, but I do."

Neither of us knew what to say. Or maybe we did but didn't want to.

"What are we going to do?" I breathed into the blackness, knowing when I spoke how he'd answer.

"The only thing we can. We say goodbye."

Emotion seized me at the truth of it, squeezing my heart out of my throat and into my stomach. "Of course," I said. "It would never work, would it?"

The stroke of his thumb on my arm had me wishing with a deep desperation that I could see his face. "I can't see how."

It was unbearable, being so close to him, my senses on fire as I mourned what would never be. I grieved the impossible future of his company, of his kiss.

The thought struck me, the proximity to him conjuring flashes of imaginings. I wished I'd kissed him before we'd known. I wished we'd had just a moment, just one moment together.

It was then that I realized I still could. Because *this* moment wasn't over yet.

I drew an unsteady breath. "If that's all it is to be, can I ask something of you?"

A pause before he answered, "Tell me what I can do."

"Kiss me," I said with a terrifying bravery.

His hands found my jaw, my cheeks, framed my face, the shape fitting in his palms as if one were cut from the other. But he didn't come closer.

"Please," I whispered. "If this is all I can ever have, please leave me with this."

I could feel the longing in his fingertips, riding his breath, in the warmth of his body against mine. But as the seconds ticked past without an answer, dejection took the place of my hope.

It was his nose that first reached me, that strong and straight nose brushing the bridge of mine, first one side, then the other. My tingling lips felt his breath, felt the space he occupied without touching as anticipation locked my lungs, fisted my hands around his lapels.

One moment of indecision or persuasion or both.

And then he gave up the fight.

A soft brush of his lips against mine, a drag of connection as if he were charting the topography of my mouth for posterity. And when he was satisfied, those lips captured mine and held them captive.

It was a kiss thick with hello and desperate with goodbye. It was a long and languid meeting of two people who would never be, a tasting determined to mark every sensation, to commit it to memory. We were a twist, his hands roaming my back, my face, my hair. My hands learned the shape of his jaw, as hard and sure as it appeared. They memorized the feeling of his hair, thick and lush, ruffling under my fingertips.

For that brief and fluttering span of time, nothing mattered in the whole world except for his lips and mine.

Though the kiss held no power over us, it was no match for the truth of our circumstance. And as that truth made itself known, our fever broke. Lips slowed, then stopped. Heavy breaths were the only sound in the room.

Our foreheads met in the dark.

I was only to feel the brush of his lips once more when he pressed a kiss to my furrowed brow.

"I'm sorry," he whispered as he stepped away.

"Me too," I whispered back.

He opened the door and stepped into the slash of light, the visage of him so striking, so right, I took a step toward him.

Toward Marcus, tall and lean and beautiful, his face etched with regret.

And then he was gone.

With a painful exhale, I leaned against the table at my back, found in the dark in my desperation to stay upright.

And it wouldn't be the first time or the last that I wished I wasn't who I was.

# Harbinger of Bloom

## MARCUS

**M**y hands weren't the only thing shaking as I rushed out of the building.

A trembling in my knees accompanied a rattle in my lungs, a tremor in my heart, a shuddering of my mind.

I shouldn't have kissed her. But I couldn't help myself, not with her asking me so painfully, so gently, a plea echoed in the chambers of my heart. If we were only to have one kiss, it had been one for the books. That kiss had cracked my rib cage open, exposing me in a bald honesty I couldn't have hidden, not from her.

I'd only just realized my general disinterest in relationships had nothing to do with my inability to care and everything to do with the girls I'd considered for the job. I'd been waiting my whole life for a thunderbolt.

When I met Maisie, I saw lightning.

But it was the kiss that struck me down to the ground.

Never once had I been consumed by a kiss. Never once had

I lost a part of myself, a piece I wouldn't get back, in the span of a hundred heartbeats. Never, not in a thousand years, did I believe desire could burn so deep that it could make a mark I'd never erase.

I'd be crazy to let her go. For a moment, there in my arms, I didn't know if I could.

But I didn't have a choice.

I stepped to the curb, held up a hand, confused and disoriented and filled with regret. Not for the kiss. But for the knowledge I'd never kiss her again.

Blindly, I slipped into a cab and gave the driver my address, uncertain I could have made my way home on the subway. My luck, I'd have ended up in Queens. So I sat in the back of the cab as it carried me home, trying to collect myself, which was as sporadic and tedious as picking up spilled marbles on a busy sidewalk.

Margaret Bower.

Margaret fucking Bower was Maisie, and nothing in my universe made any sense.

I hadn't seen a photograph of her in years. She'd tucked herself away in college on the West Coast somewhere and afterward, she left for England to work in their British division with her aunt. I only knew because my mother knew, and my mother's favorite topic of gossip was the Bower family. I knew Evelyn wanted to pass Bower on to her daughter, and we all assumed she was ready and willing to take over, if Evelyn ever let go of the reins.

Although I figured it would be more of a *cold, dead hands* situation than a *willing* turnover.

Either way, the Margaret I'd created in my mind had been groomed for this. She had studied and trained and was back in New York to take her place at her mother's side. But the cruel, evil duplicate of Evelyn I'd expected Margaret to be wasn't even in the same neighborhood as Maisie.

She wasn't even in the same solar system.

But that fact didn't change our circumstance. She was the heiress to Bower Bouquets. And I owned Longbourne, which her mother had set out to destroy. In fact, there was a very high likelihood she would.

Heavy dread settled me, steadied me, anchored me to the ground like a stake. The future of the flower shop and my family hung in the balance. And it all landed on me.

I'd known when I put all my savings into taking over Longbourne, its debts and its waning business, that it was a risk. And I was risk averse. Not in the sense that I didn't like a good gamble—years on Wall Street and day trading couldn't be stomached without a desire for a thrill—but my gambling came only after ensuring my security with heavily padded investments. Never would I have bet the farm. Until this. Until now.

My family needed me—their livelihood depended on it. So I did what I could by taking the wheel. We'd turned the shop around, finally climbing toward the black after years of empty pockets and bad accounting.

But I should have known things were going too smoothly.

If only she'd told me, all of this could have been avoided. If she'd come to me when the shop fell into decline, I could have stepped in. I could have managed the business better, fired her accountant, invested their money. I could have patched the holes to keep the ship afloat.

I could have stopped Mom from signing that contract with Evelyn Bower.

Now it was my responsibility to set things right, and I didn't take that lightly. I was the only one equipped with the tools to save them, so I rolled up my sleeves and dove in headfirst.

I'd be goddamned if I saw my family laid to waste when there was a chance I could stop it.

Even if Evelyn Bower had made it her mission to ensure we wouldn't succeed.

And at her right elbow was her daughter.

Her daughter who I'd just kissed.

Her daughter who I'd only see in boardrooms and, if Evelyn had her way, in courtrooms.

Her daughter who I wanted to take on a date. And another date. And more. So much more.

It was beyond reason, and I struggled to accept it.

When the cab pulled to a stop in front of my family's home, I had no answers. But I'd pulled myself together, and that was saying something.

As I climbed the steps to our old Victorian brownstone, a wave of worry washed over me. This house—which we just might lose—had been in my family for a hundred eighty years when my independently wealthy ancestors migrated from England to try their hand at American capitalism. They bought a handful of properties in Greenwich Village, all in a row on Bleecker, built a greenhouse in back, and turned one into Longbourne. Through the generations, the shop had been passed down to the women of the family, finally landing on my mother.

But Mom had no head for business, as she was accustomed to saying, and somehow, I hadn't known how bad things were. I counted it as one of the failures of my adult life, not picking up on the trouble she was in.

The first hole in the boat had been the internet, and the second had been Bower Bouquets.

The rise of e-commerce and online flower orders flummoxed my mother, and either out of denial or fear, she pretended like it wasn't a thing, like it didn't exist. Slowly, business waned, and she'd thought it would work out, that it was a fad. So she flat-out refused to participate, probably because the thought of figuring it out was all just a bit too much.

Evelyn Bower didn't. She'd embraced the new avenue of business, investing heavily and buying into internet distribution. And in what felt like a snap, Bower was a household name.

Bower and Longbourne had been rivals for all of living

memory, though how the feud had started was up for debate. Gram never liked to talk about it, only said they had questionable morals and an abundance of unkindness. But Mom loved to dish, and in her story, the Bower women were cursed, unlucky in love and left with bitter hearts to show for it.

It had begun with my grandfather and Felicity Bower, a notorious prig and debutante with a family tie that had them promised to each other practically from birth. It was expected of them, written in stone as far as their parents were concerned. But on some fated night, as Mom liked to say, he met my grandmother at a party, and with little more than a look, he was a goner.

The jilting of Felicity Bower became the topic du jour of their elite high society, and publicly humiliated, Felicity set out on the warpath with my grandmother in her sights.

Of course, my grandmother was an industrious, resourceful businesswoman—my mother attributed my head for business and sums to her—and as such, Felicity had no impact on Longbourne, no matter how she'd tried to interfere. It was a shortcoming her daughter, Evelyn, made up for.

Felicity married a man who would let her have her little shop and all it encumbered, and in turn, she left him to his dalliances. They were, by all accounts, perfectly content in their misery. Evelyn did no better. I'd met her husband enough times to know that I liked him, which left me wondering what the hell he was doing with the devil's daughter.

Margaret I'd never formally met.

I'd seen her across the room a few times at the big parties our families used to attend, before the Bennets fell out of fashion and favor. But I never would have connected that the teenage girl in the corner with her nose in a book was the vibrant, blushing girl who'd just barreled into my life.

The one girl in a million.

The girl who hadn't just caught my attention.

She'd commanded it.

*Of all the shitty, unjust luck,* I thought with a sigh as I unlocked the door and stepped into the warm foyer.

The house was a living thing, powered by the ample energy of my family. And it had always been this way. The grand entry had greeted dozens of Bennets over the years. The polished staircase had weathered many a thundering footfall from the small army of children who had lived here over the decades. The paneled walls and parquet floor spoke of an era long gone—elegant and stately and timeless.

It was also an unholy mess.

Baskets and paper bags stood like footmen on the stairs. Shoes and backpacks and bags lay strewn over that shining parquet like casualties of a lost battle. The hooks lining the wall were laden with layers of coats and hoodies and hats from every season. I'd bet good money none of them had ever seen a closet.

The mess had always disturbed me on some deep and elemental level. As the middle child of five Bennets, I'd somehow ended up with my own room, which had always been the only *clean* room in the five-thousand-square-foot house. Every other room, hallway, and staircase revealed a hodgepodge of scattered things, not enough to constitute hoarding or an embarrassment. Just enough to feel forever untidy—a result of so many Bennets in one place.

It had gotten worse since my siblings came home to help save the shop. Though we were all adults, I was still the only one who actually put my clothes in the hamper and my dishes in the sink. Not that my mother had ever been tidy. And not that anyone blamed her, especially since rheumatoid arthritis had gnarled her hands to near uselessness.

I gave up looking for a clean spot in the entryway and set my briefcase next to the door. My family's voices carried into the foyer, happy, cheerful, laughing voices filling a room that I was about to suck all the joy out of.

Such was my role in our family. Forever the bearer of bad news.

I followed the sound, finding them in the kitchen where I'd

known they'd be. Dad had foregone his dining room seat—a preferred spot for the small amount of solitude it provided—in favor of a seat at the smaller table in the kitchen. Surrounding him was the rest of my family. Laney at his side, eternally Daddy's girl. Luke and Kash at the end of the table, ganging up on Laney, if I had to guess by her expression. Jett stood at the stove, occasionally chiming in as he stirred something in a pot. Tied around his neck and waist was an apron the color of a lemon, dotted with big white daisies.

And my mother sat at my father's left hand, holding that hand with her eyes on his wedding band, curiously quiet. It was not in her nature to be silent, nor was it in her nature to look so solemn, so worried.

When she looked up and saw me, I knew her quietude was a direct result of what I was about to drop on them.

The room hushed when I entered. Kash met my gaze and held it, his face instantly grim.

"What's the news?" he asked for everyone, knowing none of them actually wanted to know.

"Evelyn Bower has no plans to back down," I answered as simply as I could.

The room deflated.

"Damn her," Mom hissed, but her voice shook. "There's only one reason she would do this, and it's to end us."

I nodded. "Seems that's the goal. Ben believes we can win. But Evelyn seems to be set on putting us in the ground once and for all, and she has some of the best lawyers in Manhattan."

"If she's not backing down, neither are we," Laney started, straightening up. "She's wrong. This whole thing is wrong, and any judge would agree."

"What's right and fair doesn't matter with the right lawyers," I said. "Nothing is a sure thing, not until it's done. And we are a long way from being done." I couldn't bring myself to sit, not with dread simmering through me like bubbling poison. "I don't know how long it's going to take, and I don't know what it's going to cost in legal fees. If we lose, we'll lose everything. The greenhouse. The shop. The house. *Everything*. And so I can't make this decision alone. Because if we fight, we risk it all."

"We have to fight," Luke said without hesitation. "We won't lose."

"You don't know that," I noted.

"What happens if we roll over?" Kash asked.

"We either close Longbourne's doors, or we comply to the terms of the contract—grow flowers for Bower alone, turn our profits over to them, and continue to take our monthly allowance. But the truth is, we can't survive on that allowance. We can't repay our debts and rebuild our business under these terms, and Evelyn knows it. Any way we look at it, giving in means losing everything."

"Then we have no choice," Kash said darkly. "We have nothing to lose and everything to gain."

"We'd still have to file bankruptcy if we lose, but yes. If we win, we win big." I turned to Mom. "What do you want to do?"

She was straight in her chair, her blue eyes filled with regret and tears. "I don't know that I have a say, not after putting us here in the first place."

"Of course you have a say," Laney said gently. "You have the biggest say. What do you want, Mom?"

"To go back in time. Is that an option?"

Quiet laughter filled the room.

Mom sighed. "I'd like to fight. I feel that I owe it to all of you to fight. But I want you to decide. I'll leave my fighting with Evelyn for garden club. At least there, I have shears to defend myself with."

"Does anyone object?" I asked, scanning their faces.

But they shook their heads in dissent just like I'd known they would. Because if there was one thing Bennets always did, it was stick together. Thick or thin. Rain or shine.

Especially when it came to our opposition to Bower Bouquets.

And to my sorrow, everyone in it.

Including Maisie Bower.

# Bitter Pills

## MAISIE

"**I** cannot believe you showed up to that meeting like this," Mother said, gesturing to the length of me.

"You've mentioned." I turned my gaze out the Mercedes window as we pulled away from the curb. "Would you have preferred me to go home and change first? I was late as it was."

"I would have preferred you not disobey me. This was not part of the agreement—you were to go to and from work with me, live under my roof. One year, Margaret. You have one brief year to prove you're responsible enough to do what's asked of you, and you've already failed."

"You were the one who refused to take me with you this morning."

The temperature dropped several degrees. "That meeting was none of your concern. And you should have listened to me—if you had, you wouldn't have ruined your dress. I'd ask when you were going to learn I know best, but we both know you likely won't." She ignored my sigh. "At the very least, you could have gotten a cab. But the subway?" She shuddered in my periphery.

"Millions of people take the subway."

"You are not one of them." She smoothed her skirt. "I'd almost say you got what you deserved, if I wasn't so appalled at your display this morning."

My heart lurched at the thought of Marcus and the ghost of his kiss even though I knew that wasn't what she meant. It was just that it was the only thing on my mind. The only thing that seemed to matter, if for no other reason than my mother stood in the way of something I wanted. Again.

"Of all days, Margaret," she huffed. "You know how important this is to me."

"Taking down a tiny flower shop just to be petty doesn't seem all that much of a priority. You run a multibillion-dollar company. Why you'd spend your time sinking the poor Bennets is beyond me."

My bitterness was unmistakable, and I couldn't have schooled it if I tried. Her inexplicable, small-minded dedication to the destruction of Longbourne was the reason I would never speak to Marcus again. And as a result, I had nothing charitable to say to her.

Her voice lowered an octave, sharp as a razor's edge when she answered, "Because the Bennets take things that aren't theirs. They believe themselves to be above their station, and I'd like to put them back in their place."

I couldn't even look at her for certainty I'd say more than I already had, which was too much.

"I can't see why you care," she said as stiffly as her back. "The Bennets have never been anything to you."

*And thanks to you, they never will be.*

"They're human beings," I said, knowing it was useless. "Isn't that enough reason for compassion?"

"Compassion? For the Bennets? Your grandmother just rolled over in her grave."

I watched out the window as it began to rain again. Fat droplets hit the windows and streaked like comets across a glassy sky, and I wished on one of them that I could go back to England. Having an ocean and a five-hour time difference between me and my mother had become a crucial necessity in my life. One I hadn't fully realized until I came back.

Of course, that was its own necessity. England had been a respite, a temporary stay of execution, and we'd all known it.

My mother had made herself a household name, hitched her wagon to 1-800-ROSES4U, and cashed in big. Bower Bouquets could be found in strip malls all over the country, and we distributed flowers all over the world. There were Bower books on floral design with my mother's face on the covers. The floral magazine Mother had started in the nineties was one of the largest on the market, sitting right next to *Star* and *US Weekly* in the checkout line, and unsurprisingly, she featured herself on every cover. Making appearances on the most popular talk shows and national morning shows was just a regular Tuesday, and she hobnobbed so successfully that she received annual invitations to all of the awards shows *and* the Met Gala.

Evelyn Bower was a force of nature so powerful, she single-handedly fueled an entire corporation on her energy.

And then there was me.

The great disappointment of my mother's life was that I wasn't a duplication of her, complete with a matching French twist and superior tilt of the chin. Though it wasn't as if she hadn't tried. In fact, until a few years ago, I had been the model daughter, doing all she asked in the hopes that I'd win her approval.

But my mother was no fool—she knew without question that I was nothing like her. Perhaps she thought me weak for wanting to please her so badly. Or the tenderness of my heart, which she so often criticized me for. It was no secret that I was disinterested in notoriety or fame, and I had zero desire to appear on television or write books or wear dresses to an award show that cost six times what most people spent on their monthly mortgage. But I did as I was told with a genial smile and a wish that maybe if I did things right, she'd be the mother I'd dreamed of when I was a little girl.

Two years ago, that dream had died in a fiery crash that left nothing but truth and ashes.

Evelyn Bower didn't care about anything but herself.

I'd come to Bower after college, bright-eyed and idealistic about my future at our family company. Proud of my legacy and honored to be in the line of women who had inherited it. There was good to be done in the world, and Bower had all the resources to do it.

In my hand was a project I'd come up with in school, an idea that took root in my mind and the foundation of my heart. The concept was simple—the center was a community outreach program that turned vacant lots into parks with gardens. And not only for flowers.

For food.

The vegetables we grew were then used in a soup kitchen we ran, and all of the landscaping, cooking, and management was done by volunteers and the homeless people the soup kitchen served. We taught skills and connected the homeless we served with jobs—the landscaping and construction companies hired half of the workers who volunteered in production. After that first year, some of our volunteers even ended up in management of the kitchen and groundskeeping.

Looking back, I was shocked she'd given it to me, but I saw it for what it was—a patronizing pat on the head and eventually a bargaining chip she'd use to keep me in line. But she'd let me have it without much of a fight, and it'd only taken two little words.

Public relations.

I painted the picture of the press we would get—*Charitable daughter of Evelyn Bower starts nonprofit to feed homeless*—and she was sold.

The year I worked on Harvest Center was the first and only glimmer of hope I had for my future at the company I'd been born into. I imagined myself heading up the charity division with all the energy my mother spent throwing herself in the public eye. Daydreamed about how the money allotted for the charity could help people. I started searching for properties for the next center, considered who we'd already trained and how many more we could get on board to help start it up.

Nearly on the year anniversary of the start of the project, she called me into her office and stonewalled me.

Harvest Center had served its purpose, and in the end, our nonprofit hadn't been profitable enough to expand. The single center would be all there was, and I was to be moved to marketing and advertising instead.

The fight that followed was the first and only of its kind.

My life until that point had been a long string of concessions, a gradual bending of will by her hand. The charity was the center of my happiness at Bower, the culmination of my hard work. It had consumed my life, from months of planning and building to the hundreds of hours I'd spent in the kitchens and gardens there.

It was all I wanted, and she took it from me. And for once, I wasn't going to stand for it.

Perhaps it was her shock that I'd fought back that drove her to cruelty. It was a shedding of twenty-four years of lies between us, and when the truth spilled out, it was a deluge of loathing. I told her all the ways she'd failed me, all the ways I wished she'd cared. I told her what I thought of her—that she was cruel and selfish and that I would never be like her, no matter how hard she tried.

In turn, she let me know exactly what she thought of *me*. How weak and soft I was. How my father had ruined me, how she regretted letting him have control. How stupid and naive I was—qualities that would ruin the company. That the real reason for her taking Harvest was to teach me a lesson—there was no place for gentility in this world. And if she had to break me to prove the point, then so be it.

I could very easily mark that moment as the point in my life when the world came into focus. My beliefs and dreams about what my life would be turned into a fairy tale, a silly notion of princesses and castles that was just as naive as my mother had accused me of being. And in that moment, the idealistic little girl died, and a cynical shade took her place.

A week later, she packed me off to England "to cool off." My aunt—the younger of the two Bower sisters—ran European distribution there, and I was to learn the ins and outs of that and agriculture at our farms in Yorkshire. Two glorious years of freedom, and then she'd crooked her finger and called me back. And I wouldn't have gone if not for her offer.

Over the course of ten years, she would shift her shares to me annually in a sliding scale, and at the end of that decade, I would only have one less share than her.

My counteroffer—she'd give me Harvest Center to do with what I pleased.

She'd agreed, and like a fool, I'd come running, sure of all the good I could do, the difference I could make. One board member was all that stood between me and outvoting her. It had been too alluring to pass up.

But now that I was back, it just felt like another trap. Particularly when she'd added my residence to her terms. What little freedom I'd stupidly thought I'd have disappeared with the snap of her fingers.

*The greater good,* I reminded myself. A few years of indentured servitude was nothing compared to a lifetime of opportunity.

As we ambled toward the Village, Mother continued on about some photo shoot she had planned for the two of us for the next magazine issue, some farce where we were to go out to one of our farms in Long Island and pretend to be the best of friends—probably all rainbows and sun hats with a basket of flowers between us. I'd been groomed my whole life for this, and I'd never dreaded it more than right now.

And trust me, I'd dreaded it a lot.

I didn't want photo shoots and board meetings and, least of all, legal meetings regarding the Bennets. What I wanted was to throw myself into Harvest Center and pretend like I was anywhere but back in my mother's clutches. What I wanted was the sanctuary of my room where my books and my garden waited for me. I wanted my little joys.

*Do what you have to do, Maisie,* my aunt Ava would say. *And do good where you can. The only way to survive the Bowers is through small sacrifices.*

And so I would. I'd tune Mother out. Show up everywhere she required me to be. Keep my mouth shut as often as was in my power. I'd play her game. And in return, I'd get the keys to the kingdom and do some real good.

At least I had my father to keep me company. We were two lone soldiers waging war against a tyrant. And by war, I meant we hid in the woods, stayed quiet, and hoped she kept on marching toward whatever town she was about to sack.

I watched rain streak the window, offering the occasional noncommittal noise or disinterested nod, which was all the encouragement my mother needed to prattle on about the magazine, some photographer she'd fired, butting heads with the board, a shopping excursion, and a new designer handbag she needed to pick up from Saks.

Mercifully, we pulled up in front of our home, and instantly, I exited the confined space. A deep sigh of fresh air brightened things considerably.

Ours was a beautiful home in the Village, an extravagant mansion built sometime in the late 1800s, but not by my ancestors, like the Bennets. No, this old historic home had been purchased by my mother, I suspected simply because the Bennets had something she didn't.

As big as she talked regarding putting the Bennets in their supposed place, her insecurity spoke louder. The feud was old and tired, the vengeance bred into her so deep by my grandmother, it seemed inescapable. I used to think it was competition that drove her, but now that she was after the Bennets' throats, I realized it was deeper than that. But I guessed she'd never read about the good old Count of Monte Cristo. If she had, she'd know revenge never paid off. A miserable soul was a miserable soul.

No amount of petty fuckery would change that.

She was still talking as we climbed the steps, the door opening before we reached it by our estate manager, which was just a fancy name for a butler. We had a cook and a maid too—they occupied the servants' quarters. Because this ridiculous house I called home actually had such things as butlers and servant's quarters.

"Hello, Mrs. Bower," James said coolly, warming when he turned to me and frowned on inspection. "Maisie, did you get caught in the rain? I told you to take an umbrella."

"You did, and you were right."

"You should have made her take the car, James," Mother said as she passed, never quite looking at him as she handed over her purse and coat.

"I tried, ma'am. She wouldn't have it," he defended, taking her things.

God forbid she hang her own coat. Or open her own door for that matter.

"Well, you should have made her anyway," she snapped, smoothing her hair as she strode to the writing desk in the hallway. It had a chair, but no one ever sat there. It was as staged as the rest of her but had one practical use—it served as a landing pad for mail and keys. On approaching, she rifled through a stack of envelopes on its surface.

James somehow managed to look both regretful and annoyed.

I patted his arm. "He really did try his best, Mother."

"Yes, well, we can't all excel at our jobs, can we?" She didn't look up from her task.

James and I shared a look, and once he disappeared with our haul, I made to excuse myself. But before I could escape, my father walked in, and I no longer needed to.

William Argent had always been a handsome man, though his blond hair was now streaked with gray, as was his beard, clipped short and tidy. I had not been blessed with his height, which was towering, but we did have the same dark eyes and quiet smile. In terms of warmth, he was the polar opposite of my mother, and thank goodness for that. Who knew where I'd be if not for him? Likely the duplicate of my mother, just like she wanted.

Fortunately, I had also acquired his disposition.

He walked straight past my mother like she wasn't there, kissing me on the cheek when he was close enough.

"How was it?" he asked.

"Sufficiently awful," I answered.

"Do you ever do anything but complain?" The letters in Mother's hands snicked against the wood as she stacked them, turning to lay her stony gaze on us.

Dad's eyes narrowed. "Do you ever do anything but give everyone reason to?"

She rolled her eyes and turned for her office. "Don't start, William."

"You're right—I shouldn't start. I might never finish."

Studiously, she ignored him, closing the grand mahogany doors of her office with a solid thump. The sound echoed like we were in the Alps and not a house in Manhattan.

He sighed, his eyes lingering on the office doors. "Hungry? Tillie made chicken salad."

"With grapes?"

Dad smirked, offering his arm. "Is there any other kind?"

"Not as far as I'm concerned." I slipped my hand into the crook of his elbow, and together, we escaped to the kitchen.

They said that opposites attract, and my parents hit opposite on the nose.

The attraction part was another story.

He'd told me the story in bits and pieces, and once, when I was old enough to see what was happening and protest his ritual mistreatment by my mother, he sat me down and told me the whole thing, which was really just one very simple point.

My mother had gotten pregnant, and *her* mother had forced them to marry.

Granted, Dad would have done it anyway. But their parents stood behind them disapprovingly as they walked down the aisle, threatening with trust funds rather than shotguns. Mom lost that first baby late term, something she never mentioned and Dad only spoke of in the broadest of strokes. Those were their happiest years, which I had a feeling were still miserable. But as they tried for me, they were as together as they'd ever be. If they hadn't been, Dad would have left.

When I was born, nothing else mattered. He stayed for me.

Never once did my mother tuck me in. Never did she push me in a swing or read books with me. Not once could I remember her playing with me or offering a compliment.

But my father did.

He braided my hair and sat on the floor, playing Barbies. We played checkers and cribbage, baked cookies and colored. He took me to the park and to ice skate at Rockefeller.

My father was the only reason I was who I was—to my mother's lament, which was funny. As much as she'd abhorred my grandmother's control and restraint and lack of warmth, she'd promptly turned around and did the exact same thing to me.

When I'd left for college, Dad would travel, coming home only when I was there. When I'd lived in Yorkshire, he would visit for months at a time. He owned flats all over the world and spent most of his time in Europe. I wondered sometimes if he dated or had girlfriends and secretly hoped he did.

If anyone deserved love, it was him.

But if I knew him at all, I knew he wouldn't drag anyone into his mess. Wouldn't ask someone he loved to play second fiddle to my mother.

As it was, he'd come home the same day I did, and I wondered if he could stand to spend even one night in this house with my mother alone. He had his own space, his own room and library on the other end of the house from her.

And in the middle was me.

Dad deposited me in a chair at the kitchen island before making his way to the refrigerator.

"Wanna tell me what really happened?" he asked from inside the fridge.

I sagged in my chair from the weight of it all. "She was horrid. The Bennets want to settle, and she won't have it. No surprises there."

"Not a single one. Who was there to represent them?"

My heart threw itself at my sternum. "Marcus."

His name was forbidden and familiar on my tongue. Thankfully, Dad was busy making me a sandwich and didn't see me flush.

"Well, at least it wasn't Mrs. Bennet. Your mother might have set the room on fire."

I chuckled. "Why don't you ever call her by her first name?"

He shot a smile at me over his shoulder. "And summon the devil to take me? Her name is expressly forbidden in these walls, and so is her husband's."

"Remind me one day to ask you outside of these walls."

"It's been so long since I've uttered them, I don't think I could say them for fear of being struck by lightning. Or your mother. I think she'd even manage it from another continent. Maybe have a hired man follow me around with instructions to break my nose on their mention."

At that, I full-on laughed. "I wouldn't put it past her."

"Me neither. But you know...I always was a rebel," he said with a mischievous smile, turning toward me to lean in, casting a dramatic glance over his shoulder. "*Rosemary Bennet*," he whispered.

And we burst into laughter.

"So," he started, going back to his task, "your mother will fight the fight even if it means dying on the hill?"

"Does she know any other way?"

"No. But if there's one Bennet who can beat her, it's Marcus."

"I didn't know you knew him," I said, ignoring the jolt his name seemed to inspire, now that I knew how his lips tasted.

"I don't, not really. But I've followed his career. He made quite a name for himself on Wall Street and moved on. Technically, Longbourne is his. He acquired it all, including the vitriol of your mother."

"Lucky him."

*The kiss,* my heart whispered.

The urge to tell my father what'd happened with Marcus tugged at me. But I glanced down the hall at Mother's office and found resolve to keep it to myself. This wasn't a safe place to talk about it.

I didn't know if such a place existed.

But I wondered what Dad would say if I told him, imagined the relief I'd feel on telling him. He would understand. He would tell me to stay the hell away from Marcus for my self-preservation, but he would understand. I thought he'd even be able to commiserate—our family was well known for biffing our love lives and had been for generations.

Such was our curse.

If I'd ever thought I'd shake it, I'd learned my lesson today.

"Well," Dad started, turning to me with a plate in hand, "I'm sorry you had to come back into this."

"It's only for a little while."

"Only you would call a decade *a little while*," he said on a laugh.

"And only one year of incarceration at the Bower Correctional Facility. Really, Dad. You should go stay at the SoHo apartment. No point in us suffering together."

"How can I be a human shield if I'm in SoHo?" When I didn't laugh, he sighed. "I didn't stay married to her all these years just to abandon you in your hour of need. If you're here, I'm here, and that's that."

I groaned.

"Besides. We have a host of dinners and appearances we have to pretend we're happily married for. It's convenient, staying here." The look I gave him must have been effective because he amended, "Okay, but it could be worse."

"How?" I scoffed.

"I could have to sleep with her."

I winced, and he laughed.

"I tell you what, kid—when you're free, I'm free. When you're released from all this, I'll go too, whenever that may be."

"Promise?"

"Promise."

"Then I'll pay my dues and earn us both a pardon. It seems a small price to pay. I'd pay more, all told."

His smile was warmer than a summer sun. "I don't doubt that. Not for one second. And if she doesn't hold up her end of the deal, she'll have both of us to answer to."

We laughed, but by the time I tucked into my sandwich, I was left wondering if she would dare change her mind.

But I swallowed that thought with my lunch and hoped that if she honored nothing else, she'd honor this.

The legacy.

# Hello/Goodbye

## MARCUS

The minute I stepped into the coffee shop, I scanned it for Maisie, same as I had every day for the last week.

I came here daily, sometimes twice, armed with a myriad of reasons to justify it. It was convenient, for instance, situated near Longbourne on Bleecker. I had a punch card and was working for a free coffee. It was cold out, and I wanted something to warm me up. My mother would appreciate a cup of tea.

But under all those excuses was the truth—each morning, I passed the threshold looking for her.

It was ludicrous. I found myself thankful I'd thrown her number away because had I still possessed it, I couldn't have promised I wouldn't use it. I didn't know exactly where she lived—not that I could show up at the Bower doorstep even if I did—nor did I know if this particular coffee shop was near her. But this was the only tether between us that didn't involve a lawsuit. And as such, I couldn't seem to stop myself from coming here to relive the moment we'd met in the hopes that I would find some lingering magic among the murmuring chatter and heady scent of coffee beans.

But every day, I was disappointed.

Sometimes twice.

Today was no different. Disappointment sank in my chest like a stone in a river as I headed for the line with heavy feet. Somehow, the sensation still surprised me. Somehow, I didn't expect to be disappointed, floating here every day on the hope that maybe, just maybe, I'd catch a glimpse of her again in a place where we could just be us.

I'd thought a lot about what I might say, both what I wanted to and what I should, which were two very different things. But instead, I would buy a cup of coffee I wouldn't drink and tell myself that maybe tomorrow would be different.

I wanted to see her again as desperately as I hoped it'd never happen.

It was strange, this feeling, an invasion of my very self. She crept into my thoughts in mundane moments and times when I should have been thinking about anything but her. And I didn't know why. Perhaps that was part of my obsession with seeing her again, that noisy, unshakable quest for answers. I was not a man who lost control, but when it came to her, I was a runaway train. And the desire to know why was almost as deep as my desire to know her.

These were my thoughts as I stood in line, scanning the crowd once more with a destructive affliction—the guileless certainty that I'd find her if I looked one more time.

My gaze snagged the back of a small girl with short blonde hair who had materialized at the end of the counter. Everything around me ground to a screeching halt. My heart thundered in my ears as my disbelieving feet pointed in her direction. Here she was, as if I'd summoned her, standing there like I'd imagined a hundred times. All that was left of the things I'd thought to say turned to static.

I reached out. Touched her arm. She turned to me.

And I realized with no small amount of shock that she was not Maisie.

The stranger's brows furrowed. "Can I help you?"

Now my disappointment was coupled with embarrassment. "I'm sorry. I thought you were someone else."

She gave me a suspicious look. "Sorry to disappoint."

I was about to excuse myself when someone tapped my shoulder.

The stranger looked around me, smiling as she cocked her head. "I think you were looking for her."

This time when I turned, I was rewarded.

Maisie stood before me with a timid smile on her lips, her cheeks smudged with color and her dark eyes soft as velvet.

"Hello," she said nervously, hopefully.

"Hello."

For a moment, we were silent, and when we finally spoke, it was at the same time.

"Do you want a coffee?" I said as she said, "Could we sit?"

To which we both answered simultaneously, "Yes."

With a laugh, we moved to a table, sitting first. Well, she sat. I asked her what she wanted before getting back in line. And all the while, my mind ran a rut in my skull.

There were so many things I wanted to say, and I couldn't seem to recall a single one as I stood there in what felt like an endless line, trying not to watch her. But I couldn't seem to help myself, too thirsty for the sight of her to abstain. My comfort was that she couldn't seem to either.

I took that as both a good and dangerous sign.

Once coffees were in hand, I took the seat across from her.

Her hands circled the paper cup, and her eyes struck me in the heart. "Would you think me strange if I told you I'd been coming here hoping I'd find you?"

"How could I when I've been doing the same?"

Warmth sparked between us, lit by her smile. "Really? I thought after … well, after the last time I saw you, I got the impression that you'd prefer never to see me again."

"My preference has nothing to do with it. What I'd prefer and what I'm allowed aren't in alignment."

"No. I don't suppose they are."

A heavy silence settled between us.

"I'm so sorry, Marcus, for all of this," she said. "I don't agree with her. My mother."

Judging by the sudden relief I felt at the admission, I realized I hadn't known.

"I haven't been able to stop thinking about what she's doing to Longbourne—to you—wondering *why*. It's inexplicable and small, but she's decided to dig in her heels, and when she decides"—Maisie sighed—"well, that's that. Nothing will stop her other than victory or death, metaphorical or otherwise."

A minuscule laugh through my nose accompanied the thought.

"I … I just wanted you to know that I don't support this. And I'm sorry. And I hope she loses."

"So do I. If I have anything to do with it, she will."

"I believe that. In fact, you might be the only one who can stop her." She paused, turning her cup in her hands. "You must hate me for all this."

"I don't think I could hate you even if I wanted to. Which I don't, by the way."

Her eyes were bottomless, fathomless. "I wish things were different."

"So do I."

"And I wish I could stop thinking about you, but I can't."

With a hard swallow, I said something I shouldn't, "I shouldn't want to see you, but I do."

Hope flickered across her face.

"I shouldn't keep coming here, but I can't seem to help

myself, and I doubt I'll stop. I don't hate you, Maisie. But I hate *this*. It's not often I want something I can't have."

"Because you don't often want?"

"Because what I want, I get."

"And you can't have me," she said, finishing the thought.

"And I can't have you," I echoed.

Her gaze dropped to the cup, her throat working. "It's cruel really. I don't know why. I don't even know you. Maybe it's just the injustice of it all. Maybe it's just another choice my mother has taken from me. But either way, I hate it too."

I drew a painful breath, one fraught with indecision. I knew I should go—I shouldn't have come here to start. But I couldn't bring myself to leave.

"I wish there was a way," I said. "If there were, I would have already found it. Trust me, I've looked."

For a moment, she watched me, her head shaking slightly. "I can't believe that the two of us want the same thing, that even though we're in agreement, we can't do what we please."

"Your mother would turn you out. Mine might have a cardiac event. And keeping it a secret would only hurt everyone, us most of all. It's not often I wish I had my brothers' ability to jump into a fling. Be casual. But I know myself better than to pretend this doesn't mean something. And that would be the only way. We have no future, so I don't see how we can have a present. Right now, we're disappointed, but later … later, it would hurt. I don't want to hurt you, Maisie."

"I don't want to hurt you either," she said softly. "Maybe, someday, things will be easier."

I tried to smile.

"Maybe," I answered without believing it.

Her sigh told me she didn't believe it either. "Then I guess this is goodbye again."

I didn't want to agree. I didn't want to be rational or reasonable. But they said a leopard couldn't change his spots, and

I could no easier pretend that ignoring my instincts was the answer.

"Come on. Let me get you a cab," I said as I stood, avoiding answering her directly.

She complied, standing and falling into step at my side. Without thought, my hand moved to the small of her back as I guided her out, and in that spark of connection, I imagined opening the door like this for her in a dozen different settings that we'd never see.

Neither of us spoke as I stepped to the curb, lifting my hand to hail a taxi. When one pulled up, I opened the door. Extended a hand to help her in, reveling in the feel of her soft, small palm against mine. But I held the door, held her eyes, held my breath for a painful heartbeat.

"I'll see you around, Maisie," I finally said.

"I hope so," she answered.

And with a lamentable thump of the closing door, so did I.

# What If

## MAISIE

I was on fire.

Cheeks warm. Coat too thick, too heavy. Palms damp. Heart aflame, kicking my ribs with every painful thud.

I shifted in the cab to peel off my coat, fantasizing about cracking the window to let the cool air in. Though I didn't know if it would help. In fact, I didn't know if anything could help me.

Sitting across from Marcus, I should have been focused on what he'd been trying to say—that we couldn't see each other, probably ever, and for reasons I understood all too well. I should have been bolstering myself with the reminders of what would happen to me if I were so stupid as to start seeing Marcus Bennet, starting with the defiance of sneaking away from my mother to come to the coffee shop, looking for him.

I didn't do casual either, and I certainly didn't think I could start with him.

I should have been doing a lot of things as I sat in the taxi, smart things, things that would keep me safe.

But instead, I only had one thought—Marcus wanted me.

He'd said it with regret in the depths of his brilliant eyes. He'd said it with his broad lips curled down at the corners. He'd said it like he meant it more than he'd ever meant a word he'd spoken, and I suspected Marcus didn't say anything he didn't mean. But these words in particular had been so earnest that they struck me still there in the crowded coffee shop. We could have been the only two people in the world.

Up until that moment, I supposed I hadn't known. I'd imagined. I'd hoped. I'd feared he wanted me and feared he didn't, but I hadn't known. And now that I did, I had no idea what to do with that knowledge.

What I should have done was forget it. Or perhaps acknowledge it before tucking it away in the box in my heart labeled *What If.* He was right, of course. Pursuing it made no sense.

But I wanted to all the same.

As he'd said, what I preferred and what I was allowed were not in alignment. The difference was, I found I had little interest in doing what was allowed.

It wasn't as if I had much of a choice in the matter, though. My mother would crucify me, revoke our deal, take away my little joys, business or otherwise. I could leave, of course. When faced with the loss of the only life I'd known, and—perhaps the most heartbreaking—the loss of my avenue to help so many, it wasn't quite so easy. It wasn't at all simple.

But I couldn't help but wonder if it wouldn't be worth it.

Marcus wanted me. And if there was a way, he'd be with me.

My heart sank, the flame of home streaking through my ribs. Because there was no way. Not without risking it all.

By the time we reached my mother's building, only my temperature had waned. Beneath that, I was roiling heat, brought to the surface of my soul by the knowledge of his affection. And I didn't know how to vent it off. Didn't know how to cool it down.

The closer I got to my mother's office building, the less I had to worry myself with that—proximity to her was a bucket of ice water. A snowball to the face. A belly flop into the deep end.

And when I stepped into the chaos of her office, all I could consider was what was in front of me, and I welcomed the distraction with open arms.

*Office* might have been an understatement. The space my mother bestowed upon herself was larger than most retail spaces in Manhattan. It was a corner office with a sweeping view of downtown, the rivers, the bay beyond peppered with ships, and the sky crisp and blue and dotted with cheerful clouds.

Inside, however, was a flurry of motion and people—eight, to be exact, nine including myself. My mother stood at a light board with her bold black readers perched on her nose as she looked over magazine pages with an editor at her elbow. A florist fiddled with arrangements on a table that looked to be set with samples for a spread. Two assistants I didn't recognize flitted around the room as well as one I did know—my mother's assistant, Shelby.

She smiled when she saw me and weaved around the obstacles before her with grace and ease. Because this chaos was her domain, and no one ran it like she did.

"Maisie," she said warmly. "How are you?"

"Good. Did I get the time wrong? I thought we had a meeting this morning."

She stepped to my side and surveyed the madness, saying softly enough that only I could hear, "She's avoiding her accountant."

A nod of her head directed me to a small, balding, and impatient-looking man who sat in a chair well out of the way, like a child put in time-out. His gaze alternated from his watch to my mother and back again.

I would have laughed had it not been so very much like her. "Of course she is. He's probably going to tell her to cut back on her shoe allowance, and if he can't get to her to say so, she can't be obligated to listen, can she?"

Shelby chuckled. "As if anyone could stop your mother from buying shoes."

The accountant decided he'd had enough, shooting to his feet and scuttling across the room. "Evelyn, I have another meeting, and I cannot keep waiting—"

"Then don't," she said lightly without looking up. "I'm terribly sorry, Roland. I didn't realize my meetings would run so late."

"You need to make time for this," he blustered. "There is much to discuss, and soon. We're running out of time to—"

"Yes, yes. It's just that I'm so very *busy.*" She finally looked up, offering him a mild smile. "I'll have Shelby schedule you for earlier in the day next time. Perhaps if she'd done so from the start, this could have been avoided." She shot Shelby a warning look before turning back to the light table.

Shelby stiffened at my side. I knew good and well she'd done exactly what my mother had asked of her, which was to purposely double-book her. But my mother not only paid Shelby well for her abuse, she also held the power to ruin any of Shelby's future prospects.

But rather than balk at my mother throwing her under the bus, Shelby smiled and stepped to Roland's side. "It's all my fault, Roland. I hope you can forgive the oversight. If you'll come with me, we'll get you scheduled with Mrs. Bower soon."

"*Very* soon," he insisted, scowling and smoothing his suit over his paunch as he cast one more look at my mother over his shoulder.

"Yes, of course," she said, ushering him out.

The second he was gone, my mother straightened up, taking off her glasses. "That will be all," she said, making no more eye contact as she walked to her desk and took a seat as if the room weren't full of people she'd summoned.

Confused glances were exchanged, but no one dared argue. Instead, they gathered their things and began filing out of the office in silence.

"Don't just stand there, Margaret," she said to her desk as she wrote something in a notebook lying open in front of her. "Sit down, for God's sake."

I bit the inside of my cheek to keep myself from sassing her and took one of the low-backed armchairs in front of her desk. Only when I was firmly in my seat did she look up, sweeping her glasses off her face.

"What did you want to see me about?"

"What did Roland want? He said you were running out of time—"

"That is not why you're here."

I frowned. "You want me to know the business. In fact, I already own a sliver of it. Isn't whatever Roland needs part of the business?"

"What Roland does is currently above your pay grade. Now, please tell me what you need so we can both get on with our days."

"Well, that's just it. I don't really have much to do. Part of our agreement was that I'd be able to work in the charity division, but you've kept me out of it, dragging me to pointless legal meetings, ignoring me when I try to ask. So now that I have your undivided attention, I'm calling in the promise."

She leaned back in her chair, eyeing me. "I will never understand your obsession with that silly little project."

"No, you wouldn't." The defensive ember that always flickered between us glowing brighter. "There's no power in it. Maybe that's why I like it so much—it's not about me. It's about others. But it doesn't matter why I want it. You promised it to me, and if you want me here, you'll honor our terms or I'll go," I said, meaning every word. "The lure works both ways."

Her eyes narrowed, either from thought or defiance, I couldn't tell. "Part-time," she answered without answering. "You are limited to twenty hours a week—"

"But—"

"But what? You have an obligation to me first and foremost. Your duties as my successor are nonnegotiable."

Betrayal and frustration whistled through me. "I should have known there would be a catch."

"Yes, you should have. But if you'd rather forfeit the charity—"

"No. I'll do it," I ground out the words.

Bitter blood-red lips curled into a smile. "There. That wasn't so hard, was it?"

"I'm starting today." I didn't dare ask if she had any objections for fear she'd fill my plate with tasks to rob me of my time.

"Then the clock will start too. Use your time wisely, Margaret."

At that, she turned to whatever was on her desk, sliding her glasses back on. And I was invisible to her once more.

I rose on shaky legs and carried myself out the door, blind with a confusing mixture of pride and disappointment. I'd stood up to her, gotten the thing I wanted, just not how I wanted it. She knew just how to strip my spirit, cut me down, keep me pinned. And I should have known.

I shouldn't have come back to New York.

Shelby stepped around her desk, her face touched with concern. "Are you all right, Maisie?"

"No, I am not all right," I answered with an unsteady voice. "She promised me Harvest but only delivered on half."

Shelby sighed. "I had a feeling. I'm sorry I couldn't warn you."

"Don't be. I know better than anyone why you didn't."

"Well, if I can help, I will. Are you heading down to the charity division now?"

I took a breath, reached for that joy, and grabbed it. "I am. We have to take what we can get, right?"

"That's the spirit. I'll call down and let them know you're coming."

"Thanks, Shelby."

"Anytime," she answered.

I made tracks for the elevator, leaving my mother behind me as best I could. But I was left with the unsettling feeling that all of this was to break me so she could remake me in her image. And all I wanted to do was bolt.

But then the elevator doors opened to the charity division of Bower, and I was reminded of all the reasons to stay.

Where the executive offices upstairs were a stoic, impatient array of suits and tidy hairstyles, the charity offices were their humming, happy contrast. It was all smiles, messy buns, and scruffy faces. Music floated around the bullpen. A burst of laughter rose above the murmur of chatter. I even caught sight of *denim*.

It was a whole new world.

I found myself smiling right back at everyone, light and easy, the tension in my shoulders easing with every step. As I wound my way through the cubicles, a hush fell in my wake. I'd come to expect it—the general consensus was that I was a carbon print of my mother, and everyone either feared my mother or loathed her, some both.

So I made it my mission to prove them wrong.

In the back of the floor, there were no opulent corner offices like my mother's but instead a row of smaller rooms that housed the upper management of the charity division. And in the biggest of those, I found the person I'd come looking for.

Jess popped out of her chair, bounding around her desk with arms flung wide.

"Maisie!" she said just before launching herself at me.

I caught her with a laugh. "I missed you too."

She leaned back, looking me over. "I can't believe she actually let you come down here to hippie alley."

I sighed. "It wasn't without convincing. Or a leash."

"I wouldn't expect anything less. Come here and sit," she

said, moving a stack of papers and binders out of a modest chair and onto a similar pile on the shelf behind her. "God, I can't believe you're actually here." She took a seat, her face alight.

"And I can't believe you're running the place. I always knew you'd do it."

She laughed. "It's all thanks to you. If you'd never gotten me hired at Bower, I wouldn't be working my dream job."

"Being the boss's daughter sometimes has its perks."

She scoffed. "Steep price, if you ask me."

"Not if it gets the perfect people to run the best department."

"Flatterer," Jess said with pink cheeks. "God, I'm so glad you're back. I feel like I've been waiting a lifetime to see this day."

"I didn't think it'd ever come, if I'm honest."

Her smile faded. "Another steep price?"

"Wouldn't be here if it wasn't. But I'm here, and that's what matters."

"So what's your plan?" she asked. "We got word that our budget is expanding and the request that we allot resources in whatever direction you choose."

"Well, that's where you come in. I'd like to start with a new center, I was thinking in Hell's Kitchen. We can use the model for the first, train some new people, take our best to the new center to get it up and running. Start recruitment. What do you say?"

Jess smiled, a broad and honest and beautiful expression on her face that filled me with hope. "I'd say, when can we start?"

# Settle Down

## MARCUS

"**A**gain," I said flatly, glancing from my mother to the legal pad in my lap.

"I don't see why any of this is necessary, Marcus," she blustered, adjusting the drape of her cardigan.

"It's necessary because you will be in a room with Evelyn Bower, answering deposition questions under oath. If you're not prepared, we're all in trouble."

"And Evelyn will have a field day," Luke said from my side.

I ignored him. "Now, let's try it again. When you signed the contract with Evelyn Bower, were you of sound mind and body?"

"You know very well that I was," she answered, nose in the air.

"A simple yes or no will do. Keep your answers short. Don't elaborate. Yes or no?"

She gave me a look. "Yes."

Luke snickered from my side, covering it with a cough, which bought him his own glare.

"Did you have legal counsel regarding the contract?"

Her cheeks flushed, lips flattening. "No."

"Did you read through the conditions of the contract?"

A hard swallow. A moment of silence. "It was a very long contract."

"Did you read through the conditions of the contract?"

Her brow quirked. "There were a lot of clauses and sub-thingies and—"

"Yes or no?"

She drew a fiery breath. "No! I didn't!" Her eyes shimmered with tears, her chin wobbling. "I was foolish, and I can barely admit it. How will I say the words in front of h-h-her?"

The ache in my chest twisted. "I know, Mom," I said softly, setting my pad on the chair as I stood, moving to kneel at her feet. I captured her gnarled hands with mine. "But they're going to ask these questions, and in preparation, you have to say these words until they don't hurt. Evelyn Bower will be in that room. She will witness and delight in every word you speak. So you're going to have to find a way to swallow your pride. It's happening whether you want it to or not. It's up to you to decide if you want to handle it with grace or vanity."

She sniffled, turning her hands in mine to hold them. "You're right. You're always right, you know. What would I ever do without you?"

"Oh, you'd figure it out. You always do."

"No, I don't. Even when you were little, you seemed to always know where to find my keys or my other shoe or my coat when I needed it. You knew better than I did when I needed to pick someone up from soccer practice or baseball tryouts."

Luke scoffed. "Well, after you left me there the sixth time, somebody had to step in."

She ignored him with practiced skill. "I never once had to tell you to clean your room. Tell me where you got that gene because I'd truly like to know."

I chuckled. "I liked knowing where things were, that's all."

"And being helpful. You always liked being helpful," she said, removing her hand from mine to cup my jaw.

At that, Luke snorted a laugh. "You mean he liked to be a know-it-all."

"Well, if you could find your ass in the dark, I wouldn't have to be," I shot over my shoulder.

He shrugged. "I'd argue, but you're not wrong."

"No, he's not wrong at all," she said. "It's lucky for all of us that you're here. Otherwise, we'd be in far more trouble than we already are."

"We would have had to close Longbourne," Luke added.

"Well, I haven't saved it yet," I said. "Are you ready to go again, Mom? I'm afraid there are harder questions than this to answer."

Her nose wrinkled in distaste, her eyes flicking to the door. "I could use a cup of tea, couldn't you?" She stood, nearly knocking me over. "Yes. I'll go make some tea, and we'll do this later. After, I mean."

I sighed but smiled, sliding my hands into my pockets. "Thirty minutes," I called after her.

"Hmm? Chai Rooibos?" she asked over her shoulder as she left the room, her voice disappearing down the hallway. "No sugar, just like you like it! Anything you want, dear!"

Luke shook his head from the armchair where he lounged. "She's a mess."

"It's genetic."

His smile faded. "Are you sure it's a good idea to let her answer questions? I can't see it being anything but a disaster."

"We don't have a choice." I did my best to curb my impatience. "Her signature is on the contract."

"How many months do you have to get her ready?" he joked.

"Depositions start next week," I said anyway. "And hers is the name they're waiting to destroy."

He loosed a heavy sigh. "I can't believe they've called

*everyone*. Even Dean, and he only delivers supplies. Tess is freaking out. She's had me drilling her for the last two days."

"They didn't stop there. A few women from the garden club are even on the list, and I can just about guarantee they won't be there to support Mom. Not with Evelyn running the club and especially not after last week."

A dark look touched Luke's face. "God, I hate Evelyn Bower. Our grandma *started* that stupid garden club, so what right does Evelyn have to stage a coup?"

"To be fair, I'm surprised Evelyn didn't oust Mom years ago."

"The look on her face," he said quietly, staring at nothing. "When she came home with that look on her face, I swear to God, Marcus. I could have burned that place to the ground so none of them could have it."

"It's been the bright spot in her life since she was a teenager. Damn Evelyn for taking that small joy from her too."

"Can you imagine growing up in a house like that?" he mused. "That whole family must be a pack of wolves. They don't eat turkey for Thanksgiving—they eat each other's livers."

My heart flinched at even the sidelong mention of Maisie. "Well, there's no avoiding them. Her—Evelyn, that is. She's on the hunt for *our* livers at present, and if we don't get Mom in order, I may as well hand her a—"

"Bib with a lobster on the front?"

"I was going to say a knife, but that works too."

"I heard Mom saying Evelyn was dragging Margaret around with her to all the legal happenings. Is that right? Have you seen her?"

I stilled all the way down to my veins. "Yes."

Luke didn't notice. "What's she like? A little clone of Cruella? I bet she's a toady, all Botoxed and superior and precious."

"She's ..." I didn't know how to answer. "I don't think she's anything like Evelyn."

He frowned. "No? I don't know how that's possible with a

mother like hers. She's got all the warmth of a lizard. Think Evelyn is grooming her? Think Margaret wants to throttle her mom in her sleep, or does she have a shrine of Evelyn in her closet? And most importantly—is she cute?"

"Don't ask me questions about her, Luke," I snapped. "How the hell should I know?"

He made a face and held up his hands in surrender. "Jeez, sorry. I'm just curious, is all."

"Don't apologize. It's fine," I grumbled, taking my seat again and pretending to scan the questions on my notepad in an effort to avoid looking at him. "How's Tess? Haven't seen her around much lately."

"She's good, just busy working on her book. Plus, we got another editorial feature for Longbourne, and we've been working on designs for the windows. The rest of the time, she's at home with her dad."

*Home* wasn't just Tess's—Luke had moved in with Tess and her dad a few months ago. Other than a weekly family dinner and visiting them at the shop, we didn't see much of him.

Luke wasn't the only one. Kash had moved in with his girlfriend a few blocks away, and he was the one I'd thought would never leave home, having never left in the first place. The rest of us had left the roost after high school—Luke moved to California, Jett moved uptown, and Laney ended up in Texas of all places. But Kash had stayed right here, working alongside our father in the greenhouse. And when everyone had come back to help save Longbourne last summer, I was the only Bennet not under the roof.

Though I might have moved out, I didn't go far, buying a brownstone a couple doors down. I ended up at the house for dinner almost every night under the pretense of duress. That my mother could be very convincing supported this pretense without question.

Of course, the real reason I hadn't gone far was this—I

worried over my parents, my mother especially. I'd spent my childhood taking care of her, from the smallest things, like having constant tabs on her keys, to the bigger ones, like sifting through the mail for bills I'd make sure to put directly in her hand. And so I had a deep-seated compulsion to make sure they were all right, so deep that I feared if I wasn't close by, some disaster would strike that I could have stopped.

When I'd worked as a trader on Wall Street, I'd commuted downtown. I found a way to check on Mom every day, even when my day was eighteen hours strong. It was easier once I took my F-you money earned through investments and left Wall Street behind me, keeping my income steady and high. I had enough padding to get me comfortably through a jobless decade, and after a few years of day trading, I'd doubled my money and invested *that* too.

Laney and Jett were the only ones left at the house, but the two of them were an impenetrable unit. I figured it was a twin thing, the same sort of thing Luke and Kash had even though they were of the Irish variety. Jett spent his free time—which was sparse, considering he'd become Mom's hands around the house—uptown at the book bar he managed, Wasted Words. And Laney ... well, Laney made herself scarce whenever she could, on account of the sticky business of her inheritance.

A Bennet woman had run Longbourne for nearly a hundred seventy-five years, never taking their husbands' names in order to pass the Bennet name down. Dad was so committed to the cause, he took *her* name. When Mom had a girl right off the bat, she'd been thrilled. But where the rest of us were happy in the greenhouse, cultivating green thumbs, Laney was in her room, fingers smudged with graphite and a sketchbook in her lap. It just wasn't her thing, and to her credit, Mom didn't push. She was a big proponent of letting us grow on our own, providing all the sunshine and water she could to allow us to do what we would.

But a quiet contention, though joked about and purportedly

forgiven, was a very real shadow over them. And as such, Laney kept herself busy. When she wasn't working on the marketing for Longbourne, she was running around with her old friends or skipping off with Jett to Wasted Words.

As much as I hated to admit it, now that all my family had come home, I'd miss them when they left again. There was a comfort in their chaos, a steadiness I found in anchoring them. I could be helpful, useful to the people I loved most in the world.

For the foreseeable future, the *only* people I loved in the world.

My last real girlfriend had been in college. Post that, my life was too busy to fit anyone in but the occasional date, usually with a convenient colleague, and my family. By the time I'd managed to slow down, I'd extricated myself from social circles for no other reason than lack of time. Any friends I had left were either still killing themselves in the Financial District or were married and having kids, and the only single guys I knew were related to me. *Knew* being the operative word. The only one left was Jett, and with Laney as his wingman, I had no practical use.

Mom used to set me up on dates with the daughters of her one-percenter garden club friends, and they foamed at the mouth for a shot. Not at me, I'd realized quickly, but at my money.

Now that I'd sunk all my money into Longbourne, I was no longer appealing. I wasn't even mad about it. Those girls could never be my person. It seemed impossible to think my person could ever exist in that sphere.

Maisie flitted through my mind, as she so often did. God, how I wished I were anyone else, just for a chance to know her. I'd been unable to shake my incessant wondering over what could have been and the frustration that came along with it. I hated not having answers, hated walking away without even trying. I hated not having a choice, and I hated the loss of possibility.

I hated that I couldn't just sneak around and do it anyway. That was what Luke would have done.

A book whistled toward me, hitting me square in the cheek with a smack when I turned to the sound.

"What the fuck, Luke?" I snapped, snatching the book and chucking it back at him.

He caught it like a jerk. "What? You weren't listening."

"Giving me a black eye before I have to represent our goddamn inheritance won't help any of us."

"Nah, but it sure would be funny."

I would have whipped another book at him had one been within reach.

"What were you even thinking about? I thought your eyebrows were going to merge into one big super-brow."

I weighed my words carefully, weighed the burden on my mind, and found a gray enough answer to say aloud. "How'd you do it? Date without any expectations. No attachments."

Luke's face quirked. "That is not what I expected you to say."

I laid an unamused look on him.

He sighed and shrugged. "I don't know. Partly, I think I just wanted to eat the whole world, see it all, experience it all. You know?"

"I don't."

A chuckle. "No, I guess you wouldn't. It's … I don't know how to explain it," he started, pausing to think. "It's like … a hungry sort of search. Like I couldn't stop looking, couldn't slow down, but I was hunting a ghost, chasing a thing I couldn't name. I had to try everything, collect experiences. Find the one thing that would satisfy my insatiable thirst."

"That sounds exhausting."

"It was, but it was fun too. Point is, I never *wanted* to settle down, not really. Not until Tess." The earnestness from my cavalier brother disarmed me, his eyes soft and voice prone. "So, really, if you don't want to be casual, you won't. And when you find the right girl, you can't."

I sighed. "That wasn't particularly helpful, but thank you."

"You're welcome. But I want to know why you asked."

"I bet you do."

"Oh, come on, Marcus. I answered your question. My turn."

"I didn't agree on an exchange."

He held up the book like a gun, closing one eye as if he were looking down a sight. "I can give you that black eye if you really want it."

I huffed, knowing he would. "Because I'm too busy to date," I lied.

"And you're *looooonely*," he cooed.

"This is why I didn't tell you," I said coolly as I stood, buttoning my suit coat.

"Too bad the garden club girls are off the table," he lamented. "Those girls are easy and convenient."

"Please, I was off the table the second my money was no longer liquid. And if I'm not careful, what's left will potentially end up in Evelyn Bower's hands. I doubt she'd take kindly to any of her cronies consorting with the enemy."

Especially not the crony I wanted to consort with.

"But see, that's what makes them so perfect—you wouldn't *want* to settle down with any of them."

I rolled my eyes.

"God, you're such a baby. Just get on Bumble like everybody else."

"Thank you, Luke," I said pointedly as I walked past.

"Anytime. Let me know if you need any help setting up an account," he called after me as I exited the study.

I trotted down the stairs and into the kitchen where my mother hadn't even put the kettle on in an obvious attempt to stall. So I gave her a temporary stay of execution by postponing our preparations until after dinner. You'd think I'd told her she'd actually been acquitted of a murder sentence, as relieved as she was. And with a kiss on her cheek, I left.

The day was crisp, the trees finally budding after a long, bare winter. It was one of those days where a jacket was only needed until the sun peeked out, but I'd forgone it, shoving my hands in my pockets to keep them warm on the short walk to my place.

My brownstone was just down Bleecker, next to Blanche's, the coffee shop with featherlight donuts and pastries that my siblings and I had practically grown up in. The upside was that my house always smelled sweet—not enough to be cloying. Just enough that a delicate, sugary scent hung in the air, welcoming me home.

I dropped my keys in the dish next to the door, heading for my room. I hadn't seen the value of paying someone money to help me furnish my own home, so instead, I'd spent a long time browsing the internet to build a repository of furnishings. Curtains and couches, dressers and sideboards, everything had a purpose and a place. It was neat and tidy, cleaned and dusted weekly by a maid simply because I didn't have the time to do it myself. Especially not now that the fate of our family rested firmly on my shoulders.

Familiar fear rose in my chest at the thought of my failure. We would lose it all if I made a single misstep. For all my planning and all my organization, I had precious little control. And there was only one way out.

Through.

So I'd do what I always did. I'd rise to that challenge and look my fear in the eye. And then I'd beat it before it could beat me. There was no other choice. In the battle of fight and flight, I would go down swinging every single time before exposing my back to the thing, to leave a target for a knife.

Again, Maisie flittered into my thoughts, the thing I couldn't fight for. The only thing I couldn't look in the eye and conquer. I couldn't even try. Instead, I ran. And oh, how I hated to run.

Maybe one day, I'd forget I had to.

But I doubted it.

# Snares

## MAISIE

Tess glared at my mother's lawyer with the fire of a thousand suns. That look was so hot, I was surprised steam wasn't climbing from his collar. But he was cool as a cucumber. Or a snake, more like, with predatory eyes and body coiled in preparatory stillness to strike.

"And would you say that Rosemary Bennet was reliable?"

"How exactly do you mean?" she asked, her voice tight and angry.

"In your general opinion, would Rosemary Bennet ever be described as reliable?"

"In my definition of the word, yes."

"Merriam-Webster states, *Consistently in good quality or performance.* Would you say that Rosemary Bennet was consistently in good performance?"

"Yes, I would." Tess swallowed, belying her confidence.

And the lawyer knew it.

"What about on the twelfth of March when she failed to open the shop at its appointed time?"

"I don't recall that."

"Hmm," he said to the papers in front of him, shuffling through them in show. "How about the sixteenth of March? The twenty-second? How about last week on the fourth of April? Might you recall that?"

Discomfort slithered through me with every serpentine word.

Tess stiffened, her face a mask. "I opened the shop those days."

"Might I remind you, Ms. Monroe, that you are under oath."

"But I did open the shop those days," she insisted.

He gave her a condescending look. "On time? Or because Rosemary Bennet failed to open it herself?"

The room fell silent, all eyes on Tess as she simmered in her seat, grappling for a suitable answer but finding none. Because she answered, "The shop did not open on time."

"Because Rosemary Bennet failed to open the doors."

"Yes," she ground out.

He smiled. "Thank you, Ms. Monroe. I think we have all we need."

The room exhaled, some with pleasure and some with pain, as Tess rose, her eyes finally releasing the lawyer—whose name I'd chosen not to remember—in order to throw a savage look at my mother and an objectionable look at me. But when she turned to her side of the table, her fury abated instantly, and the regret on her face when she locked gazes with Marcus was total.

He was still, so still as Tess exited the room. His lawyer leaned in to speak to him, and whatever he said tightened Marcus's face, darkened him to shadows.

"I told you this would be easy," my mother said, smiling as she slipped her hand into her stupid, flashy purse to retrieve a tube of red lipstick and a compact I was almost positive was solid gold. "She shouldn't have been so stupid as to sign a contract with me. I'd call it dumb luck, but there was no luck involved. Only dumb."

I swallowed, shifting in my seat, fighting the urge to either shove her or run out of this room like I was on fire. I said nothing.

"I mean, really. That she didn't realize I put a leash on her is the most naive thing she's ever done."

"You're awful," I said, soft and still.

Her compact snapped shut. "I'm resourceful, Margaret. And you'd do well to pay attention. Someday, you'll be sitting right here, just like me, unless you're as naive as poor, softheaded Rosemary."

*Never*, I screamed in my mind. *I will never be like you.*

"Why am I here?" I asked again.

Something in her tightened, hardened. "Opposition to the Bennets is a bone-deep Bower credo. And until you embrace that, you'll witness every step I take toward their downfall."

"Why won't you admit that they're no threat to you? Why won't you just own up to the fact that you're petty and that this whole thing is outrageous?"

She turned, laying the full weight of her gaze on me, and I struggled not to buckle beneath it. "Maybe it is, and maybe it isn't. Either way, I will finish what my mother started and erase them. And should they somehow rise again, you will do the same. I'll bend you until you break, Margaret. Because this is just one of many things you were born to do."

Dissent rumbled up my throat, heading straight for her, but we were interrupted by the entry of the next Bennet. And once again, the room stilled, all but my mother, who leaned forward like her lunch had just arrived.

Rosemary Bennet was a small woman with apple cheeks and creases on her face etched from joy. Her hair was big and wavy, cut short and brushing her chin, a shade of graphite framing creamy skin. She wore those brilliant blue eyes of Marcus's, or he wore hers, and though she didn't have a stitch of makeup on, no one could possibly call her plain. She was a light, a soft and shining light that was felt by every heart in the room, my mother and her lawyer excluded.

They didn't have hearts to begin with.

Though you could see she generally wore a smile, she had misplaced it today. When she reached to pull out the chair, her gnarled, knobby hands came into view, applying force in an unconventional way to make do with what she had.

Something in my chest ached and sank at the sight. I'd known she'd had to stop working at the shop for her arthritis, but never had I imagined it was so bad as that.

Those big blue eyes of hers didn't chance a look in our direction, and I hoped to God they wouldn't. Because my mother was poised to devour her, and I wanted to throw myself in front of Mrs. Bennet like a human shield to stop it. She seemed too gentle for this place, for this room.

My mother might as well have licked her lips when she smiled and said under her breath, "Now, here we go."

# MARCUS

The second my mother walked in, the room held its breath.

My impassive mask was belied only by my eyes, tethering me to her.

*It's going to be all right. We prepared for this. Don't let them win. I'm here, I'm here, I'm here.*

She folded her hands in her lap and sat up straight, putting on the best smile she could muster. It was brave, that smile.

After the way today had gone, I knew only one thing.

They were about to decimate her, and there wasn't one fucking thing I could do to stop it.

"Please state your name for the record," Thompson, their lawyer, said to his notepad as he scribbled what I suspected was nothing more than doodles. A show of tedium to lure her into letting her guard down.

"Rosemary Bennet," she said with a sturdy voice, her eyes darting to me.

I offered an encouraging smile.

"And you owned the Longbourne Flower Shop and greenhouse. Is that correct?"

"Yes." She relaxed a hair at the question. "For twenty years."

"And in August 2019, you sold that business to your son Marcus Bennet."

"Yes."

He flipped the pages of his notebook back like he didn't know exactly what he was going to ask. "In February 2019, you were approached by a lawyer from Bower with an offer to purchase flowers from your greenhouse. Is that correct?"

"Yes, it is."

"Describe to me your understanding of the terms."

Her throat worked as she swallowed. "Bower would purchase a minimum of five thousand dollars monthly in wholesale flowers for five years."

"And what was your understanding of the clauses in the contract?"

"That they were legal mumbo jumbo to support that basic term."

"Did you read the contract yourself, Mrs. Bennet?"

Color crept up her neck to settle on her cheeks. "No."

"Did you have a legal representative read it?"

"No."

"Did *anyone* read it before you signed?"

"No, but—"

"It seems outrageously irresponsible for you not to have read a contract that you entered your business into, but you have a history of irresponsibility, don't you, Mrs. Bennet?"

I straightened up, propelled by my fury, which had nowhere to go.

"I don't know that I'd say that," she started, trailing off.

Thompson gave her a small, sarcastic smile. "For instance, we were just talking to Tess Monroe about your inability to open the store on time. She thought it irresponsible."

Mom jerked like she'd been struck.

*Don't take the bait,* I willed, drilling a hole in her with my eyes. *Don't listen to them.*

He smiled, having hit his mark. "But that's just one example among many of your mismanagement of Longbourne. We also have the tax issues. The misplacement of money. The absence of bookkeeping, no financial investments, and the lack of business to even fund your upkeep, driving you deeper into debt with every year. Can you tell me what you did to address any of this?"

"I … well, I …" She looked to me for an answer, but I had none to give.

"Yes, that's what I found too," Thompson said. "You allowed your shop, which has been in your family for a hundred seventy-one years to fail. And along the way, you ruined any possibility of a future for your business. So when Bower reached out, would you say it was a lifeline?"

"I w-would."

"And how did you feel when you signed that contract?"

"Relieved."

"And yet you are contesting the terms of that very agreement. Is it the fault of my client that you failed to read the contract that you signed?"

"No."

"Would you say that it's another example of your irresponsibility?"

Her anger flared. "Now, wait just a minute—"

"Mrs. Bennet, do you deny that you failed to file your taxes on time for ten of the twenty years you owned your business?"

"But that wasn't me, it was my accountant!"

"Whom you hired, correct?"

"Yes, but—"

"Do you deny that you held contracts with various distributors that never delivered to you?"

"Well, no, but I just didn't realize—" she rambled, crumbling.

"Do you deny that you do not keep regular hours?" he charged, voice rising. "Do you deny that your staff has consistently been delivered late paychecks? Do you deny that in your twenty years of running Longbourne, you have bankrupted it? Do you?"

"That's enough," I spat, ready to fight.

"It's only the truth, Marcus," Evelyn said, and I gnashed at my name on her lips.

"The truth is that you trapped her into the agreement in the hopes that we'd end up right here."

A slash of a smile. "You know as well as I do that she has hammered every nail into the coffin herself."

"And you handed her the last one," I bit.

Her eyes lit with gratification. "I was trying to *help* her."

"Bullshit. You were trying to ruin her."

Ben laid a hand on my arm and whispered my name, but I shook him off.

"Why should I try to ruin her when she does such an admirable job on her own?" Evelyn cooed.

"Evelyn Bower," Mom said, drawing the room's attention, "do not pretend you didn't know what you were doing."

"And don't pretend as if you didn't know this was coming," she shot back.

"Mother," Maisie said, her worried eyes pleading, "please. Let it go."

"You are meant to be an observer only, Margaret," she warned. "I suggest you leave this to me."

"I think it's been left to you long enough," Maisie answered.

Thompson said, "Ladies, if we could—"

Screws tightened in Evelyn as she laid a disdainful look on her daughter. "Now is not the time—"

"It feels like exactly the right time." Trembling rage wafted off Maisie. "You have done enough to this family. The least you can do is keep your thoughts to yourself while you destroy them."

For a handful of heartbeats, Evelyn Bower was silent and stock-still. When she stood, it was with a calculated grace that left her looming over her daughter like a vengeful god.

"That is nowhere near the least I can do," Evelyn said, her tone even and deadly. "You will shut your mouth, Margaret Bower, and you will shut it right now. If you don't, she won't be the only one I ruin."

Maisie's cheeks were crimson, her eyes shining, jaw tightening with her small fists by her side. The only other motion was the shallow rise and fall of her chest as she looked for a refusal and found none.

Maisie's color rose a shade as she turned to face forward again, her shining eyes staring a hole in the wall.

An inexplicable, unbound rage rumbled through me, a stampede of fury at the sight of Maisie being restrained, at the sight of her pain, at the sound of Evelyn's noose sliding around Maisie's neck.

I fought the desire to turn the entire room inside out. To flip this table and tump Thompson out of his chair. To shackle Evelyn to a post and burn the building down. To grab my mother and Maisie Bower and get them the fuck out of here.

My hands trembled with defiance, stayed only by some well of self-control I hadn't known I possessed.

"Now, where were we?" Evelyn said, smiling as she lowered herself into her chair with grace she shouldn't be allowed.

My mother sat across from us, lips pinned between her teeth and chin bent. "What has happened to you, Evelyn? You have always been cruel, but I didn't know you'd be so horrible to your own child."

"And I always knew you were this stupid," she snapped. "Bovine and soft and chewing cud, not realizing you're going to slaughter."

Mom shook her head, her voice tight with emotion. "You sound just like your mother. And I am so sorry for that."

Evelyn shot out of her seat, and the room erupted in noise once more—Evelyn's lawyer trying to stop her, Maisie yelling at her to let it go, Mom yelling at Evelyn with tears in her eyes, Ben calling for me to calm down. I realized then that his arms circled my chest, and I relaxed enough that he let me go.

I rushed around the table and put myself between Mom and everyone. Held her face, forced her to look me in the eye. "I'm here. It's all right, I'm here."

She choked on a sob, sinking into my arms, and I folded her up, shielding her as best I could. I threw Ben a look over my shoulder.

He answered with a dark nod, "That's enough for today. These circumstances are untenable, Thompson. My office will call to reschedule, and in the meantime, I suggest you leash your client."

Thompson breathed a sharp sigh. "I recommend you do the same."

I didn't hear anything else that was said, only my thundering heart as I ushered my mother out. Kash, Luke, and Tess popped out of their seats and rushed toward us, asking over each other what happened.

"We're rescheduling," was all I said, moving us out of the common area in the hopes of avoiding Evelyn Bower and whatever poison waited on her lips.

Over the top of Mom's head, I watched them file out, Maisie last.

Pained. She looked pained and small. Hurt and angry. And sorry. She looked so sorry, it took everything I had not to move for her.

Her name from her mother's mouth was the crack of a whip. Maisie jolted, turning to follow with shoulders curved from the weight of it all.

I kissed the top of Mom's head before leaning back to look at her.

"Are you all right?" I asked, knowing she wasn't but unsure what else to say.

She sniffled, swiping at my coat. "Your suit. Look at what I've done to your suit."

"I don't give a damn about the suit."

She tried to smile, but it broke into a sob. "You told me it would be worse, but I didn't know. I mean, I knew, but I didn't realize. And sitting there, across from her ..." Her breath hitched. "Here, in this place with no one to see her act like an animal, I don't even recognize her. I walked into that room and saw her mother, and that's perhaps more terrifying than anything."

"Don't worry," I said without expecting her to stop. "We're going to start over, and I'm going to request Evelyn not be present. I'll do what I can."

"I know you will. You always do."

I deposited her into Kash's arms, sharing a look that promised we'd talk about it all later. "Get Mom out of here. I'll meet you outside," I lied.

They nodded as Tess took Mom's free hand and started to say something about Evelyn and a crowbar and the tightness of her asshole, but I didn't wait for the punch line.

I turned on my heel, stalking down the hallway, looking for Maisie.

The impulse overwhelmed me, commandeering every thought. The moment she'd stood up for my mother only to be pinned by hers, something in me had come unleashed, a prowling beast that would rather see the world shredded to ribbons than witness her pain. And I didn't even consider tethering that feeling down.

I was a reasonable man. But not when it came to her.

A plan clicked together in a neat little row in my mind. I would find her. I would pull her aside, separate her from her mother so I could make sure she was all right. So I could be sure she was safe.

It was the best I could do right here and now.

And it wasn't nowhere near enough.

I found her alone in a sitting area, face in her hands and body curled into her palms. Her shoulders bounced in even intervals.

She was crying, I realized.

The beast in me roared.

"Maisie ..." It was a rasp, rough and pleading.

She shot up in her seat, blinking and swiping at her face when she saw me. "Oh! Oh, I-I ... I'm ... God, I'm s-so s-s-sorry, Marcus." The words dissolved, and she pressed her hand to her lips as if to stop them from spilling out.

With little more than a step, I was at her feet, taking her hand. "Please. Please don't cry. It's all right."

"It's not. Nothing is all right." She seemed to remember herself, straightening up. Her eyes darted around the perimeter, and she jerked her hand back. "Oh God. My mother." She moved to stand, and I did the same. "I don't want to make it any worse for you or your family, and if she sees me with you ..."

"I don't give a goddamn what she sees," I growled.

"Don't say that," she begged, her eyes deep with sadness. "I couldn't bear to be another reason for her to hurt you. Please, for me, Marcus. You have to go." She nudged my arm. "Hurry, before she finds you."

A thousand rounds of no sounded in my mind, and against every instinct, I stepped back. "Meet me tomorrow."

She blinked. "Wh-what?"

"Tomorrow. Eight in the morning at the coffee shop."

Her brows quirked. "But why?"

"Because I want to talk to you, and I can't do that here."

Footsteps approached with Evelyn's voice floating above them. Maisie panicked, a rabbit in a snare.

"Please, Maisie."

She shook her head to clear it, her eyes snapping to mine. "Y-yes. Yes, of course."

I breathed, my lungs stretching in relief. "Good. I'll—"

"Margaret?" Evelyn wielded her name like a knife. "Excuse me, Mr. Bennet," she spat, reaching for Maisie's arm.

But Maisie's face twisted in anger, and she tore herself free. "Let me go."

Evelyn paused, laying a cold look on her before turning her attention to me. "That was quite a show. Better than I could have imagined. Such a shame you'll have to pay for another deposition."

Something in her tone struck me first with curiosity and then understanding. Because Evelyn Bower had baited my mother knowing exactly what would happen.

"You did this," I breathed. "You did this on purpose."

Her smile was all the confirmation I needed. "Careful for hasty accusations. We've seen how well those work out for your kind—just ask your mother." She shifted her gaze to the nothingness in front of her and walked away. "Come, Margaret."

Maisie's gaze bounced from me to her mother to me in indecision. But I gave her a nod, and with a sigh, she followed her mother toward the elevator.

I watched with blind desperation as she walked away, my heart stopping when she looked back.

And I rattled my cage with fury and frustration that she could never be mine.

# The Why Of It

## MAISIE

"**W**hat in the hell were you doing talking to Marcus Bennet?"

I sank into the back seat of the Mercedes, miserable and wretched. "Nothing," I lied. "You interrupted before he could say what he wanted."

She watched me. I kept my eyes trained out the window without seeing anything but red and black.

"You are not to speak to him. Not under any circumstance or for any reason. And if you ever address me that way again, I will take back every single thing I promised you."

"I have no doubt."

She stared a hole in my face, fuming. "I cannot believe your nerve."

"That makes two of us."

"Oh, please, Margaret," she spat. "Nothing that took place should come as a surprise. If you haven't deduced that we are going to strip Rosemary Bennet down to the studs, you haven't been

STACI HART

paying attention." With a shift, she turned to face forward, folding her arms. "Your father has always coddled you. You're soft. Weak. Perhaps I've made a mistake in counting on you."

"I've been telling you that since I was in grade school. You never listen to me."

"*Margaret.*"

Slowly, my face swiveled in her direction. She seethed from the seat beside me.

"That is *enough.*" Her tone was deadly and sharp, the kind of tone that only a stupendous surplus of arrogance could relay. "I'm sorry that you're so tender and feeble that you couldn't see the slightest pressure applied to Rosemary Bennet, of all people. Pull yourself together. Another outburst like that, and your little project is on hold until you earn it back."

Instantly, my cheeks flushed. "I am not a child."

"Then stop acting like one. I expected very little from you to start, but your tantrum was beyond the pale. I'd still love to know why you're so incensed by the lawsuit."

"I'll tell you if you tell me why you hate them so much."

She scowled but said nothing. I shifted my gaze back to the window.

"I didn't think so," I said flatly. "You probably shouldn't bring me to another of those meetings."

"Wouldn't you like that? No, I think you'll be going to *more* legal meetings. Perhaps we'll toughen you up in the pits. Maybe the only way for you to learn is by doing, and I can think of so many things I could have you do."

Though I had much to say, I didn't speak, knowing the conversation wouldn't end until either she'd gotten the last word or I'd blown everything to hell.

Blowing everything to hell sounded so nice though.

I asked myself what I was doing here, just as I had a hundred times. With a well-worn list of reasons in hand, I silently recited each point in the hopes that I'd convince myself the abuse was worthwhile.

She honestly had no idea why I was upset, couldn't understand how I wasn't on board the crazy train, shouting, *Tallyho*. She couldn't see that watching her hurt good people hurt me. Not only for the injustice of it all, which on its own set me on fire.

The Bennets' circumstance was a mirror, a reflection of my relationship with my mother. A tugging of strings, a careful setup. A web of deceit and manipulation, woven to snare all the things she wanted. What she was doing to the Bennets, she had done to me my whole life. For a long time, I hadn't even realized it. And when I finally discovered it ... well, they said you couldn't unring the bell. And though I'd gotten away for a moment, I'd never truly escaped.

Standing up for the Bennets had felt like standing up for myself in so many ways. Not that it did either of us any good.

But it sure felt good to try.

The rest of the ride was endured in indignant silence. When we walked through the front door, we split like a fork in the road, her marching to her office and me hurrying up the stairs on a path to my room. The door closed too loudly behind me, and the second it was shut, the second I was alone, my thin shell of defiance cracked and crumbled, and there was nothing left to hold me together.

I sank into bed, pulling a pillow into my lap to wrap my arms around and squeeze. To bury my face in and cry. And I made myself as small as I felt, as inconsequential as I was.

I had been born to be her puppet, to do what she wanted, say what she wanted, be who she wanted. And if I didn't, she would take it all away. My shares and my trust. My power and future. My charity and joy. She would lay it all to waste, including Marcus, if she suspected I cared for him. If she couldn't ruin him, she'd find a way to make him hate me, just to prove a point.

My tears ebbed as a familiar rebellion rose in me. Because I didn't have to participate in this.

In fact, disengaging from all of it sounded like a sublime idea.

I'd rather be poor and alone if it meant my life was my own. The alternative was to fall in line, and I honestly didn't know if I could do it.

I didn't have it in me, like she'd said. And I, for one, didn't consider that a bad thing.

The snick of my door opening marked my father's entrance, and on seeing me, his face bent in worry and fury.

When I was firmly in his arms, a fresh wave of tears surged. I was grateful for his warmth, for his love. Thankful that I didn't have to hug my pillow.

I had him.

As I was tucked into his chest, he stroked my hair and let me cry without asking questions. He just let me be what I was. Who I was.

It was a good while before I finally calmed down. With a sniffle, I removed myself from Dad's arms even though I didn't want to.

Grim concern colored his face. Not the cursory sort of concern, but a disturbed distress that troubled me right back.

"What did she do?" he asked darkly.

"Nothing I didn't expect."

"Don't do that. Don't make excuses for her behavior."

"But it's true. She did exactly what I knew she would. She made a ruthless show of it all, prodded and jabbed at them until they fought back. I knew she would, somehow. But knowing a thing and living it isn't quite the same, is it?"

He sighed, dragging a hand through his hair. "No. No, it isn't. Is Rosemary all right?"

"No, I don't think she is. It was awful. It was so hard to be in that room, to listen to her lawyer strip down every person who sat in that chair until they betrayed Mrs. Bennet, undermined her character, even using them against each other. The second Mother saw an opening, she took her shot. I wish I hadn't been there. I wish she hadn't made me go there with her to tear those people down. And in the end, I'm just left wondering *why*. Why is she this way? Whatever did they do to her to deserve this?"

His jaw clenched and flexed, his brows drawing tighter. He glanced at the closed door, and something about the look on his face set the hairs on the back of my neck tingling with anticipation.

"I suppose it's time you know. She's threatened me with everything she could throw at me if I told you."

"Tell me what?" I breathed. "What happened?"

A heavy sigh. A pause.

And then he spoke, "It feels like a million years ago, like another life. A story of someone who only exists in memory. The man I was then and the man I've become are so distant, I don't even know how to connect them." He shook his head and met my eyes. "Before I dated your mother, I was with Rosemary Bennet."

My mouth fell open.

"And your mother was with Paul Bennet."

"*What?*" I asked stupidly, the question falling out of me in shock.

He ran a hand across his chin to the sound of stubble against skin. "Well, he was Paul Christy at the time. I can't tell you the blind rage your mother flew into when he took Rosemary's name."

I blinked at him.

"Your grandmother didn't approve. He was no one by their measure, a boy from the prep school we all went to. He'd gotten in on one of the few scholarships they offered, the son of a plumber. You can imagine what the Bowers thought of him. But Evelyn didn't care. She loved him, back when she still had love to give, back when she was soft and smiled with her eyes. Defied her parents' authority to see him. It was a whole thing."

"I'll bet."

"Rosemary and I dated our junior and senior year, and your mother dated Paul through the same time. We didn't mix much, ran in different crowds. But the summer after graduation, the four of us were dragged to a charity ball. Your mother was strictly forbidden to bring Paul, and Rosemary came up with an idea at garden club—we'd all switch dates, and Paul would sneak in with Rosemary. And the second they arrived, Evelyn and I took one look at the two of them and knew. Something about the way they looked at each other. Something about the way he held her close." Another sigh, a shake of his head. "Your mother was furious, detonated on the spot. Launched herself at Rosemary and took her down in a screeching bundle of arms and legs. The blast radius grew to her parents intervening, then to Paul getting kicked out of the building. And Rosemary and I watched on because there was nothing we could do. She broke up with me in the cab on the way home."

"Did you love her?" I asked quietly.

But he laughed, a small, breathy sound. "The way any teenage boy loves a girl. She wasn't the love of my life, though after your mother, I suppose she was the closest I've ever gotten. I was crushed, but truth be told, I'd been wondering about our future myself. Where we would go next, if we'd even end up in the same city. No, Rosie was meant for Paul. I don't know why it took us all so long to figure it out."

I frowned, shaking my head. "But then how did you ..."

His smile faded. "Looking back, I know your mother falling into my arms had more to do with making Paul jealous than it ever had to do with me. At the time—God, I can't believe we were ever so young ..." A pause. "I thought it just made sense. We were grieving together, looking for comfort after a heartbreak. I didn't realize it when she got pregnant, didn't understand even when we walked down the aisle. I was dumb enough to think I could even learn to love her. She watched Rosemary and Paul get married and run Longbourne and have all those kids. And all your mother did was build her business and spend her spare time resenting me and her mother and Rosemary. Evelyn went after her fortune, and I've always held a suspicion that all that hard work was to spite Rosemary. Maybe she thought money would make her happy. Maybe she thought she could put herself above Rosemary, to look down at her and feel like she'd won. Either way, Evelyn was wrong. The Bennets might not have money, but they have everything she wants."

I sat for a moment in stunned silence.

My past and present fluttered like a flip book, every picture flashing to make a whole. Her bitter rivalry. Her determination to ruin the Bennets. Her mistreatment of my father.

And in that understanding, I found a solemn sort of peace.

Dad watched me. "Are you all right?"

"I feel like you just threw open the curtains and illuminated the room. Why didn't you ever tell me?"

"Aside from your mother's threats? It never mattered before. But now that you've been dragged into the middle of it, you should know why."

"Why didn't she want me to know?"

"Pride, if I had to guess. There aren't many people who knew or cared enough, and I think your mother would prefer no one know she lost a man to Rosemary Bennet."

I sat for a silent second. "I didn't think it was possible to be more opposed to this lawsuit, but you've done it."

"I'm sorry. I'm sorry for all of it. I'm sorry for agreeing to the whole thing in the first place."

"Why did you?"

"Because she was pregnant with my child. Because I thought it was the right thing to do. When she lost the baby … I don't know. We found each other in our grief, held on to each other to survive the loss. It was a girl. Elizabeth, we named her. Evelyn was in her last few weeks."

A shock of emotion gripped me, squeezed my throat, stung my nose. I'd never heard my mother mention her first pregnancy, and my father had only spoken of it a few times, never in detail.

I'd never heard my sister's name, and the pain in his voice when he spoke it shook me to my core.

For the first time in my adult life, I imagined my mother having a heart. The thought was astonishing, unnerving. Like peering into the window of a stranger's life, though I'd known her all my life.

"After that, we were trying for you, and again, I thought ..." He trailed off. "Those were the happiest years we had. I think she tried. But your mother never loved me. I was a means to an end. A warm body. A contractual obligation. Nothing more. When you were born, she shut me out. Shut you out. Shut out the world. She wouldn't see a doctor for her depression, wouldn't let me help her. And things just ... disintegrated. When your grandmother died, I think your mother stepped into her life as a way to cope, not realizing she'd replaced Felicity in all ways. And here we are. I'm not at all surprised she's still trying to hurt Rosemary. Two Bower women in a row were jilted by the Bennets, and it made the Bowers miserable. They call it a curse. I say it's self-inflicted." I must have looked worried because he added with a teasing smile, "Don't worry. I think it'll skip your generation."

"I don't think it has," I said softly, my heart lodged in my throat.

"Why do you say that?"

I looked up, met his eyes. "A truth for a truth. I owe you one."

His gaze darkened. "The truth about what, Maisie?"

"I ... I kissed Marcus Bennet."

He stilled.

"Well, I mean, he kissed me, but I asked him to," I rambled, "so I'm not really sure who kissed whom, but we did. We kissed."

"How ..."

"It was chance. I ran into him in the rain. Literally ran into him, and he took me to a coffee shop and asked me out. Well, I asked him out. And a half hour later, he walked into the boardroom, representing his mother."

He ran his hand over his mouth in a long, slow stroke. "Maisie, you can't—"

"I know. I know we can't, and he does too. But I hate it, Dad. I hate it so much." The catch of my voice prompted me to swallow. "And after today, I'm not altogether convinced I shouldn't just pack my things and leave. Forsake it all because what kind of life will I live if it's under *her*?" My breath hitched, and I swallowed a sob. "I don't want to end up like her, Daddy. I can't."

"Oh, sweetheart," he said, pulling me into his arms again. "You will never end up like her."

"Even if I end up loveless? Will I spite and resent her so much that I become her, just like she became her mother?"

"No. You won't end up like that. I promise."

"You can't promise that."

He didn't argue.

I backed away, wiping my cheeks. "I can't live like this. I can't."

"Then don't."

"You would support me leaving?" I asked hopefully.

"I'll support anything you want, but that's not what I meant. You have something she wants, Maisie. She's doing an awful lot of negotiating, considering it's *you* she has to convince to stay."

I sniffled, thinking it through. "So I should try to bargain with her?"

"Your mother doesn't bargain. She demands, and so should you. Because here's the thing—there *is* a place for you here. Think of all you could do with this company when those shares are in your hands. If you play it right, you can inherit a vehicle to elicit change and good in the world. You can reshape the company. And most importantly, you can stick it to your mother."

I couldn't help but chuckle.

"If that isn't enough for you to stay, I understand. If you don't want to be yoked to your mother for another minute, I will back you up. If you're ready to go, say the word and I'll take you anywhere you want to go. But before you give up for good, I think you should put up a fight."

"Do you really think it would work?"

"You're ready to walk away, right?"

"I am," I answered with certainty.

"Then what do you have to lose if it doesn't?"

A feeling arose in me, a slow rise of light, of hope, of purpose and freedom. Because she had nothing left to hold over me that I wasn't willing to give up. The power shifted to me, slid into my waiting hand and blazed in defiance.

I would make my stand. Make my demands.

And for once, she would give me what *I* wanted.

"All right," I said with a bold streak of rebellion fluttering in my belly, "I'll do it."

He smiled, cupping my cheek. "Attagirl." He made to stand, pausing to press a kiss to my forehead. "I believe in you above all, Maisie. You can do anything you put your mind to."

"Thank you. For believing."

"You're welcome," he said, turning to go. "But do us all a favor and stay away from Marcus Bennet."

And I laughed like that was possible.

Because there was one more rebellion I'd make.

And he'd be waiting for me in the morning.

# Satisfaction Guaranteed

## MARCUS

I walked up to the coffee shop the next morning with determination I shouldn't have, considering I had no plan.

Winging things was not in my nature. I came into every moment of my life equipped with a plan and a contingency plan. Nothing was left to chance—not if I could help it—and if it had to be, I planned even for that.

But when it came to Maisie, there were no steps to take, no outcome to predict. There was no logic to apply. Only the undeniable intention to unearth what was between us.

This, coupled with the knowledge that I couldn't have what I'd found.

The risk was too great for her, and I knew I should warn her off. I should refuse her for the sake of her future. But then the reminder of what that would mean for her well-being to stay would rise within me, and the compulsion to save her would overshadow all reasoning.

This was not my decision to make. It couldn't be. Because if it were, I would defy all consequences and claim her for mine.

Fuck the rules if the rules involved Evelyn Bower telling anyone what to do.

The coffee shop was warm, or maybe it was just me. I scanned the room for her in vain, both disappointed and unsurprised—I was early, unable to stall, too anxious to get here. Too ready to know what would come next.

I ordered coffees for us both—I remembered what she'd ordered, remembered what she'd said, remembered every moment I'd spent with her. And once drinks were in hand, I took stock of the available tables, looking for the perfect one. Something close enough to the window but without the exposure, something private enough without being tucked away in a dark corner.

Of course, a dark corner didn't sound like the worst idea I'd ever had.

My mind buzzed with eager dread as I took a seat at a table for two, putting my back against the wall so I could see when she entered. If she entered. But she would. I didn't know how I knew, but I did.

A few minutes after eight, I basked in my rightness.

Maisie was the portrait of loveliness. A streak of light illuminated her hair, illuminating the golden curls like a halo. Her face, small and shaped like a heart, was alight from within, her eyes locking on mine the moment she passed the threshold. With a longing smile, she floated in my direction, our gazes never disconnecting.

"Hi," she said softly, adjusting her bag on her shoulder.

"Hi," I echoed, too struck to be clever.

She drew a breath to fortify herself and set her bag next to the chair. "Is that for me, or did you need that much of a pick-me-up this morning?" Her eyes flicked to the table, but I was too busy watching her slip off her tan wool coat, revealing a crimson dress that somehow managed to be both sweet and suggestive.

Something about the cut maybe, the tasteful V of her neckline, the swinging grace of her skirt.

"Hmm? Oh," I started, glancing down at her coffee. "I got you a flat white. That's what you drink, right?"

"It is," she answered with a smile as she sat. "Thank you."

I watched her fingers wrap around the cup as she took it, watched her lips as they met the rim of the cup for a sampling.

"I'm sorry I'm late," she said. "My mother had a hard time taking no for an answer when I made excuses so I didn't have to ride with her to work."

"I imagine she did." I tried to school the distaste out of my voice without luck. "I'm glad you came, Maisie. We have a lot to talk about."

A flush rose in her cheeks, her eyes lighting with hope. "Like what?"

*Like how I can have you. What would it take? What would it cost you? Would you even want me?*

"Like what exactly your mother has over you," I said instead, wondering first what I was up against. "There has to be some way I can help."

"Oh." She looked down at her hands. "I … I thought that maybe …" She laughed rather than finish, waving her hand in dismissal. "Never mind. What exactly do you propose to help me with?"

My pause was pregnant with uncertainty that I had any reason to hope. "What did you think I wanted to talk about?" I asked quietly.

Her fair cheeks flamed. "Nothing."

"Did you think I wanted to talk about us?" I chanced.

"I'd be lying if I said I hadn't hoped."

Relief bloomed in my chest, a leap of my heart, a rush of deliverance. "I'd be lying if I said I didn't come here to. If you and I had been alone yesterday when I found you crying, this conversation would be very different."

"How so?"

My eyes fell to my hand as I reached across the table for hers. "For starters, we wouldn't be here."

"No?" she breathed.

"No. We'd be at my place, and you'd be wearing less than this."

"Oh," left her lips as a whisper. "And what would we be talking about?"

I traced the shape of her knuckle with my thumb. "How to see each other with all of this between us."

"What's stopping you now?"

"Only that there's no solution, not one where you don't give up more than I would ask. What would you lose?"

She turned her hand, threading her fingers with mine. "What if I told you it didn't matter? What if I told you I was ready to walk away?"

"I'd say you were crazy. And I'd tell you to do it."

A chuckle. "Well, my mother inspires crazy in people." She paused, and for that moment, we were preoccupied with the sight of our hands entwined on the café table. "I came back from England because she promised me almost half of her shares over the next ten years, provided I do exactly what she wants. And she gave me the charity I started after college, though she hasn't held up her end of our deal. But yesterday ... yesterday, I realized I *can't* do exactly what she wants. I have to find out if there's a way to do what *I* want inside of what she wants. And if not, I can't stay." With a breath and a sad smile, she said, "I have nothing to lose and everything to gain."

Recognition and pride struck me. "That's exactly what I told my family when it came to fighting your mother."

Her dark eyes snagged mine. "I think we have a lot more in common than we realized, Marcus."

"I think you might be right." I shook my head. "I won't stand by and watch her destroy everything good in my world. Including you. I'll do whatever I have to do to strip her of her power. So tell me how I can help, and I'll do it."

"I hope you won't have to. I can't pretend for another day that I can do this. And so, today I'll raise my bet and see if she antes up."

"Do you think she'll fold?"

"Not a chance in hell," she answered bravely. "But then that will be that. And I'll do what I please with no one left to stop me."

"And your inheritance? Your future?"

"Well, if I know my mother, my money, home, and relationship with her will disappear, as will my place at Bower along with any opportunity to do something meaningful there. I suppose I'll get a job in public service somewhere, another charity maybe. Anywhere, as long as it makes me happy. That's really all I want—to be happy. And as for my future, well"—she looked up at me with timid hope—"that depends on you."

*Sweet God, when you look at me like that* ... I thought, pressing down hope of my own, reluctant to accept the implication that she wanted me until I knew for sure.

"If your happiness depends on me, I could deliver as soon as right now. Every thought since I first met you has been chased by the memory of you. But what I want is secondary to what you need. Maisie, you need to be sure. I can't ..." *let you in, lose you, lose myself* "Are you sure?"

She considered the question for only a heartbeat. "When I think about walking away, I don't feel afraid. I feel relieved. Would you be on the other side?"

"I would be," I said quietly.

Worry gathered her brows. "I'm not the only one who has something to lose. What about your family? Your future? The lawsuit? Wouldn't I put you in danger too?"

"It's nothing I can't handle. The lawsuit would likely get harder, yes. But it would be easier to ruin your mother if you weren't in the room—I can't deny that."

She chuckled.

"My family will love you, and renouncing Bower would go a long way in terms of brownie points."

Her lips curled up in a smile. "You said *will*. Not would or could, but will."

"I did, didn't I?" My mind raced with possibility, my smile light with the fantasy of having her after believing I never would. But that smile fell as I searched for pitfalls. "What happens if your mother accepts your terms?"

The weight of that question made itself known.

But she answered, "Then I suppose I'll have to add a term to that ultimatum. You."

I could have burst out of my skin and taken flight. "But not yet," I amended, stroking her hand, watching her lips. "Don't put yourself on the line for me, not until you know. In the meantime, we'll keep it a secret."

"Until after the lawsuit," she added. "It'll give us time to figure out what this is, and we'll know where the chips fall. If she finds out before …" Her face fell. "If we think she's bad now, she'll be impossible once she finds out. And your family will pay for it."

"Don't worry—we'll do our best to make sure she doesn't find out until we're ready, until all this is over. It'll make it easier to break the news to everyone if we know who's won and lost."

"Exactly, and it won't put any more stress on your mother."

"What about yours?" I asked.

"I couldn't give a good goddamn about what stresses her. And if today goes like I think it will, it won't matter."

"And the lawsuit? Will she keep forcing you into the middle of it?"

That smile of hers widened. "I'll give her that, because it will allow one very useful thing—I will be privy to every move my mother makes. Which means you will be too."

"A spy, huh?"

"Why not? It's one of the few ways I can help you. Because what she's doing is cruel, and if I don't do something to try to stop her, I won't be able to live with myself."

"Maisie," I started, my heart thudding painfully in my ribs as I gave her a final out, "I don't want to be something you regret."

"If I can have you, it's because I've made a choice for myself. And I could never, ever regret that."

"Come here," I said, my throat tight as I tugged her hand and leaned back to make room for her.

She took the signal, standing to make her way to me. I snagged her waist the second she was within reach and guided her into my lap.

Her arms wound around my neck, her eyes on my lips and breath shallow. And I looked into her eyes, cupped her face, and wondered if I was already lost.

"Maisie?"

"Yes?"

I thumbed her bottom lip, savoring the feel of her weight in my lap. "I'm about to kiss you, right here in this café, in front of all these people. I'm about to taste the lips that have haunted me since I tasted them last. I'm about to kiss you, Maisie, and when I do, I'm—"

Her lips crashed against mine, hard with determination, mine firm from surprise. But a heartbeat was all it took for the sweetness of her mouth to soften, to open, to meld in a seam that sealed more than our lips. It sealed a promise, a wish, a longing I'd believed would never be satisfied.

And if I learned anything from that long, languid kiss, it was that satisfaction was guaranteed.

The kiss slowed, stopped, and when she leaned back with heavy lids, she laughed. "I'm sorry, but I thought you'd never shut up."

I stole another kiss. "Come to my place tonight. I'll make dinner, and you can tell me what happened with your mother."

Her smile faded, the light in her dimming at the mention. "At least it'll give me something to look forward to."

"Yes, it will. Whatever happens, I'm here. Just say the word."

"Thank you. For all of it, Marcus. Thank you."

"Don't thank me yet."

But she smirked. "Don't tell me what to do. I think I've had enough of that."

"Should I ask you to kiss me again?" I baited with a tilted smile.

"Oh, no—you can tell me to do that anytime you want."

And she granted my wish, just like I'd hoped she would.

# Pavlovian

## MAISIE

**A**gainst all odds, I found myself kissing Marcus Bennet, curled up in his lap like a cat, boneless and braindead in his arms. At eight-something in the morning. In front of twenty people.

And I couldn't have been happier about it.

We parted with a sigh, the blue of his irises barely visible for his wide black pupils. Both of us smiled sheepishly.

"Tonight at eight." His words came out rough and hot, words that said we would be doing a lot more than eating dinner and talking about my mother.

My stomach flipped at the thought.

"I don't want to leave," I said, fiddling with his lapel.

"I know. But go do what you need to do. I'll send you my address. Just let me know what happened when it's all said and done."

"I'll probably be on my way home to pack my things," I joked, not at all joking.

"You never know. Maybe she'll surprise you. She's good at that."

"It's one of her special gifts." I slid off Marcus's lap, ignoring the looks from a few surrounding tables. When I turned, I bit down a smile at the sight of him discreetly adjusting his pants before standing.

One dark brow rose with the corner of his mouth when he caught me looking. "Can I get you a cab?"

"I suppose we can't share one," I lamented, pulling on my coat.

"Probably not. Anyway, I'm heading home to help Mom prepare for our next shot at her deposition."

"Your poor mother." I hung my head, wishing there was more I could do. "I couldn't even stand it yesterday. I had to say something. I was going to burst into flames if I didn't."

"It was the bravest, most perfect thing you could have done. If I hadn't wanted you before that moment, you would have changed my mind right then and there." He laid a broad hand on the small of my back, stepping into me. "I wanted to grab you and steal you and kiss you."

"I would have held on and gone quietly and kissed you right back."

He pressed a lingering, promissory kiss to my lips before guiding me out.

Marcus walked me to the curb, and with a final brush of his lips, he put me in the cab.

The second the door thumped closed, it cut me off from my joy, leaving it with Marcus there on the busy sidewalk.

Dread settled over me, into me, sinking into my stomach, weighting my lungs. It was the tingling sense of danger, the knowledge that I was about to walk into a fight that could set my life on a course I'd never expected. I had no map, and the road before me disappeared into craggy mountains, the path unfamiliar, uncertain when my life to this point had been planned out so precisely by my mother, charted and mapped and visible from space.

It was unnerving. But it was exciting too, and the promise of what was around the bend fueled my confidence as I stepped out of the cab and into the building my mother occupied.

She didn't occupy the whole thing, of course, only five meager floors of the towering building in Midtown. But she might as well have filled all seventy floors for the space her ego took up.

With every open and close of the elevator doors, my anxiety climbed, my hopes shrinking under the shadow of what I was about to do. Through the bullpen of her floor I walked, enduring the occasional *Hello, Ms. Bower.* But my eyes were on the office down the hall, and my mind was consumed with a ticking countdown to my fate.

Shelby popped out of her seat when she saw me, her brows drawn. "Maisie? Did you have an appointment this morning?"

"No, but I was hoping to talk to her for a minute. Does she have time?"

"She has twenty minutes until Roland arrives for take seven of the elusive finance meeting, so I'm sure she'll welcome the opportunity to avoid it."

I couldn't even laugh. Or smile. Or even remember what she'd said, my eyes on the doors to her office. "Good. Thank you."

"She'd kill me for not insisting, but do you want me to announce you?"

"No, thank you. May as well make it a surprise all the way around."

Shelby's head cocked, but she waved me on. "Well, good luck."

"I'm gonna need it," I said under my breath as I opened the door.

My mother looked up from her grand desk, somehow managing to appear both surprised and annoyed. "Have you come to explain where you've been going every morning? Because you've exhausted my patience where that is concerned." When I didn't immediately answer, one of her brows rose. "No? Well, I hope you've enjoyed it, because that ends as of today. What do you want then, Margaret? I thought you were down at your little project today."

"Well, there's been a change of plans."

She glanced at my dress. "Perhaps you should have considered a change of plans regarding your dress as well, dear."

I ignored the jab, walking up to her desk with my chin up and shoulders back. My heart, however, did not have such confidence. It beat so painfully fast, I wondered briefly if I was about to have an anxiety attack.

"Sit," she commanded.

"I'd rather stand, thank you."

At that, she took off her glasses and leaned back in her chair, assessing me coolly. "Well then, go ahead."

I took a breath, my dry throat working to swallow. *You have nothing to lose. It's about to be over one way or another, so jump, Maisie. Jump.*

So I took a breath and did just that. "I think we both knew that my return to Bower wouldn't be smooth or easy. But I expected at least the most basic respect."

"And I expected you to do as you were told."

I drew a long breath to keep ahold of my temper. "Had you not taken my charity from me, I probably would have. But there's no repairing what's happened between us, and though I know you don't believe it, there's no amount of force that will change that. We find ourselves here, and I'd like to remind you that I'm not a toy. I'm not a doll for you to play with or a pretty little handbag for you to show off. I've allowed you to dictate what I can and can't do. But not anymore."

Her eyes narrowed, but she didn't speak.

"It seems to me that I have something you want, and you have nothing I require. You want me to head this company, to be a replica of you, and you want it so badly, you've lured me back to do just that. But I certainly have no interest in being your plaything, nor am I willing to be berated by you anymore. No amount of money or power will change that."

"So what do you propose?"

I lifted my chin. "If you want me to be your successor, then it will be on my terms."

"And if I refuse?"

"Then I'll go."

A long, silent moment passed.

"I see. And what *are* your lofty terms?"

"The charity will be mine to do with as I please with all the funding I wish and all the hours to devote to it that I like. You will not force me to do what isn't necessary—including monitoring my comings and goings—and otherwise, you'll stay out of my way."

Her face remained unchanged, which was perhaps most terrifying of all.

"Tell me, Margaret—what do I get out of this deal?"

A bubbling tension simmered in my belly, one both hopeful and averse. "You will acquire the heir you so desperately want. I will also concede to a short list of required tasks, such as attending board meetings and shadowing executives, but we'll define boundaries to determine what's considered *necessary*. If I'm to run Bower one day, I need to know how it all works, but you'll give me the freedom to participate on my terms, which we both know aren't unreasonable."

Tension crackled in the air between us.

"You came in here prepared to leave, didn't you?"

I drew myself taller to mask my fear. "I did. I am."

I waited for her to thrash. To yell and fume and sling everything she could at me. My trust fund. The life I knew. My home. My father. Bower. The charity. Braced for impact, I held my breath and waited for her to stand up and fight me.

But instead, she smiled.

It wasn't a kind smile or a smile of pride. It wasn't maternal, and it held no empathy.

Hers was a smile of triumph, as if she'd won a battle I hadn't known we were fighting.

"That, Margaret Bower, is exactly what I have been waiting for."

I blinked, confused. "Y-you've been waiting for me to leave?"

"I've been waiting for you to fight. To decide what you want and demand it. You've been so useless to me since your return, I was beginning to think there was no hope. Do you know why I brought you here?" She didn't wait for an answer. "One day, this will be yours, and it's my duty to prepare you for that. Your disapproval of my methods doesn't matter in the end, not if you rise to the challenge as you have today. For perhaps the first time, you've given me a reason to be optimistic."

My stomach turned as she flipped open her notebook and picked up a pen.

"Let's discuss these *boundaries*, shall we?" she said as she began to write. "You will attend *all* promotional appearances and board meetings regardless of whether or not you want to attend. That is nonnegotiable. As is your attendance in the Bennet proceedings."

"All right."

I must have answered too quickly, too boldly, because she looked up at me with a narrow, scrutinizing gaze.

"You are willing to attend the Bennet meetings without causing a scene? Without arguing or undermining me? You will be the picture of compliance regardless of what is said?"

"Yes. I knew you'd demand it of me." *And I want to know what you're plotting.*

"A well-thought-out deal. You surprise me."

I kept my head up and hands still, but my thoughts were a bumble of buzzing bees as she went on to note a few more requirements from her, none unreasonable. Otherwise, I was free to do what I wanted without interference. All I had to do was keep up my end of the bargain.

Of course, we'd done this dance before, and we both knew who was leading.

We said our goodbyes, and I left the office on shaky legs, my disbelief and discomfort dimming my surroundings. I breezed past Shelby with a cursory nod, heading for the elevator that would take me down to the charity division where I planned to spend my day.

As the elevator doors closed, a thought unnerved me.

I'd pleased her. And nothing about it felt good.

It wasn't the happy approval I imagined other mothers gave. Nothing about the exchange made me feel warm or tender.

Had she been holding me down to force me to fight? Was my assertion a response to something she'd planned? Had I been trained against my will to do what she pleased, like Pavlov's dog panting for its dinner when she rang the bell?

Would I end up like her whether I wanted to or not?

As much as I flexed and fought, could I ever win? Or would that cycle continue on and on, our history destined to repeat itself? Perhaps I'd lose a man to the Bennets in a whole new way and disintegrate into bitter remains, just as my mother had.

*No*, I told myself. Because I would hold on with both hands to what I wanted. I would do my duty here in the hopes that I would someday earn the power to push back. I'd fight that future. I'd fight her until the bitter end if it meant I could avoid her fate.

And I assured myself I knew what I was doing even though I had my doubts.

## MARCUS

I couldn't escape the clock.

From the second Maisie and I had parted ways, the day crawled past. First with the clock in my mother's study, ticking incessantly as I attempted to coach her on deposition questions. Then it was the time on my phone while I worked on billing, the screen flashing every thirty seconds with messages as my siblings blew up our group text with a string of shit-talking. While I worked out, the clock on the wall moved at an infinitesimal speed in a defiance of the laws of science.

Even now, as I checked the temperature of the pork loin I knew wasn't done, the time on the oven was right there in my face, the colon blinking at me like laughter. The microwave clock was no better, an aggressive shade of red that reminded me she wasn't here yet.

So I paced around my house, straightened the silverware and place settings on the table. I refolded the blanket on my couch, hanging it artfully on the back in a drape that suited me a little better. On inspection, I noticed there was dust on my TV stand, so I beelined for the kitchen for supplies to right that infraction before somebody saw it.

But before I could, the doorbell rang, and my heart shot into my throat.

I hurried to the door, partly because I wanted to see her that badly, partly because the longer she waited outside, the higher the chance that someone in my family would pass by and see her standing on my doorstep.

When I opened the door, I found Maisie on my stoop, conspicuously looking over her shoulder. In fact, everything about her was conspicuous—the big, floppy hat and sunglasses that obscured most of her face, her tan wool coat, which was buttoned up tight, the lapels clutched in one small fist.

She whirled around in surprise, smiling sheepishly, her flush nearly masking the tiny freckles on her cheeks and nose.

"You look like Carmen Sandiego," I said on a laugh, reaching for her hand to tug her into my entryway.

The door shut behind her.

And then we were alone.

The relief was instant, the separation from the world beyond that door tangible. Because here, we could just be Maisie and Marcus, not a Bower and a Bennet.

"I feel more like Inspector Gadget, clumsy and jumpy and getting by on sheer luck," she said on a giggle, pulling off her glasses first, then her hat.

I helped her out of her coat, grateful to find her still in that red dress I'd been thinking about since this morning. "Was it hard to get away?"

"Not too bad." She shook out her curly hair with her fingers. "Mother usually ignores me when she doesn't need something from me. She ate separate from Dad and me, as usual, so I told Dad I was having dinner with a friend. He didn't ask questions."

"I told my family I was working late. I'm pretty sure they

bought it." I headed toward the kitchen, snagging her hand on the way.

She frowned. "But you live alone."

"We have a family dinner every night. Not everyone makes it nightly, but I've only missed a handful of dinners in the last couple of years."

I deposited her on a stool at the island, finding her smiling when I walked around. "I've always dreamed of a family like that."

I snorted a laugh. "You've clearly never had dinner with my family."

"I can't imagine it would be worse than mine." She said it lightly, as if it were a joke, but I heard the edge of a long-worn scar beneath the levity.

"Mother lives in her office, takes her meals there, spends every waking minute behind those doors. I wouldn't be surprised if she occasionally sleeps there. That big, grand house, and she only uses one room." She shook her head. "Anyway, Dad and I usually have dinner together. As anxious as I was to get here, I hated to leave him to eat alone. He eats by himself too often as it is."

"That sounds very lonely."

"It is," was all she said.

So I changed the subject. "Red wine or white?"

"Either is fine."

I reached for the bottle of pinot noir I'd set out, popping it open and pouring into waiting wineglasses. When hers was in hand, she extended it for a toast.

"To the things we want. May they all be ours."

I brought my glass to hers in a click of agreement, and for a silent second, we drank.

She set her drink on the shiny quartz surface and smiled up at me.

"Tell me about your day," I said with an answering smile, leaning on the island across from her.

"Well, I don't think a single thing happened the way I thought it would, not from the second I walked into the coffee shop. It exceeded all expectations."

I watched her take a sip of crimson wine, watched it slip past her lips. Something so small, so mundane, and I found myself consumed by the sight, imagining those lips against mine again. Imagining the feel of her in my lap, here in my house where I could do something about it.

She sighed, an expression of contentment on her face. "My mother surprised me even more than you did, I think—I'd hoped we would end up here, even if I didn't believe we would. But I never could have guessed that she'd be compliant. I expected threats. Shouting. The squeeze of her control. Instead, I told her what I wanted, and she agreed. I'll have full control over the charity and time to manage it, and in exchange, I accepted a list of terms she devised. And not a single one of them was excessive. It'll be bearable though, I think." Another sigh. "We'll see. You know what the most upsetting, unnatural part was?"

"Everything about her is unnatural, so I can't imagine."

"She seemed pleased with me. And not in some *good for you, chuck on the shoulder* kind of proud. It was ... I don't know." She shook her head. "It's probably nothing."

"Tell me," I urged.

Her brow furrowed. "I think she planned it. I think she pushed me until I stood up to her to teach me some sort of lesson, and I complied without realizing she'd manipulated me. I didn't feel good about it when I left. But I got what I wanted, which, all in all, leaves me confused."

I rankled at the thought of Evelyn exacting any more control on Maisie.

"Some days, I wonder if I even have a choice," she said, half to herself. "Maybe turning into her is inevitable."

"You always have a choice. And you are nothing like her."

"Maybe, maybe not. Maybe even now I'm more like her than I realize. Maybe somewhere inside of me, she's there, waiting to be let out. What if it's all a setup? And one day, she'll pull a rip cord and let the monster she bred out of me."

"Never. She has no real power over who you *are*. Nothing she could do would change who you are at your core, the woman your father raised."

Her smile was one of resignation, one that said she wasn't so sure. "Thank you."

Neither of us spoke for a moment until I asked a question that'd been on my mind since the beginning.

"What's keeping you at Bower? What about that place compels you to stay?"

She thought, her eyes on the claret wine in her glass. "Mostly I've stayed because, as the heiress, I have a vested interest in Bower. As a child, I was largely sheltered from her. She was just a person who was sometimes around for holidays and the occasional weekend, like having a parent who's a surgeon. A busy, distant presence in my life, one that I idolized simply because I didn't know differently. But she was a stranger to me, and it wasn't until I worked there after college that I really saw her for who she was and what I meant to her, which was nothing. But it's more than that ..." She paused, searching for words.

When she found them, she took a breath and met my eyes. "When I was a little girl, we didn't go to church—we worshipped Bower Bouquets. Bower has been the lifeblood of my family for generations, the cornerstone of every decision we make, personal or otherwise. It isn't a company, not to my mother. It's a religion. And that religion has shaped every part of me—my ambitions, my work ethic, my relationships, even my major in college. It's shaped me in ways I probably don't even realize. I've been conditioned to be a part of Bower. No," she corrected. "I suppose it's a part of me. And even though I'm ready to walk away, there's this ... I don't know. It's a fear, I guess, one that goes beyond money or family. There's this irrational sense of foreboding, as if walking away will somehow upset the balance of the universe."

The weight of her words settled on me.

"You must understand, as close as you are to your family," she urged. "It's a sense of devotion, though for me, that devotion is born of obligation."

"I do understand. Longbourne is so tied up with our relationships, I don't know how to separate them. That flower shop is another member of our family. The thought of it ending or closing is unfathomable. We'd be lost without it."

"Exactly, though your commitment is founded in your love of your family. Mine is rooted strictly and deeply in fear."

"When did you realize it?"

"Before I left for England. Out of college, I had this starry-eyed daydream of my future, the kind of thing only a kid would believe. A fairy tale. I'd come to work with my mother at Bower. I'd find a happy little nook, do what I'd been born to. Worse ..." She hesitated. "I ... I thought I'd win her approval. Sure, my mother was bitchy and overbearing, but wasn't everyone's? That first year that I worked for Bower, I was filled with blind hope. But when she took Harvest Center from me, something in me snapped. It was like rubbing sleep from my eyes—when she came into focus, I saw the unfairness of it all for the first time. She only serves herself, and I'm just a little, inanimate cog in her machine. An important cog but one without rights all the same."

I shook my head. "People like that aren't born. They're bred. I can't imagine what happened to her to make her this way. I always assumed it was indoctrination by her mother—that, or the Bowers had some genetic predisposition to cruelty. But then I met you."

Her face softened, first her brows, then her eyes, then the line of her lips. "I think much of it *was* bred by my grandmother, but Mother hates her for it. Which is funny, seeing as how alike they are, particularly where their daughters are concerned. But ... well, from what I understand, my mother wasn't always like this."

"What changed?"

Maisie squirmed, avoiding my eyes as she took a drink. "I ... I'm not supposed to know. Dad wasn't supposed to tell me."

I frowned. "Tell you what?"

Her throat worked as she swallowed. "Has your mother ever told you about when they were young?"

"Only that they went to school together but weren't friends. Apparently, they weren't enemies either—they left that war to their mothers until they were older, right?"

"That's part of it." Another pause, and I officially needed to know. "Did she ever tell you that my mother used to date your father?"

A hot slash of refusal hit me in the gut. "Impossible."

But she said nothing, only looked at me with deep, dark eyes.

"No. There's no way she could keep that from us, even if she'd wanted to. Even if she'd tried."

"But it's not just that. My father dated your mother too."

I set down my glass with a clink, gripping the counter with damp palms as she told me the story of our parents. The real heart of the rivalry. She told me how her parents ended up married and why her father stayed.

Thoughts pinged around my skull like gravel in a vacuum cleaner. My father with Evelyn Bower. No universe existed wherein that statement could be true. But it was. I could see it on her face.

"I didn't believe it either," she said quietly. "I knew about my parents and the baby they lost, but not how your family was involved. He only told me now because my mother has put me in the middle, and he thought I should know why."

I scrubbed a hand over my mouth. "It would explain ... well, it would explain just about everything. But goddamn." After a pause, I joked, "Bright side—you won't lose a man to the Bennets."

She didn't smile. "But I could. One day, you might be asked to choose, and I don't think you would choose me." Before I could argue, she continued, "And if not, she might lose *me* to the Bennets. I can't imagine that would be much easier for her."

I stepped around the island to her. "I knew telling you what I wanted would put *you* in a position to have to choose. How could I ask so much of you?" I shook my head. "I couldn't. I still don't know if I should."

"Well, that isn't your decision to make, is it?"

"But isn't it my responsibility?"

She shifted in her seat, face upturned as she took my hands. "Is there anything I could say that would convince you that you aren't responsible for my feelings, for my happiness?"

"Nothing."

With the shake of her head, she said, "But you aren't."

"Maybe I want to be."

She stood, stepped into me until our bodies were flush, her hands on my chest and mine on her waist. "I love that you want to be. So few people in my life ever have."

"And fuck every single one of them who haven't. You deserve everything, and I want to give everything to you."

Her cheeks flushed. "You don't even know me, not really."

"You don't believe that," I whispered, sweeping her jaw with my knuckles. "I may not know your favorite color or your middle name, but I know you, somehow. I know you are filled with goodness. I know what you do is for others before yourself. I know your life has been hard for being so privileged, and I know you have not received the love you've given to the world. And as far as I'm concerned, that ends right now."

Her lips parted to speak, but I swallowed her answer with a kiss, unwilling to let her speak, knowing I'd said too much. I kissed her, not understanding the fierce devotion I felt for someone so new to me. All I knew was that no one had ever protected her, and she didn't know her worth.

And I was exactly the person to show her.

It was a compulsion, a deep and instinctive impulse to keep

her safe. To make her happy. To show her a better life than the one she'd been living in the long shadow of her mother. I understood her, and I believed she understood me.

I'd spent my life feeling separate from the family I loved, different, unlike them in almost all ways. I'd found my place by being useful, dependable. And though we knew each other well and loved each other unconditionally, we never understood each other.

I hadn't realized just what that meant, to be understood. I hadn't known just how much it meant, not until that moment, holding Maisie in my arms, knowing she saw me just as distinctly as I saw her.

In my world, this was a rare and impossible gift.

One I didn't intend to waste.

I kissed her to prove that point, kissed her until we were noisy breaths and thundering hearts. Kissed her until her hands were under my suit coat and mine sought the hem of her skirt.

Kissed her until the goddamn timer on the oven went off.

I broke away with a pop and a swear on swollen lips. She sank into her seat as I marched to the traitorous oven and temped the stupid pork loin, which was inconveniently done.

"Dinner's ready," I said flatly, glancing at her when she laughed.

Her face was bright, her cheeks high, chin resting in her palm. She gazed at me like I was the most wonderful thing in the world.

With her looking at me like that, I even believed it.

I let the meat rest while I plated the vegetables, then carved the loin into juicy medallions, lining them up in the center of the tray. And once it was all ready, she followed me into the dining room with our wine in her hands.

"Blue," she said as she sat, taking the servingware to fill her plate. "And Ann."

My brow quirked, and she laughed.

"My favorite color and my middle name. What are yours?"

"Also blue, though I prefer the darker shades, navy or cobalt. And Antony."

Her fork paused midair. "Marcus Antony? Mark Antony? As in Cleopatra's lover?"

I sighed. "My mother is a romantic with a penchant for Roman names."

"I hope that's not a bad omen. I'd hate to end up in a double suicide."

I snorted a laugh as I served myself. "I don't think we'll ever be in it so bad as all that. And please, don't ever call me Mark."

"Don't ever call me Margaret, and you have yourself a deal."

She popped a bite into her mouth with a teasing smile that dissolved into a moan. The sound sent a wave of heat through me. "This is incredible."

"Thank you. I derive odd pleasure from physically putting food on the table." I took a bite of my own, savoring it for a moment. "Does anyone call you Margaret other than your mother?"

"My grandmother did, but that's all. Everyone else calls me Maisie. My mother hates it."

"I can imagine she does."

"Just another thing she blames my father for."

"I don't know how he does it. How he stays with her. Thirty years," I said to myself. "That's no life to live."

"No, it isn't. I've tried to convince him to leave, but … he's afraid to leave me with her, even now. Anyway, it's always been the two of us. The truth is, he's only been around Mother for a year out of the last eight. When I left, so did he, and we only came home on holidays to pay our dues so we could leave again in peace."

"When I was a kid, I always daydreamed about being an only child," I said as we ate.

"That's funny because I always daydreamed about having a big, rowdy family."

"It's not all it's cracked up to be."

"And how about now? Do you still wish you were an only child?"

"Not for a second. I spent my childhood trying to control the chaos that is my family. Five kids in four years didn't help my mom's general lack of organizational skills, and I'm smack in the middle of us in age. Jett and Laney have their twin thing. Kash and Luke have their Irish twin thing. And I'm just ... well, just in the middle, is all. But it makes me happy to help them. It fulfills me to see their happiness."

"And you all get along?"

"We do. I mean, don't get me wrong—we fight but not with teeth. I might punch Luke in the kidney, but I don't mean it any more than he does when he choke-holds me for not telling him who I'm dating."

Her eyes widened.

"Don't worry, I haven't told him who I'm dating."

She swallowed what was in her mouth and said, "I'm more worried about the punching and choke holds."

I chuckled. "No real harm—it's just roughhousing. You can't have that many boys in one house without some brawling. It was never over anything important, just seemed like a joke turned into a swing, which then turned into grappling."

"I somehow can't imagine you getting in a fight. You're so ..."

"Stiff? Aloof? Formal?"

"I was going to say refined. That, and I can't picture you fighting in a suit."

"Would it help if I told you I usually took my coat off?"

"A little," she said on a laugh. "I think I would have taken the occasional busted lip over being alone all the time. My house is big and cold and empty, and my only happiness as a child was school and my father. Isn't that sad? My best friend growing up was my dad."

"I don't think that's sad at all," I said quietly. "He must love you very much to go through what he's gone through."

"He does. He's sacrificed his happiness in love for me. I wish he'd get a girlfriend, but I don't think he wants to drag anyone into the mess."

"Think he'll ever leave her?"

She sighed. "He says he will. In a year, I'll be out from under her, and he promised me he'd leave too. Until then, he insists on being a buffer between me and my mother. Speaking of," she started, setting down her fork, "my mother has a plan I thought you should know about."

The pork turned to dust in my mouth. I swallowed it in a lump and took a drink.

"I was in the room for a conversation with her lawyer as they outlined their strategy, which currently consists of them doing what they can to bankrupt you in legal fees."

I took another pull from my wine without speaking.

"The plan is two part—delay and interfere with depositions so you have to pay to redo them and run you around for excessive information for discovery. They're going to call for depositions of every single person you've talked to or worked with in the last decade. They'll ask for paperwork and records they don't need just to bury you in costs."

I sat back in my seat, eyes on my wineglass, hand on the stem. "I can't say I'm surprised."

"Is there anything you can do to stop her?"

"I'll have to talk to Ben, but I think so, yes. We can file a motion to have the judge intervene."

Her bottom lip slipped between her teeth. "That might not be easy. The judge's wife is one of her friends, if you can call it that. They're on a few charity boards together, which is how they've been able to get this case taken as far as it's come."

I swore under my breath. Because if the judge wouldn't do his job, Evelyn Bower would most *definitely* bankrupt us in fees alone.

We'd be stopped before we even started.

"I'm sorry," she said sorrowfully.

"Don't be sorry—you aren't her keeper. *I'm* sorry you're in this situation in the first place."

"I'm just glad there's something I can do to help. Possibly help. Maybe help?"

At that, I smiled. "You definitely help."

"Good," she said, relieved as she picked up her fork to finish her dinner.

And for the first time since we'd been in each other's company, we fell silent.

Music played over the speakers wired throughout the house—no matter what I did, I couldn't deprogram from the noise of my childhood. In fact, quiet drove me a little crazy, and in that moment, I was thankful for the habit of keeping music going.

Something crackled between us in the sweet silence, questions and thoughts, wonderings and anticipation. What were we doing, and why couldn't we help ourselves? How would tonight end, and where would we go from here? What would we do together, and how would we spend our time? Could I really keep her safe, or would I just be another complication in her already complex life?

"Is this crazy?" she asked, reading my mind. "Are we crazy?"

"Without question. Do you care?"

"Not even a little. I know I should. I just … don't."

"I won't lie to you and say I'm not worried about what will happen to you because of me. I can't pretend I'm not selfish and self-serving for wanting you. I won't take away your choice, but I don't want to willingly put you in danger either. And refusing you seems to be beyond my ability. Past that, I've never wanted to lose my mind more."

I earned a small laugh. "You trust me, don't you?"

"Why wouldn't I?" I asked.

She shrugged one shoulder. "You don't seem to be the type to trust easily."

"No, I'm not."

"And even though we might feel as if we know each other, we don't. You don't *know* me, Marcus."

"I know you well enough to know you're different."

"Why? I'm just plain old me. Why would you trust me without a reason?"

I cocked my head as if inspecting her, a tilted smile on my face. "By my count, you've defied your mother, decided you're willing to walk away from your life and inheritance, and you are currently spying on your mother for the sake of my family. You stood up to her in front of all of us, defended what you felt was right. Your actions have spoken nothing but trust. Why do *you* trust *me*?"

"I don't know. Because we're allies, that's part of it. Because I can't stand by and watch her decimate your family over some tired, pointless grudge she's held on to rather than moved on from. But mostly because when I'm with you, the world seems full of possibility when I've lived without hope for so long. I trust you because I want to trust you, and you've done nothing but prove you're worthy."

I watched her for a protracted moment, one spent searching for words. "I have never met anyone like you, not in my whole life. And that you're sitting here, that you're with me, is the most terrifying and satisfying thing that's ever happened to me."

She rose from her seat, her eyes locked on mine as she approached. Reaching for her, I pushed my chair back to make room, and in a single, fluid motion, we connected in a slide of her arms, the slip of her body into my lap, the sweetness of her lips against mine. We were a mingling of breaths, a seam of lips, a tangling of tongues, the bounds of the world shrinking to just us, just this. My hands roamed as the kiss deepened. The silken strands of her hair in my fingertips. The soft curve of her jaw. The dip of her waist. The shape of her thigh beneath my palm. Her skin, hot and smooth, my curious hand seeking the end of her thigh like a cartographer seeks the shore.

When the curve of her ass rested firmly in my palm, I squeezed and was rewarded with a moan into my mouth. There was little I could do with her sidesaddle in my lap, but when I skimmed the hem of her panties, she shifted to grant me access.

The heat of her mouth arrested my senses, leaving my hands to act on their own, and they took that opportunity before I could consider. My thumb slipped into the cleft of her ass, the silken fabric barring me from more than a delicate exploration. I traced that line down until I found her heat with my thumb, nestled in the valley of her body, found the peak of her and stroked. The arch of her back rocked her in the crook of my hand, my thumb holding steady and fingers splayed on her ass.

She held on to my neck, the weight of her intoxicating, the kiss hard, her body alive. A desperate mewl purred in her throat, and I broke away, panting.

Another handful of minutes, and I'd have her saddled up in full. And that was not how this was going to happen, not this time.

I removed my hand from the cradle of her body, sliding it over the curve of her thigh, down the back of it until my fingers hooked her knee. Looking up at her left me stunned—her hair fell toward me in golden waves, her eyes lust-drunk and parted lips bruised from kisses.

"Please, don't stop," she said, her voice raspy.

"I don't plan to."

I scooped her up to a whoop and a giggle, striding through my living room and up the stairs, and she took that time to press tender kisses to my neck, along the line of my jaw, the dip behind my ear, the dart of her hot tongue Morse code to my cock, which strained against the confines of my pants. And when we were finally in my bedroom, the air grew heavy and thick with anticipation.

I laid her down, held close by the loop of her arms around my neck. But her gaze rested on my lips as I settled on top of her, aligning our hips, flexing to test the connection—her gasp told me I'd hit the spot. And I descended to take her lips before I took the rest of her.

My hands were occupied with the curve of her neck, down to the curve of her breast, and hers were just as busy—maybe more as they made quick work of my shirt buttons. But she stopped halfway, impatient to slide her fingers inside, seeking the planes of my chest, the ridges of my stomach.

When she broke the kiss to look down at her fingers, I rose to my knees and spread them, spreading hers. As I unbuttoned my shirt and shucked it, I cataloged every detail of her. Her red dress against the white of my sheets. Lily-white thighs slung over mine, parted to expose a sliver of her panties. Her hands riding her panting ribs, her fingertips threaded absently. Her face, framed by flaxen hair, tilted to the side. She tracked the motion of my fingers as they unbuttoned my pants, lowered my zipper.

She rose, her hands taking the place of mine, her lips connecting with my abs. I cupped the back of her neck, heart thundering as she snagged the hem of my pants and underwear and slid them over my ass, down my thighs, releasing my cock. First her hand, soft and warm around my shaft. Her breath, humid against the tip. The shock of her tongue drew my desire from deep within me, the hot chamber of her mouth the single point of awareness in my universe.

A moan rumbled through me, echoed by her. A languid lick, a slow suck. The rush of pleasure was intense and immediate, not only for the silken feel of her, but for the way she tasted me, as if I were a discovery, a wonder, and she wanted to know every bit of me as best she could.

When I finally pulled myself away, it was to lay her down, pinning her to the bed with my hips, meeting her lips as soon as they were within reach. The cool shock of air against my slick cock was gone when I settled between her thighs, resisting the impulse to move her panties out of the way and drive into her.

If I stayed there, I would. But I had other plans.

I leaned back and kicked off my pants, scanning her body, dragging my hand in the wake of my gaze. "Too many clothes," I mumbled, flipping up the skirt of her dress, pressing my palm to the flat of her stomach, kissing the V of her neckline. And then the cumbersome dress was gone in a frenzy of hands and lips and whispering fabric.

And with a kiss that ended with foreheads joined, time stretched thin and long before stopping completely.

There was the sound of our breaths, the heave of our chests. The thumping hearts and drumming pulse. There was Maisie, soft and lovely, snowy white but for the pale of her nipples and the flush of her cheeks. And there was me, dusky and hard and nestled between her thighs. She was perfect, and not for symmetry or size. But because no one and nothing had ever been so right as she was in that moment.

It was an alignment, a clicking into place of a thing we knew was there but hadn't seen. That rightness settled into me, occupying a space I hadn't realized was vacant. Not until here. Not until now.

Not until her.

I kissed her both to forget what I felt and to brand the truth of it on her lips. My throat was caught in a vise, a desperate ache in my chest. A longing, not for her. A longing to keep her.

Something in her kiss told me she felt it too.

I broke away to move down her body, to ebb our connection while I still could. But she stopped me with her hands on my jaw and a crane of her neck, a stretch to capture my lips again and keep them against hers. Her thighs split wider, her hips shifting in search until she found what she sought—the aching tip of my crown, caught in the slick heat of her. With a hiss, I withdrew, putting enough space between us that I wouldn't thoughtlessly take the invitation.

I reached for my nightstand drawer, her hands stroking my

ribs, then my chest as I tore open the condom and rolled it on, kissing her. Kissing down her. Spending a long moment at her breasts, tasting the tips, learning their shape. And then my patience was lost. Hastily, I slid off the bed, dragging her to the end by her thighs. Spreading her open, touching her to find her wet and wanting. Falling to my knees to bring my lips to her, to discover the taste of her. A gentle shake of my head, buried in her heat. A lick, a lap, a suck left her impatiently tugging my shoulders, whispering my name as a plea.

A final taste, and I stood on legs weak from desire. Blindly, I gripped my base, my eyes on the rippling flesh between her thighs. A flex, and I disappeared inside her to the sound of a gasp that parted her lips, shuddered her legs.

And when I could go no further, when my heart hammered in its cage, when the whole of me drew tight, reaching into her depths, I realized that rightness had become a fact, as tangible as the heat of her body sheathing mine.

With a shift and drive of my hips, I emptied and filled her again.

A long, relieved sigh echoed in the room. I wanted to kiss her but refused to leave her warmth, rolling my hips to retreat and advance in waves. Starving eyes devoured the sight of her breasts, jostling with every drive of my body into hers. I wanted to bask in the heat of her, in the feel of her, the sight and sound and smell of her. I wanted to fuck her until she fell apart, and I wanted to love her down for hours.

Her chin lifted, her hands scrabbling at the bed for purchase, the sweet sounds of pleasure slipping out of her, sliding over me. One desire rose above all else. To feel her beneath me. To cage her in my arms where she was safe, where she was wanted, where I could keep her.

I felt the loss of her body the second I left it and found my way back inside as quickly as I could, climbing up her body, filling her up, kissing her with my palm on her neck and fingers gripping her chin. And I stayed right there, buried inside her without moving, occupying her mouth, consuming her as she'd consumed me. Pinning her with my body, a cage she couldn't escape, and she went boneless, not wanting to.

When I pumped my hips again, it was with intent.

Our bodies fit together in such a way that I didn't have to seek the places she needed me. With the arch of her back, the flush of color from her chest to her neck to her cheek, she whispered something I couldn't understand. Braced herself. Tightened around me painfully, her lips stretched in a silent cry.

A gasp, and she came, drawing me deeper, deeper with every pulse, every squeeze.

Heat gripped my chest, spreading through me, overtaking me. And with a heady pull from the very depths of me, I followed her down in a blind spiral of pleasure to the aftershocks of hers.

I collapsed, burying my face in her neck, her hair stuck to my panting lips and the scent of gardenias in every breath. Her arms looped my neck, both of us damp from exertion, our bodies still linked with no intention of upsetting the fact. I lay languid in her arms, heavy and spent and relishing in the feel of her fingertips in my hair, on my neck, my spine to a trail of goosebumps. I could have stayed right there forever, lost in a timeless haze with her.

But awareness rose again like a gnawing nag, reminding us that life was happening somewhere out there.

I turned to press a kiss to her neck, pushed myself up so I could see her.

My God, she was beautiful, the tiny freckles on her nose and cheeks glistening. Her face was soft and sated, without a line of tension or worry to be found. I'd done that, I thought with arrogant pleasure.

If only I could keep her in this state forever. But the world wouldn't wait for us, and I couldn't save her from everything.

"Stay tonight," I said, cupping her cheek, knowing her answer.

She leaned into my hand. "I wish I could. I don't know what

I'd tell my mother, and somehow, she'd know I was lying. She always knows."

A string of curses whispered through me at the woman who had Maisie so firmly under her watch. "We're looking for an apartment. Tomorrow."

She chuckled like I was kidding. "I can stay for a while though."

"Good, because I'm not through with you." I kissed the tip of her nose. "If I can't have you all night, I suppose I can make do."

"Would you like to have me tomorrow too?"

"I'll have you tomorrow, tomorrow night, the morning after. I'll take you whenever I can get you."

Her smile made me feel like a goddamn king. "I'm going to have to come up with a story. She won't believe I'm out with friends every night. I don't have enough friends to constitute a busy social calendar."

"Not even friends from high school?"

She shrugged. "A few, but they moved away. And remember—I've been living with sheep for the last few years."

"Ah, and I can't imagine they'd be entertaining dinner guests."

"I don't know. They have their charm," she teased.

For a moment, we just smiled at each other across the inches that separated us, alive with possibility. Because this was the beginning of something—I knew it in my marrow.

Hang the rest. Because Maisie was mine.

And I wasn't about to let her go.

# Perfection Defined

## MAISIE

It was nearly midnight when I floated out of Marcus's apartment and into a cab, tossing my coat and hat in without a care in the world. The city rushed by, but I didn't see it, smiling stupidly at nothing with every thought consumed by Marcus.

Consumed, all of me, as if I'd been swallowed up by feeling.

Leaving was the actual worst. I'd have given my right arm to stay the night, but I was already pushing it with midnight. Didn't want to risk anything more. Staying out all night would be grounds for the inquisition to lay its heavy eyes on me.

Nobody wanted that.

This late, Mother wouldn't be awake, and thank goodness. One look at me, and she'd know more than she should. I didn't think I could pretend I was the dejected girl I'd been this morning.

Not after Marcus.

*Marcus.*

Good, sweet God, my imaginings—of which there had been many regarding Marcus Bennet—had paled in comparison. And yet it somehow came as no surprise. It just felt *right*, exactly as it should be. As if for the first time in many, many years, the stars had aligned, and I was given a perfect moment.

A flash of fear dimmed my smile.

It was *too* perfect, too good to be true. Was I being blind? Crazy? How could he hurt me, what could he do with my trust?

But I took a breath and pushed the thought away. Because that was the influence of my mother, and I refused to be influenced by her for another minute of my life.

When my thoughts wandered back to him, my smile returned, and absently my fingers rested on my lips as I thought of his.

Tomorrow seemed a world away.

Deciding I needed to be more productive than all that, I tried to come up with a story for my mother—a problem that needed an immediate solution. But it was no use. Instantly, my thoughts flitted like book pages back to him.

*I think I'm twitterpated.*

A giggle bubbled out of me, and the cabbie gave me a look in the rearview. But I didn't care. It was blissful, this feeling. Was this what it was like to be happy? Had I lived my whole life thinking happiness was oatmeal, the misconception falling apart now that I'd had a steak dinner?

I told myself it was just brain chemicals. And/or that it'd been a while since I'd seen anyone. Dating was a hassle, a string of awkward dinners with the vaguest of intentions, especially in York. Plus, there had been no reason to put in too much of an effort when I knew I wasn't staying.

For the first time, I was glad I hadn't.

We pulled up to the curb, and once I paid, I stepped out into the brisk spring evening. Up the stairs I went, my heels clicking on the concrete stoop. Noting the sound, I slipped them off, hooking them on my fingers so I could unlock the door.

The house was chilly and silent as a tomb, the shadows

swallowing everything on a moonless night. Goosebumps raced up my arms, down my spine.

When the light clicked on, I discovered they had nothing to do with the chill.

My mother stood in the entry, her pajamas stiff and her slippers pointed at me. In fact, everything about her pointed at me—from her glasses to her glare to the aggressive shift of her hips and square of her shoulders.

"Why are you home so late?"

"Why are you up so late?" I countered.

"I was working."

I stopped myself from scoffing. Since we were both lying, I said, "I was out with friends," and headed for the stairs in a vain attempt to bypass the conversation.

"I wasn't aware that any of the three people you knew were in town."

"You are not entitled to every corner of my life. Only Bower." I marched up three steps before she stopped me with a single word.

My name.

It was the swing of an ax, never spoken with love or tenderness. It was a weapon, wielded for control. And as she'd trained me, I stopped and turned.

"Where were you?" She was the only human I knew who could order someone with a question.

"Why do you want to know? Your adult daughter was out like *adults* do. I don't see how it matters to you."

"Adult," she mocked. "Adults accept their responsibilities—they don't run and hide. They don't keep secrets."

My eyes narrowed. "Funny, because I have a feeling you have a secret or two of your own."

Fury smudged her cheeks with crimson. "You will not keep secrets from me. Are you seeing someone?"

"It's none of your business." I turned to walk away.

"*Margaret Bower.* You will answer my question."

With slitted eyes, I looked down at her. "Or what?"

"Do not test me," she seethed.

"I'm not doing this with you." Again, I turned.

But she laughed. "I'm almost proud, seeing you pretend your power. Just a little taste, and look at you."

A shock of dissent wheeled me around. I opened my mouth to tell her the many ways she could go to hell, but she headed me off with a triumphant look on her face.

"I shouldn't worry. Whatever your little fling is, it won't last. How could it? Oh, don't look at me like that, Margaret—you have no ambition, no backbone, and ... well, take a look at yourself. You don't even try, not for anything worth something in the world. It's why you've never had a boyfriend worth a damn. So have your fun while you can. And if it makes you feel better to pretend I won't find out, go right ahead."

The bald cruelty stung, the slap painful. "Thank you for the permission," I snapped, doing my best to steady my voice. "Now, if you'll excuse me—"

Her flippancy twisted into something tighter, darker at her realization that I wasn't going to fold. "Don't be stupid, darling. If you think you can keep this from me, you're mistaken."

"And if you think I give a shit, so are you." I spun around, desperate to leave.

Something close to disdain struck her face. "You have always been weak, but at least you used to be respectful."

"You've always been a miserable bitch, so at least one of us is consistent."

I marched up the stairs with furious tears in my eyes, ignoring her calls, hoping to God she didn't follow me. The last thing I needed was to assault my mother in the middle of the night, on my perfect night.

But when I slammed my door and found myself in my old room, the gravity of the situation laid its full weight upon me. Because perfect would only find me in fluttering, fleeting moments.

*Not forever*, I reminded myself.

Because if things didn't change, I would leave. And if Marcus and I went like I thought we might, I'd tell my mother about us, and I'd *have* to leave.

Either way, fate would decide.

But my mother would not.

# Whistling Maisie

## MARCUS

I walked through the turquoise door of Longbourne, a tray of coffees in hand, cheerfully whistling my way inside.

Jett glanced up at me from the register, double-taking when he really got a look at me, head cocked and dark brows drawn.

"Morning," I said, nodding at the customers in the shop as I passed, heading for the counter. "Got you a coffee from Blanche's."

He took it, confused and suspicious. "You're awfully chipper this morning."

"What can I say? I got a great night's sleep."

His eyes narrowed. "I'm trying to think if I've ever heard you whistle."

"Oh, look at that. A customer." With a smirk, I moved out of the way for the woman behind me, turning the corner into the workspace.

The shop was bustling, as it always was these days, even on a Wednesday morning. Over the summer, Luke and Tess had renovated the storefront, planning weekly installations that brought people through the front door in droves. We sold out of her market bouquets daily, our deliveries were up four hundred percent, and our greenhouse was booming with blooms.

Business was good. Excellent in fact, our income making steady work of the debts my mother had accrued.

If we could only get rid of Evelyn Bower's lawsuit, we could save this place in full.

I made my way through the work tables, passing coffee to Tess and Luke, who were chatting about something he was constructing for a display as she arranged a bouquet.

"Thanks," Luke said, taking a sip, subsequently swearing as he burned his mouth.

"Never were patient," I said.

Luke rolled his eyes, but like Jett, he gave me a second suspicious look. "Something's different." He inspected me. "Did you tie your tie in a full Windsor knot instead of a half or something?"

"Look at that. I didn't think you even knew what a Windsor knot was. Color me impressed."

He made a face. "Seriously, what's with you?"

"He was just whistling," Jett tattled from the front.

That earned me a full-blown stare-down from Luke and Tess both.

"Whistling?" Tess asked.

"How about a, *Thanks for the coffee, Marcus. How did all the legal bullshit you've been single-handedly dealing with go yesterday?*"

Luke's brows flattened. "Pardon us for noticing you're not wound up like a—" His face shot open. "You got laid."

"Oh my God, he did," Jett yell-laughed over his shoulder.

I turned for the greenhouse so I didn't pop one of them in the nose. "Fuck you, ingrates."

"Oh, don't let them get to you, Marcus." Tess chuckled. "Good for you."

I threw a look at her. "Not you too."

"Forgive us for wanting to see you whistling." She leaned into Luke, who was still laughing as he wrapped an arm around her.

"Was it one of Mom's garden club girls?" he asked. "Did you get on Bumble? I was wondering if you'd figured out how to use it."

But I kept on walking toward the back. "I don't need an app to get laid."

"Coulda fooled me," he called as I pushed the swinging greenhouse door open.

The scent of fresh, wet earth hit me like a humid, familiar wall. I loved this place despite my tendency to stay away—greenhouses were no place for Italian suits—but when I did visit, I always promised myself to come here more. We had grown up here, running barefoot and filthy through the rows of flowers. I remembered when Luke used to toddle around in my rain boots and a diaper. I remembered dirty hands and dirty clothes and sunshine pouring in through high, lead-veined windows. I remembered Mom teaching us the genus and species of each flower, prompting us to taste the ones that were pleasant and a few that weren't, just for kicks.

This place was just as much home as our house was. More maybe. Because unlike at home, the greenhouse was *supposed* to be dirty.

A chuckle exited my nose.

I didn't see Dad but found Kash in the wide center aisle, shirtless and sweaty as he shucked dirt from a wheelbarrow to a bed of irises.

"Hey," I called, holding up my last cup of coffee. "Broughtcha something."

But he didn't smile or greet me. Instead, he frowned, brows together and eyes accusatory.

I frowned right back as I stopped in front of him. "What's the matter with you?"

With a furtive glance of a predator over his shoulder, he

snagged me by the elbow and dragged me toward the basement storage.

"The hell is wrong with you, Kash?" I removed my arm from his grip and stopped, squaring up. I was an inch taller than him, and I drew myself up to it.

He glared at me. "I saw *somebody* leaving your place last night."

I froze, lungs locked. Under my breath, I hissed, "*Fuck.*"

"Yeah. So if you'd follow me, *Your Highness*," he said, sweeping a dramatic hand toward the basement.

Questions and lies and a dozen excuses pinged around in my skull as I headed down the ramp, stopping just inside the basement. Kash did a cursory inspection to make sure we were alone before hanging his hands on his hips in a stance that could only be called aggressive.

"Put your shirt on," I said. "I can't take you seriously with your nipples out."

He rolled his eyes but pulled a tee out from its tuck in his back pocket and tugged it on. The words *Weed 'em and Reap* stretched across his chest before his arms folded over them.

"Got something to tell me?" he asked, his voice low.

I slid my hands into my pockets. "Depends on what you saw."

"You know what I fucking saw. You know *who* I saw. What the fuck, Marcus? I mean it. What in the actual fuck was Maisie Bower doing at your apartment?"

"*Maisie Bower?*" Luke blurted from behind me.

I gave Kash a look. "Way to go, man. Way to fucking go."

"Hey, I'm not the one sleeping with a *Bower*," Kash noted. "Of all the girls in Manhattan, you would pick the one you can't have."

"Who said I'm sleeping with her?"

"You were *whistling*," Luke said as if that explained everything.

Kash made a sour face. "Whistling?"

"You'd think I walked in here in a goddamn cocktail dress."

Luke shook his head, waved a hand, and blinked a handful of times in a second. "Stop. Back up. How'd *you* find out, Kash?"

"Yeah, how'd you find out?" I asked, folding my arms.

His cheeks flushed above his beard in an expression wholly unlike him. "I, uh … well, Lila and I were walking home."

Luke and I swiveled to face him as a unified front.

"Walking home from where?" Luke asked, smirking.

"At midnight?" I added.

"We were just out, okay?"

"But why were you over here?" I asked. "You guys live—"

"This isn't about me. It's about you fucking a—"

"Hang on," Luke started, pausing to belt a solid laugh. "You brought her to the greenhouse, didn't you?"

When he sputtered, Luke and I both broke into laughter.

"Oh my God," I said. "What are you, sixteen again?"

"It's none of your goddamn business why Lila and I came here—"

"Where'd you do her?" Luke asked, nearly giggling. "Tell me it was in the hay."

"Nah, that's all you and Tess," Kash shot, not at all amused. "*Any-fucking-way*, we saw Maisie leaving your place with sex hair and her makeup all smudged, and if you try to tell me you were having a legal meeting, I swear to God—"

"*Shh.*" I glanced toward the ramp. "Shut up. Mom can't know yet, and you know she's always snooping around. She's as nosy as Luke."

Luke frowned. "Wait, I'm the metric for being nosy now?"

I gestured to the two of them rather than explain.

"Just try not to say her name," I said, taking a breath, looking into their disapproving faces as they waited for me to elaborate. "You're not wrong, Kash."

I didn't have a chance to say anything else before they started talking all at once, asking questions and making accusations and generally being a couple of barking dogs in the echoing basement.

"*Oh my God, would you shut the fuck up!*" I whisper-hissed at them.

Mercifully, they pulled themselves together.

I raked a hand through my hair, mad as all hell that I had to explain this within hours of it happening. But I shouldn't have expected any less.

"I met her before the meeting with … *them* a few weeks ago. Literally that morning, and I asked her out. Or she asked me out, but I asked for her number, and—" I waved a hand. "It doesn't matter. And when I walked in the boardroom, there she was, sitting next to *Evelyn Bower*," I said under my breath. "I didn't know who she was, but I liked her. Liked her enough to … anyway, I knew better than to get involved. I fucking knew better. But I couldn't help myself. Especially not after she stood up to her mother, on the record and in front of all those people, for *us*. For Mom. She doesn't belong there. She doesn't belong under her mother's thumb."

"What do you mean, under her thumb?" Kash asked.

"I mean that her mother has a leash on her. Everything Evelyn Bower does is to try to heel Maisie."

"Maisie?" Kash's face was bent in confusion.

"Margaret Bower. Maisie."

"I don't understand," Luke started, his brows stitched together. "You *like* her? Who gives a shit, man? She's a goddamn Bower, Marcus. Out of all of us, you are the one who, without question, would shut her down immediately. What you think of her doesn't change who she *is*."

Kash nodded his agreement.

My teeth ground together in my skull so hard, my jaw hurt. "Would you still act like a dick if I told you she was spying on Bower for us?"

Both of their mouths popped open, and I wasn't even gonna pretend like that didn't satisfy me.

"She's not who you think, and she is not one of them.

Yesterday, she walked into Bower prepared to quit—not just the company, but her mother. Her inheritance. If she sticks it out, that company is hers. Think about that for a second. What if they weren't our enemies? What if they were allies?"

"And how the hell do you think that's ever going to happen with Evelyn at the helm?" Kash asked. "I bet she lives to a hundred-and-eighty, fueled by nothing but spite."

"Ten years, and Maisie has only one share less than her mother," I answered.

"That feels like a long time from now," Kash countered in disapproval.

"But in the meantime, she's still our ally as long as she stays in that hellhole. She's gonna help us stay a step ahead when it comes to the lawsuit."

"How do you know she's not spying on *us* for Bower?" Kash asked.

"Because I know," I answered simply. There was no other way to explain.

"I don't know if that's good enough," he said, his jaw sharp and eyes stony.

Fury rose in my chest at the audacity. "When have I ever put this family in danger? Whenever have I done *anything* but take care of you? Of Mom? Of this shop? I put every fucking penny I own into saving Longbourne, and if you think I would fuck that off for a girl, you're mistaken. And you know it."

Kash still frowned, but the tension in his shoulders eased. "You can't blame me for asking."

"I don't. But also, fuck you."

They chuckled, and the tension between us eased too.

"So what are you gonna do?" Kash asked. "What's your plan?"

"Right now, it's to lay low until the lawsuit is over. We'll tell Mom once it's said and done and things are settled. No way can I drop that on her until then."

"And then?" Luke asked.

"And then ... I don't know. We'll have to come clean to her mother at some point, but I have to leave that to Maisie—she's the one with everything to lose."

Kash eyed me skeptically again. "It's fishy, that's all I'm saying. Why would she risk all that?"

"Thanks for the vote of confidence," I said, trying not to sound petulant.

"I mean it, Marcus. It's her whole life she's putting on the line, and I don't think it's unreasonable to ask why."

"Think about growing up under Evelyn Bower. You'd turn out one of two ways. Either you'd be exactly like her or—"

"You'd be the exact opposite," Luke finished.

I nodded. "If you think we hate that woman, we've got nothing on Maisie. You either trust me on that or you don't. But I'm not gonna sit here and convince you—I know a brick wall when I see one."

Kash finally understood, unhappy as he seemed about it. His forehead smoothed, and he let loose a mighty sigh. "I'm sorry. We trust you. Don't we, Luke?"

Luke nodded, rubbing a hand over his lips. "You know what you're doing better than any of us. It's just hard to override a lifetime of conditioning against them, that's all."

"I know. Trust me, I know."

"You're gonna have to be more careful than you were last night," Kash warned. "The second Mom hears you whistling, she's gonna know you're seeing someone—"

"God, you guys and the fucking whistling—"

"And when she figures *that* out," he said over me, "your secret won't be safe. She'd burn down hell to figure out who it is, and you know Luke can't keep his mouth shut."

Luke punched him in the arm hard enough to knock him off balance.

"Don't tell Laney." I pointed at Luke.

"Why would I tell Laney?"

"I don't know, why would you tell anybody? Jett either. And Kash, not a word to Dad."

"Like Dad and I gossip about you assholes all the time? Please. I think combined we utter a paragraph a day. And even if he knew, he'd never tell Mom. Not unless she asked him point-blank with Marga—*Maisie* Bower's name in her hand. Just make sure you stay ahead of it until then."

I nodded once. "In the meantime, we've got plenty to figure out. The faster we get through this lawsuit, the better things will be for all of us." I checked my watch. "I've got to meet Ben. Bower is going to try to bury us in legal fees, so we've got to come up with a plan to head them off. If we can stay ahead of them, the whole thing will be behind us real soon."

"Hopefully, Mom survives depositions," Luke said. "If last time was any indication …"

"She'll be fine," I assured him. "Don't worry. I've got it under control. *All* of it."

And God help me if I didn't.

# One Look

## MARCUS

**M**aisie giggled, delving her chopsticks into my orange chicken. "She did not, Marcus Bennet."

"I swear," I said on a laugh. "Mom had us all lined up by age like the von Trapps and spanked us, oldest to youngest. Not one of us ever started another mud fight again. Not with the greenhouse dirt anyway."

She kicked her head back, and the sight kicked my heart into my sternum. "God, there must have been mud everywhere."

"After Luke made a Slip 'N Slide out of mud in our foyer? I think there's still dirt behind his ears from that. You should have heard him crying, waiting for his turn to get put over Mom's knee."

"Aww," she cooed. "He was just a baby."

"Don't worry—she barely popped him. I think he cried more worrying about what was coming than the spanking itself."

I watched her take a bite of chicken, the piece too big to eat gracefully. Her lips closed over half of it, and the display inadvertently bordered pornographic.

We were stretched out in bed, wearing almost nothing—me in a pair of jersey sleep pants and her in one of my tailored shirts, unbuttoned so low, I couldn't keep my eyes off the V and the occasional glimpse of her breasts when she did things like lean over me to dig in my food.

I never shared food with anyone, but Maisie could have whatever she wanted. I'd share it all, especially when there was a view involved.

I'd enjoyed that view for nearly a week, every morning, every night—a view I couldn't seem to get enough of. She'd become a regular fixture at my place, and every night when she left me to go back to her warden's house, I watched her go with the determination to boost her from that particular prison. If for no other reason than to have her in my bed for a whole night.

"I can't believe your brothers found out already," she said, swiping her hair out of her face with the back of her hand, the one with the chopsticks.

When it fell right back in her face, I tossed my chopsticks in my carton and tucked the errant lock behind her ear. "They're nosy as all hell, so I can't say I'm surprised. I just hope they keep their mouths shut."

"Are you gonna spank them if they don't?" She smirked.

"In the nose with my fist," I answered, digging a bundle of lo mein out from her container. "Is your Mom still going crazy?"

"As is her way. Too bad I can't spank *her* in the nose with my fist." Poking around in her noodles, she glanced down. "I spent the entire day at one of our farms in Long Island, pretending to like her while we took eleventy billion photos."

"And you've got the sunburn to prove it." I booped her rosy nose.

"Longest day ever. But she wasn't so bad today. The worst part was the car ride home. At least at the farm, we had fresh air. Sharing a confined space with her for hours was the actual worst."

"I'm surprised you didn't suffocate."

"Trust me, it was touch and go for a minute there. Listening to her garden club drama is mind-numbing. Whose daughter is sleeping with whom. What so-and-so said to whomever about the state of their begonias. As if any of them grow their own flowers." She snorted, rolling her eyes. "I especially don't want to hear another recount of her overthrowing your mom."

Anger bolted through me at the mention, gone as soon as it appeared. "I hate them. All of them."

"All of them? Because I heard you dated half the members' daughters," she said bashfully, casting her eyes down.

"I went on dates. I never dated them."

"No?"

"Not a single one. I didn't even kiss any of them."

When she met my eyes again, hers were smiling. "Not even Verdant? She kisses everybody."

"Nope. That one was all Kash."

With a laugh, she turned the conversation back to her mother. "Honestly, Mother has been on her best behavior. For the most part, she's kept her composure since that first night, but I can't shake the feeling that things are a little too calm, a little too easy."

"I wish this wasn't so hard. I wish you didn't have to deal with her."

"I've been dealing with her my whole life. At least now I have something worth the trouble."

"Who, me?" My smile rose on one side.

"Yes, you." Maisie leaned in to press a kiss to the corner of my lips. "It's driving her crazy not to know what I'm doing, who I'm seeing, but rather than admit it, she just makes snide comments about how it won't last."

"She's wrong."

Chin down, she looked up at me with a sweet shyness that made me want to throw my Chinese food over my shoulder and get her out of my shirt.

"About what?" she chanced.

"Everything," I answered.

I was rewarded with a flush of her cheeks and the happiest of sighs. "When you say it like that, I believe it."

"Good, because I'm generally right."

She swatted at my arm, laughing, and I feigned flinching.

"How's the property search going for Harvest Center?" I asked, changing the subject before I really did end dinner early.

Maisie lit up like a lightbulb, lowering her forgotten carton to her lap. "It's going well. There's one in particular that I love, if we can get the permits and permissions we need from city council."

"Where is it?" I popped a piece of chicken in my mouth.

"Hell's Kitchen. There's a vacant lot next door to a commercial building that I think would be perfect. I'm going to see it tomorrow, and I ... I don't know. It just feels right, you know?"

I swallowed hard and smiled sideways. "I know the feeling. One look, and you're a goner."

That flush again. God, she was so pretty when she blushed.

"I wanted to go today, but I was so busy with meetings and paperwork. Oh!" she exclaimed, rolling out of bed while somehow keeping her food upright. She did not, however, keep my shirt in place. The flash of the cleft of her ass and the shadow of promise beneath it stirred my attention.

I set the carton on my nightstand without any plans to pick it up until I had dessert.

She knelt to rummage in her bag rather than bend at the waist—a tragic loss—and when she found what she'd been looking for, she bounded back, leaving her dinner on the floor next to her things, chopsticks on display like bunny ears.

Maisie climbed back in bed, crawling toward me with a packet of papers and an envelope in her hand. She handed over the envelope first, and as I opened it and unfurled the letter inside, she nibbled on her lip.

"When I came home yesterday, I saw this in her trashcan

next to her writing desk in the foyer where she opens her mail. I figured it was nothing, but then...well..."

I frowned as I scanned the letter from the judge's wife to Evelyn, recounting all the ways she'd convinced her honorable husband to side with Evelyn in our case. This was followed by a full page of garden club gossip.

"A letter? Who even writes letters anymore?" I asked, flipping it over curiously to see if there was anything on the back.

"They've always done it. Mother said it started as an exercise through cotillion. Thank God they didn't make us do it when she made me go through the debutante ball."

One of my brows rose, amused. "You were a debutante?"

"How on earth does that surprise you?" She laughed.

"I need pictures of you in a white ballgown and satin gloves."

"Not on your life. Those photos will never see the light of day."

My eyes found the papers in my hand again. "This isn't good."

"No, it's not. Surely he won't take her side. Will he?"

"I hope not. We'll find out soon enough. If we build a compelling enough argument, I think he might have to. I can't imagine he'd be willing to tarnish his reputation as a judge for his wife's place in the garden club pecking order." My lips flattened. "You don't think she'll miss this, will she?"

Maisie smirked. "I put a dummy envelope in the trash just in case she noticed it was missing."

"Look at you. See, you're more Carmen Sandiego than you think."

"It's the trench coat. Pretty sure it has magical powers."

Her smile faded as she offered me the pack of papers still in her hand, and I took them, immediately worried again.

"So I was going through some paperwork, trying to get myself reacquainted with the finances for the center, and I found these," she said, sitting on her feet, knees together. "I don't know exactly what to make of it."

I frowned, skimming the details of the invoices and fund reporting. "That's because it makes no sense." I flipped the page. "Where did you find these?"

She tucked that lock of hair behind her ear again, and it almost immediately slipped loose. "Jess had finance send over 'light records,' which ended up being four banker boxes full of paperwork. I've been digging through them for a week, trying to get my head around the monthly costs and income, making notes, and I realized these didn't match."

My frown deepened, bringing my brows together as I added up the missing money. "This has to be a bookkeeping error. Did you find more than this?"

"No. But I can't help but wonder if there's more."

I made a noncommittal sound. "Did you ask Jess?"

"Not yet. I will though. And I'll talk to accounting too. Someone has to know. I'm sure it's nothing."

"That's very trusting of you," I half-teased. "What if someone is misappropriating funds?"

Her eyes widened. "Jess? Do you think she'd do that?"

"I don't know her, so I couldn't say. Would she have a reason to?"

"I ... I don't know. I want to say no, but ..." She shook her head. "There's some reasonable explanation, I'm sure. I just wanted to make sure I wasn't crazy before I went accusing anyone of anything. If my mother caught wind that someone was stealing from her company, she'd flay them in the lobby, and I'd hate to be some poor accountant's executioner."

She took the papers from my hand and tossed them off the side of the bed with a thump. A wanton smile curled her lips as she crawled over, affording me a convenient view of her body in the gape of my shirt, and before I could fully appreciate that, she slung one leg over mine, settling into my lap.

My hands slid up her thighs until they rested in the juncture of her hips.

"Had enough work talk?" I asked, my thumbs finding another juncture, the one split over the hard column of my shaft.

"Mmhmm." Her hips rocked in a long stroke, and mine rose to meet her.

"Good, because I was about to pop every … single … button … of my favorite shirt," I said, unfastening each one with a snick until she was naked.

And I spent the rest of the night doing another sort of work altogether.

One that involved far less math.

# Ace in the Hole

## MAISIE

**A** few days passed, marking a long and lovely week spent working in the charity I loved and luxuriating in Marcus's arms.

Almost every day, the second I could get away from work, I headed straight here. Marcus had given me a key since twice he'd had to detain his mother to make sure I got in unseen. A few hours at night, one in the morning, and the occasional extended lunch. In the mornings, I'd sneak into his place with the sun—Mrs. Bennet was not a morning person, apparently—and at the last possible second, I'd hurry off, catching a cab only once I was around the corner and out of sight of Longbourne.

Life, at present, was goddamn glorious. And for the first time in a very long time, I found myself blissfully, blindly, blithely happy.

Just as I was at the moment.

I sighed, leaning back into Marcus the second he righted the zipper of my dress, eyeing the potted ivy on his dresser.

"That little guy needs a drink. Look, he's wilting."

"He sure does."

"And your palm over there is being overwatered. Look at the tips of its leaves," I said with a sorrowful sort of tone.

He kissed my neck, chuckling through his nose in puffs against my skin. "Maybe you can help me get them on the road to recovery."

"Nurse Maisie, at your service." With wistful longing, I said, "I wish I'd woken up here instead of coming this morning."

"You can *come* here every morning as far as I'm concerned." Another brush of his lips at my neck, this one coupled with a hot sweep of his tongue.

"Be careful what you wish for. I'd hate to become a nuisance."

"You are many things, but a nuisance could never be one of them."

I turned in his arms, smoothing his tie. "Will I see you tonight?"

"I'd hate to break the cycle. I'm afraid I've become accustomed to having you here."

"It's only been two weeks," I teased.

"Sure, but what do *you* think about skipping a night?"

My lip slipped out in a pout.

"Exactly."

"I hate sneaking around. Last night, Mother was in rare form. I don't know what's gotten into her, but I swear I thought she was going to follow me. So I took the subway. She'd never step foot in a station, never mind getting on a train."

"Smart thinking. Was she waiting up for you?"

"Yes, but so was Dad. They alternated between glaring at each other and Dad shutting her down. I escaped to my room, unscathed."

"Bless that man," he said.

"Amen to that. One of these nights, I'm going to spend the night here and give her a stroke." I glanced at the clock. "I wish I didn't have to go, but she's been impossible about my not going to work with her. I can't wait to tell her about us and get it over with, come what may."

"You've decided to tell her?" Marcus asked carefully.

I didn't miss the note of hope and smiled.

"Oh, I was always going to tell her. I was sure before, but now it's indisputable."

"What?"

"How I feel about you."

He descended for a kiss, a kiss touched with depth that defied words. It was a pact and an appreciation, one that I met in full.

I broke away, smiling up at him. "Any more of that, and I will be very, very late."

"If it wouldn't get you in trouble with the devil, I'd say fuck it before fucking you."

The word from his lips sent a scandalous streak of heat straight between my legs, a space only just empty of him. Never before had I dated a man who would openly state his intent with that kind of language, and I found I liked it very much.

"Well, in eight to ten hours, you can fuck me all you want."

"I'm glad you said so because I was already planning to."

With a laugh, I stretched up to press my lips to his. And regretfully, I left his arms in search of my shoes.

I found one on the stairs, another in the entryway, my panties somewhere in between. My shoes I slipped on. The panties I tossed at him.

"Something to remember me by."

He tested the fabric between long fingers, smirking. "As if I need a reminder. But I'll take one all the same."

My thighs clenched as I watched him slip the silk into his pocket, leaving his hand right there with them.

"I don't want to go," I whined.

"How about you text me when you leave Harvest Center?

We'll call it a long lunch." He stepped into me. "We can meet here."

"By the time I get here from Midtown, I'll only have"—I did some quick math—"twenty minutes."

"I can do a lot with twenty minutes."

The kiss he laid on me promised the truth of that statement.

That beautiful jerk kissed me until I was wiggling against him with my arms locked around his neck.

He pulled away as much as he could for my death grip, smiling down at me like he knew exactly what he was doing. "Now, there's something to remember *me* by."

"God, you're the worst, you know that?"

"As a matter of fact, I do. Now, put on your disguise and get out of here before somebody sees you."

I chuckled, pulling on my long coat and donning my silly hat. Glasses were last, and with a few final cloak-and-dagger looks out the window, I left, turning in the opposite direction of Longbourne to get off Bleecker as quickly as I could. And moments later, I slipped into the cab and gave the cabbie the address to the center, sighing happily as I removed my *disguise*.

Between my time with Marcus and my progress at work, I found myself feeling more productive and whole than I maybe ever had. Mother upheld her promise to let me do what I wanted with the charity, and so far, I'd used that time to find a new site for our first expansion and pull together an initial proposal. She dragged me to legal meetings, and I passed on every little scrap I'd learned to the Bennets. Marcus's lawyer filed a motion to have the judge step in on discovery and leash my mother's team, and our dreaded hearing on the matter rapidly approached. I despised the thought of being in that courtroom, sitting next to the herald of hatred, on the wrong side of Marcus. My only hope—the only hope any of us had—was that the judge would see reason and side with the Bennets.

Otherwise, we were all screwed.

And my mother would win.

That constant companion of my anxiety piped up, as it so often did. When we were together, nothing else seemed to matter. Nothing else existed. In the safety beyond his front door, it was just me and Marcus and the magic. But we lived under the shadow of our circumstance.

And that circumstance was a house of cards.

No one could find out, my mother least of all. And not for my own neck. For the sake of the Bennets. She might make my life miserable, but she would reduce the Bennets to rubble. For the time being, she was using legal channels, but God knew what lengths she would go to. I'd spent far too much time considering just what she might do to punish them, and my imaginings covered everything from permit meddling to arson.

And then there was the subject of Mrs. Bennet.

I knew exactly how my mother would react when we were found out—with the vitriol and vengeance of a flaming, fallen angel. But Mrs. Bennet was a mystery to me. I didn't know if she would accept or deny me, and the thought of her disapproval did something undesirable to my stomach. Maybe she would accept me if things were different, if I were just any girl. Literally any other girl on the planet.

But there was a secret I held, one kept quietly in the deepest chamber of my heart. A secret that couldn't even be acknowledged, certainly not aloud and barely to myself.

I desperately wanted her approval because without it, I could never be a Bennet.

It was silly and childish. It was indulgent and decadent and a thing I wasn't allowed to wish for. But the little girl I once had been, the little girl who lived in my heart, listened to stories of the Bennets with the longing and hope I'd felt in fairy tales. Theirs was a model family, the kind I'd dreamed of as a child and believed with unwavering cynicism didn't exist as an adult.

The theoretical plans Marcus and I had discussed, should I

decide to tell my mother, was more of a flow chart than a list—
each avenue existed as a result of the action before it. If his mother
found out, then we would sit down with her and try to explain.
If my mother found out after the trial, we would see where her
wrath left us, and I would likely leave her once and for all. If she
found us out before the trial, our hope would be lost. She would
ruin us, the Bennets most of all. At least if we waited, it'd just be
me who would pay.

That I could live with. The alternative I could not.

The only faint chance at a happy ending we had was that my
mother would somehow accept what I'd done—what I'd keep
doing, if I had my way. Maybe she'd assume it was temporary, a
rebellion, a thing to work out of my system. That I'd get bored and
fall back in line. This was likely the best outcome I could hope
for—acceptance based on disbelief of my dedication to the cause.

Our worlds were shaped by perception, and hers was so
wildly skewed that our Venn diagram didn't even overlap by a
sliver. In fact, we existed in such a state of deep misunderstand-
ing, there might have been space between the circles.

As such, we all knew anything but nuclear warfare was a long
shot.

But for now, I'd keep that hope quietly shining in my back
pocket. I'd work at the charity. Help the Bennets escape my
mother's clutches. Plan for two futures—one with Bower and
one without. And if I didn't get to keep any of it, at least I would
have Marcus.

When we pulled up to Harvest Center, every other thought
slipped out of my mind and into the ether.

I didn't know what struck me most about the sight of this
place that I'd missed so much. The sunlight dappling the gardens
or the twitter of spring birds in the air. The warmth of the day
after an endless winter or the people coming and going from the
place I'd helped create. But any way I colored it, I was struck with
a bolt of rightness that this was the place I belonged.

It felt nearly identical to the feeling Marcus gave me.

Eyes followed me as I entered, but I didn't recognize any of the faces I found as I took happy stock of the full tables and soon-to-be full stomachs. It had been so long since I left. A pang of sadness struck me at how far away I'd drifted and a covetous sort of joy at the prosper here that I'd been no part of.

Jess stood at a stock pot next to an older man I barely recognized, but when I heard him laugh, I knew.

"Jacob?" I said, and they turned to smile at me.

Two years hadn't aged him at all. In fact, he seemed to be aging in reverse. When I knew him before, he wore a scraggly beard shot with white, tattered and thinning clothes, an expression of exhaustion so deep that the lines of his face seemed to be etched all the way down to his soul. He'd started by coming for food. Then to volunteer. Just before I left, he joined our support group and stopped drinking—a road I'd hoped he reached the end of.

By the looks of him, he had.

Now he wore a clean-shaven jaw, neatly combed hair, fresh clothes. And those lines of strain were no longer deep, smoothed by his health and erased by his levity.

"Miss Maisie, I can't believe it. Will you come give an old man a hug?"

I laughed, moving to fill his request. "Look at you. Look at you! I ... I can't believe my eyes."

We parted, and he rubbed the back of his neck, his cheeks flushed and lips smiling. "Been too long since we seen you down here. Jess said you were back, but I thought she was pullin' my leg."

She shrugged. "Nobody ever believes me. I don't know why."

"Maybe it was all those whoppers you told, trying to hide Clint's surprise party."

"Well, they don't call it a *surprise* for nothing, Jacob."

"Still. Can't blame us." He turned back to me. "You can't be here to cook or garden, not in that pretty dress."

"Says who?" I hung my coat and bag, exchanging them for an apron. "What are we working on for lunch?" Slipping the loop over my head, I peered into the pots.

"Chili," Jess answered. "The tomatoes are from our hydroponic garden in the basement."

Surprised, I asked, "How'd you finagle the money out of my mother?"

"We didn't." Jacob gave his pot a stir. "We had a fundraiser."

My heart fluttered with pride. "Bikini car wash?" I joked.

A laugh shot out of Jacob. "In your dreams, Miss Maisie."

Jess bumped his hip with hers. "We had a bake sale. Everyone pitched in back here, and a few of us canvassed local vendors to see if they'd be willing to help. Some sponsored, some donated goods, and nearly all of them put up fliers in their windows."

"We sold outta banana bread in two hours," Jacob crowed. "Two hundred loaves. When'd we sell out for good?"

"Four in the afternoon." Jess let loose a happy sigh. "We're lucky to be in a neighborhood that cares so much. Harvest is kind of a legend around here, if you didn't know."

"You never told me," I said on a laugh, but a pang of sadness struck me. I'd been so cut off, I hadn't known.

"Dennis—from our division at Bower, the one always in flannel? His degree is actually in agriculture. We came here every night and weekend for two months to get the basement garden set up and planted. That was a year ago."

Pride and longing plucked at my heart. "You have done so much. I knew you would."

"Well, there's always more to do," Jacob said. "We're 'bout to plant the spring garden outside."

"I did hear that," I said. "And then we move for solar. I've been working with our team on the proposal and set aside the money in our budget, so as soon as we have our permits and plans together, we'll go green energy."

"Heard you're openin' a new Harvest Center," Jacob started tentatively. "Where's it gonna be?"

"Hell's Kitchen," I answered with a smile. "I've found the perfect building, and once we have all our plans and blueprints ready, we'll propose them to the city and make a bid on the property."

"Figure you'll need help over there? Getting things started and all?"

With a fond glance, I said, "Why, are you offering?"

The earnest expression on his face stopped me. "I'm offering. If it weren't for you and Jess and everybody, I don't know where I'd be—I only know it wouldn't be good, assuming I was still alive. I got my life back, and in exchange, the center will get anything it needs from me. So you just tell me how I can help, Miss Maisie. I'm ready."

It took everything I had not to either cry or launch myself at him for a hug. "Thank you, Jacob," I said quietly.

"Don't you thank me. I didn't do anything good in my life until this, and who knows if I'll do anything good after."

"Oh, you will," I promised without a single doubt in my mind.

The morning flew by in a rush. Jacob was right—there was always something to do, whether it was loading or unloading the industrial dishwasher or setting dishes out at the window to the cafeteria where we served. Moving lunch to the window or prepping for dinner. Mopping up or wiping down. And I settled into the rhythm with the ease and contentment that came along with busy hands and helping others.

When the lunch hours were over, I made my way back to my bag, checking my phone for the first time in what felt like ages. My plan had been to text Marcus—I'd been looking forward to getting off my feet for a little while now—but instead, I found a string of messages from my mother.

They started off cursory, shifted toward brusque, leaning into impatience before reaching her final stage—infuriation. Was I at my adorable little soup kitchen? How long of a lunch *was* I taking? Ignoring her wouldn't get me any favors, she'd reminded me. And the final messages were a string of demands regarding my mandatory presence at a board meeting I'd never heard about.

With a sigh, I gathered my things and said my goodbyes, hurrying to the curb to hail a cab. I'd missed my lunch date with Marcus, too busy to message him, so on my way to whatever doom my mother had in store, I texted Marcus with my apologies and to chat about my day, lamenting over my mother in between. And by the time we pulled up to the building, I'd been sitting still in the quiet cab long enough to leave me exhausted, body and mind.

As I exited the taxi, I gave myself an inward slap to wake myself up.

Who knew what I was about to walk into, but I couldn't imagine it would be pleasant. Not after ignoring my mother all day.

I wished terribly I was headed anywhere but to her, a wish not quieted by the opening and closing of the elevator doors that gave me glimpses to other floors, happier places. In a particularly mocking gesture, the universe made sure to stop at *my* floor—the charity floor.

I gave it a longing look until the doors closed again.

That tease was a direct representation of my mother's intentions—give me a taste of what I wanted before taking it away.

The stark administrative floor hummed, its elitist occupants and the air they breathed sharp with pretentiousness and condescension. There seemed to be a permanent upward tilt of every nose paired with side-eyes and side-talk. Fitting that my mother had hand-picked every employee on this floor. I was sure she felt right at home.

I, on the other hand, felt the slime of this place clinging to me well after I'd gone.

Shelby greeted me, the only decent thing on the entire floor.

The concern on her face was not reassuring.

"She's been waiting on you to get here. The front desk saw you and called up, so she knows you're here. I—"

The double doors of Mother's office flew open in a dramatic whoosh, and we flinched, turning to find her in the threshold. "Good," she said on seeing me. "Come with me."

Shelby and I shared a look when Mother's back was to us, and I followed her as bidden. The doors closed behind us.

"I trust you're enjoying yourself? Spending all day at that dirty, old building, feeding the unwashed masses." She stilled, assessing me. "You're filthy."

I glanced down, noting an almost imperceptible splatter of sauce. I swiped at it uselessly. "We were making chili."

With a disdainful look, she sat behind her desk, gesturing for me to take a seat of my own. "I've complied, let you do what you want."

She waited expectantly.

I hesitated, unsure how to respond—she hadn't exactly asked a question.

"Well," I started, "it's only been two weeks, but we've made a lot of progress. I think I've found a new site and appointed—"

"So you're pleased with our bargain?"

I paused, recognizing a trap when I saw one, but there was no way out except through. "Yes," was all I allowed.

"Unsurprisingly, I find myself disappointed." Flat red lips to match her flat and furious voice. "Against my better judgment, I've stayed out of your way, given you the room you asked for. I've given you've all you've asked for. But you haven't given me what I want."

My brows inched together. "I've sat in every meeting required of me, even when it conflicted with my schedule. Like today, for instance. What is this board meeting, and when was it called? Because it wasn't on my calendar. But I came when you commanded, just like we agreed."

"Never mind that." She waved her hand, and I realized she'd lied to get me here. There was no meeting.

Only another manipulation.

"As much as you like to believe I'm overbearing and malicious, all I have ever done is to protect you. To protect my company. What you believe is exercised control is not to confine you. It is to *save* you from yourself. I let your father have too much influence, and the result is this." She gestured to me. "A martyr without the constitution to run Bower. But there's no choice for either of us. This is what you were born to do. And it's my job to teach you how. Because you will never, ever survive without my deconstructing what your father has done to you."

"What he's done?" I asked, lungs locked and defenses ringing. "He gave me love. Hope. A heart and a conscience. Only you would see those as liabilities."

"Because they are. You are so naive, Margaret. And the only way to teach you is to strip you of what makes you weak."

"Of what makes me *me*. Your answer is to break my spirit? To strip me of the things I want?"

"You don't know what you want," she said.

"And you do?"

An angry flush climbed up her neck, her jaw. "Better than you. You will learn to bend. You will learn to kneel. And then you will learn to fight for this company properly, or you will fail miserably."

I swallowed my emotion and shook my head, confused. "What does any of this have to do with our bargain? What have I not done? Because from where I'm sitting, I've bent just as much as you have."

Everything about her hardened, her eyes most of all. "You are keeping something from me."

My eyes flicked to the ceiling for the briefest request for divine intervention. "That has nothing to do with what I do for Bower, nor does it apply to our agreement."

"I disagree. Your secrets are my secrets, and my secrets have everything to do with Bower. You love to remind me you're not a child, but the only way to condition you is through the most basic consequences. Time-outs. Earning your rewards. Transparency. You are not allowed secrets because you are not smart or wise enough to be trusted, not even with something so simple as which shoes to wear with that dress."

The jab was nothing next to her crooked perspective.

"How novel that you'd take interest in mothering me now, given that you were absent when it counted. How fascinating that we would fight like a domineering mother and a rebellious teenager. I was always obedient—*always*. And then you tore my world apart and sent me away."

"If your world hadn't been fairy tales and gullible denial, I wouldn't have had to tear it apart. I don't blame you, Margaret. I blame myself for not training you from the start."

"Oh, I blame you for so much, but not for who I am."

Her eyes narrowed to slits. "It's my mess to undo, starting with this—I've allowed your affair to go on long enough. Either you tell me who you're seeing or you put an end to it."

"You've *allowed* me?" I asked, my voice shaky, low, furious. "I don't think you're in a place to give me ultimatums. And while we're on the topic of transparency, let's not pretend this has anything to do with the company or whether I'm fit to run it. It's *you* who wants to know and for no other reason than I won't tell you. Does it drive you crazy, not knowing something I do? Does my defiance drive you mad? Because I guarantee you, that will never stop."

Her face wrenched in indignation. "I will not have secrets under my roof. If you're this obstinate, it must be worse than I thought. Tell me who you're seeing," she said through her teeth, "or our arrangement is void."

My eyes narrowed as I rose from my seat, my body screaming with adrenaline and ready to fight. "If our arrangement is void, I'll see myself out."

"God*dammit*, Margaret," she shouted, slapping the top of her desk loudly enough to jolt me in surprise. "Your future is contingent on *my* good will. Do you think this is a game? Do you think that I'm bluffing?"

"You very clearly think I am," I shot back, unwilling to back down. "And your future is contingent on mine. You think you're so clever, luring me back with the power to fight you and the charity I love. I'm not the only one who's naive, Mother, if you truly believe you've tricked me into a bigger cage. You still don't understand that there is no cage. There is no key. The door is open, and so far, I've *chosen* to stay inside. For now. I see you, Mother. But do you see me?"

A moment of silence.

"I *will* find out who you're seeing and what you're hiding. And when I do, you should hope that I approve."

"I wonder, have you ever gotten anything in your life without a threat?"

Her nostrils flared.

"I didn't think so. Think long and hard about how badly you want me here. Because I will play along for the sake of the company, but I will not be bullied by you."

The blaze of anger in me was doused the second I heard those words pass my lips.

Because they sounded like hers.

The urge to run pulled me toward the door. Every minute spent locked in battle with her brought me one step closer to becoming the one thing I feared more than anything, even losing Marcus.

I could not become her. I could not let her shape me in her image.

Mother fumed. "The little power you think you have is an illusion. You will not leave, nor will you forsake your mother, your duty, your company. All of this was built for you, you spoiled little horror. You did *nothing* to contribute to this empire that I am handing to you without any of your effort. And if you want it, if you want this kingdom I have constructed, you will do what you're told. Enjoy your freedom while I deign to give it to you."

"I'd be glad to," I snapped, turning on my heel, waiting for a parting insult that never came.

Shelby looked concerned as I passed, but she didn't get up or speak, which was wise. Had my mother, in her rage, heard Shelby utter a word in my direction, she likely would have been fired on the spot.

Wouldn't have been the first time.

I had nearly reached the elevator when it opened, and out spilled Roland, my mother's accountant. He seemed to be in a rush, his eyes darting around like he had a briefcase full of stolen cash rather than a briefcase full of financial statements. He was so preoccupied, he didn't see me as he hurried past, pulling a hand-kerchief out of his pocket to dab at his glistening forehead.

The most curious thing about the encounter was the question of where the hell he'd gotten a handkerchief.

Into the elevator I went, heading down to the place I wanted to be, the place *I* had molded and shaped. I walked into the charity division to remind myself of all the good that could be done, all I'd worked for. I was greeted with that lighthearted cheer that accompanied doing things for others, my meager office awaiting me and my mind shifting to all the ways and steps I could take to make a difference somewhere, anywhere, while I could.

Because though I could do so much good, it wouldn't be here. When this lawsuit was over and the Bennets were safe, I would tell her I'd made a choice, and that choice was not Bower. I would walk away from her and into a new life, one that was mine and mine alone.

And there was nothing she could do to stop me.

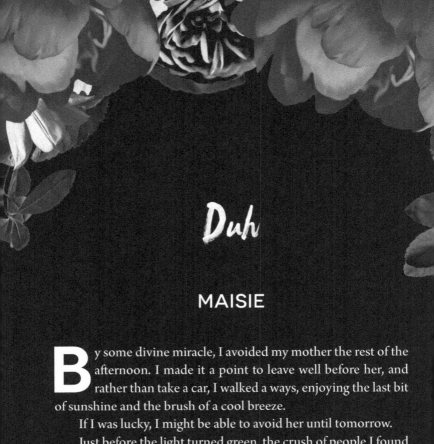

# Duh

## MAISIE

**B**y some divine miracle, I avoided my mother the rest of the afternoon. I made it a point to leave well before her, and rather than take a car, I walked a ways, enjoying the last bit of sunshine and the brush of a cool breeze.

If I was lucky, I might be able to avoid her until tomorrow.

Just before the light turned green, the crush of people I found myself in the midst of flowed across the street like a school of tuna. And the feeling it left me with was blissful normality.

Little by little, the shine of my mother's offer had worn off. Less and less was my altruism more important than my happiness, and today, I'd discovered the uncrossable line and stepped over it.

Every minute I stayed was a minute closer to becoming my mother.

I reveled in this normality as I walked through the city, craved a quiet life without butlers and cooks and private cars. A charming little apartment with a shoebox for a bedroom. A regular old job where I was nobody instead of somebody.

Shares or no shares, the more I thought about dealing with my mother for the many years until she retired, the more I knew I wanted to stay in that stream of people and disappear into my own life forever.

A breeze shot between the buildings as we passed, licking at skirts and bringing hands to stop their hats from tumbling into 8th. And on that breeze came the consequences of me leaving. I thought of all the people at Harvest Center, all those who depended on that place. Sure, there were other kitchens, other places for people to go. But to those who had set down roots and to the community where those roots had spread, closing would be a loss, leaving a gaping hole where something wonderful had once been.

Because if I knew my mother, she would dismantle Harvest Center the second I left.

I'd endangered them either way with my affair—Harvest had been placed on the chopping block the moment my mother made it a bargaining chip. And to save it, I'd have to set myself on fire.

So that would be what I'd have to do. If she shut it down, I'd find a way.

I'd open another on my own. And to hell with my mother.

It was Wednesday, which meant dinner out with Dad. Before I left for England, we would go out for greasy fries, burgers, and milkshakes, and whenever we were both in New York, we upheld the tradition. Predictably, Mother despised it, which probably had something to do with our making it a habit. Sometimes, we'd even bring home a takeout bag of oily fries and plop it on her writing desk in the entryway just to piss her off. Which it inevitably did.

Little rebellions. They were all we had even if they were as fruitful as shooting blow darts at a tank.

By the time I reached the diner, the sun had slipped behind the buildings, casting everything in their cool shadows. The bell over the door chimed, and the old jukebox stood in all its neon glory in the corner, playing the records that had probably been in rotation since the sixties.

Dad sat at our favorite booth with a book in his hand, his readers perched on the end of his nose. When he looked up, he smiled, and "Love Me Do" floated in the air around us.

"Hey, Dad," I said, leaning in to press a kiss to his cheek.

"Hey, honey. How was your day?"

"Don't ask," I said as I slid into the booth, dumping my things in the seat next to me.

"That good, huh?"

"Worse."

The waitress swung by with coffees, and we chose our dinner without menus, having memorized it years ago.

Dad picked up his coffee. "So your mother is losing her mind."

"Yes. Yes, she is." I tore open a sugar packet and dumped it into my coffee. "Did something happen last night?"

"She grilled me about who you're seeing, and we ended up in a fight that shredded my vocal cords."

My brow furrowed. "I'm so sorry, Dad."

"Oh, don't be sorry for that. I've got your back, kiddo."

"It's all so pointless. Nothing short of complete submission will make her stop, so why fight? You should just go. I'm right behind you."

His head cocked with a silent question, but I didn't stop talking.

"I'm tired of answering her questions and submitting to her demands. Sure, she's stayed out of my way to the best of her ability—which is sadly lacking—but she certainly isn't happy about it. And God knows she can't keep her mouth shut when she's happy, never mind when I'm keeping something from her. And I'm just fed up."

"You really *did* have a bad day." He paused. "Does the quality of your day have to do with her disapproval of your nocturnal activities?" he asked with a dusty blond brow arched.

"What else? But it's not just the fight, Dad." I paused, searching for the words. "Every time we fight, every time there's even the smallest confrontation, I ... I don't act myself. I become *her*."

His levity melted into dissent. "Don't ever say that, Maisie. You're nothing like her."

"Everyone tells me that, but I'm not so sure. I don't recognize myself. I say things I'd never say."

"Because she pushes you."

"And I not only put up with it, but I engage. And isn't that what she wants, aside from my compliance? She wants me to fight. She wants me to push back. And when I do, I can't get the stink of it off me." My eyes found a fleck in the formica tabletop and held it. "The only alternative is to leave. And I'm close. I am so close, I could quit right now. But ... well, if I need to hold out a little bit longer. I just need to get through—" I caught myself before spilling the truth, choosing my next words carefully. "There's just one thing to resolve, and it's almost over. Once that's behind us, I'm through."

He said nothing for a stretch. "You sound very sure of yourself."

"If I stay, I can help save someone very important to me. If I leave now, I'm almost certain to ruin them."

"Does this have anything to do with Marcus Bennet?"

My gaze snapped to his as I fumbled my mug. "Why would you say that?"

His smile tilted. "If I hadn't figured out Marcus had the potential to be the mystery man the second you told me you kissed him, I'd have sorted it out just now. Honestly, the second I told you to stay away from him—I mean it, the moment those words left my mouth—I knew there was no stopping you. You're trying to help the Bennets, aren't you? With the lawsuit?"

"I am," I breathed, split with equal parts relief and shock. "Why didn't you say something? Why didn't you tell me you knew?"

"I wanted to give you the space to tell me. Only said something now because I'm impatient."

I chuckled at my coffee before raising my eyes. "You aren't mad?"

"Mad? No. Your mother's the one with that particular grudge, not me. And I trust you. I could never be angry with you for finding someone who makes you happy. He makes you happy, right?" His eyes narrowed in mock suspicion.

"Very. He makes me feel ... equal. I feel equal to him and seen for who I am. And the only other person to make me feel that way is you."

His eyes went soft. "It's called respect, and I am very happy to know I won't have to teach him any lessons on the subject. Maisie, if this is how you feel, then I have no arguments. I'm more worried about what your mother will do when she finds out. You know she'll find out, don't you?"

"I do. But if she finds out before this lawsuit is over, she will ruin the Bennets just to spite me. She's a black hole, set to destroy all of us before seeing us happy. You'd think her therapist would have made some headway in the last twenty years."

He snorted a laugh. "Psychiatrist, and his only use to her is his prescription pad."

"Since I'm stuck there with her, I thought I could use the opportunity to collect information for the Bennets about the lawsuit. Help them head her off."

"A spy, huh?" Dad asked with amused pride. "Look at you."

But I didn't smile, didn't laugh, didn't feel good about it. "Just another thing I've inherited from her. I like to think that it's different because I'm using my deceit for good instead of evil."

He opened his mouth to object, but I changed the subject.

"I'm ready to move out. I'm ready for you to divorce her."

"Trust me, honey, I'm ready too. I've had the paperwork filled out for years—all I have to do is add the date and send it to my divorce lawyer." He watched me for a moment, tracing my face with his gaze as if to note the years that had passed between us. "The first time I ever held you in my arms, I knew my fate and stepped into it. If I'd left, she would have taken you from me. I would not have won custody, and if I had, it would have been the most minimal contact that she could manage. And all that time, every minute I couldn't be there, you'd have been alone with her. I couldn't do it, Maisie. I just … there was no way I could give you up, and if I'd left your mother, I would have had to. So I stayed."

I stilled, a lump of emotion clamped in my throat. "Daddy …"

But he smiled. "I don't regret it. Raising you was the best thing I've ever done." With a shrug, he continued, "After you graduated high school and left, I just couldn't find a way to file for divorce, not without making your life harder. Anytime you chose me over her would have been a fight. Every Christmas, every birthday, every single moment you came to see me instead of her, she would have taken it out of your hide, not mine. Past that, we all knew you were going to have a role in Bower, and things between you two needed to be as smooth as possible in order for that to have a chance in hell. My leaving would have been another hurdle for you, and I couldn't knowingly put that on you. Plus, who else would annoy her when you came home? The more I antagonize her, the less she bothers you. Not to mention that I like seeing her all frothy."

"Me too," I said on a giggle. "If you need another reason to walk away, do this for me, just like you stayed for me."

Dad sat back, heaving a long sigh through his nose. "I think I've been waiting on you. Someday, you're going to be steady. You're going to find a track for your life and slip into it, a track your mother can't bully you down. I want to see you start that life. I want to know you're going to be okay. And you know what? I think you're very nearly there."

"I think I might be too."

"How much does Marcus Bennet have to do with that?"

I let out a laugh, my cheeks warming up at the mention of Marcus. "Most of it, I think. Not directly. It's only that being with him opened up some window in me I thought had been painted shut. He makes me brave, and he gives me hope. And I won't let Mother take that away from me."

"Remind me to thank him for that, if I ever get a chance."

"I will."

"I'm glad you found him, but I'm sorry it's like this. I'll cover for you when I can, but there's only so much I can do. So promise me you'll be careful. Maybe slow it down a little, take some space. Because she'll figure it out even if she has to hire somebody to do it for her. Play along. Play her game while you keep your secret. And when all this stuff with the Bennets is over, blow her to smithereens."

"As if I'm the one with the bazooka."

"Dating a Bennet isn't a bazooka. It's a goddamn nuke," he said on a laugh as our waitress swung by with our food—a drippy hamburger with fries for Dad and big, fat waffles with whipped cream and strawberry sauce I was one hundred percent sure did not have natural ingredients.

As we tucked into our dinner, I was filled with renewed hope that I could have all that I wanted. I would protect the Bennets. I would walk away from my mother and my legacy and into Marcus's arms.

And nothing had ever felt so right.

# Wildfire

## MARCUS

**T**he courtroom held its breath.

On his bench, the judge frowned at his hands as he flipped through the paperwork Ben had just given him, outlining all the ways the prosecution had pushed the boundaries of acceptable requests.

No one but our lawyers should have been here—this type of hearing was generally handled by mediators and for exactly the reason we were here in the first place—we were at each other's throats and unable to make progress on our own. But I'd known Evelyn would insist on being present and that she'd bring Maisie.

And since Maisie was here, I was too.

Thanks to Maisie, we'd known what Bower was doing the second they first started asking for tangential and then irrelevant information. Without the tip, we likely would have gone along with the requests for a little while before more requests filed in. Instead, we'd almost immediately filed a motion for the judge to step in.

And here we were. Whatever the judge decided would determine how the rest of our case would go, including whether or not we'd be financially able to keep fighting.

Maisie sat on the other side of her mother, which kept her out of my view but for the occasional glimpse of her hand or the gold of her hair. The moment she'd walked into the courtroom, a thread plucked between us, the thrum of it still vibrating in my chest. The effort it took not to look at her was so intense, my collar steamed from exertion.

She didn't seem to be faring any better. On the few glances I allowed myself, she was tense and straight and visibly uncomfortable—a far cry from the soft, smiling girl I knew.

I hated every fucking minute of it.

My shoulders and neck had been coiled for so long, a headache bloomed at the base of my skull, inching its way toward my temples. God, I wished Maisie weren't here. But Evelyn wouldn't show up without her, the deep-seated desire to impart her opinions on her daughter predictable at best and cruel at worst.

All I wanted was for this to be over so I could get Maisie out of this room, away from her mother, and into my arms.

The judge closed the folder with that impressive frown still on his face, his eyes sliding to the Bower side of the room. "Can you give me a reasonable explanation as to why you need a deposition from an eighty-year-old vendor who has been retired for fifteen years?"

"A character witness, Your Honor," Thompson said, slippery as all hell and smiling like Satan himself.

The judge looked bored. "You have fifteen character witnesses already. In fact, you seem to have enough information to put together two cases against the defendant." He picked up a pen and began to write. "I have given enough concessions to this case, but with this, you have pushed the boundaries of what I will and will not allow in my courtroom. The remaining discovery requests are unnecessary and frivolous. There are no reasonable grounds for requesting records of the net mulch delivery from 2012 to prove the disputed clause of this contract. As such, discovery is from hereon considered closed. Mediation will be scheduled for—"

"Excuse me," Evelyn blustered.

Thompson tried to hush her, but she stood.

"Your Honor, if I may . . ."

Slowly, the judge raised his eyes to pin her like a bug. "You may not, Mrs. Bower. I suggest you listen to your counsel and sit down." He didn't wait for a response before looking back to whatever was on his desk.

Evelyn sat so slowly, she could barely be considered in motion.

"You will schedule mediation with the county clerk within thirty days. Do you understand?"

"Yes, Your Honor," Thompson said.

"Good. Do not waste any more of the court's time or resources."

His gavel clacked the block, dismissing us.

He didn't so much as glance up at us, but Evelyn Bower stared him down so fervidly, I was surprised he didn't catch fire.

We rose nearly in unison.

"That was fast," I whispered to Ben as we gathered our things, both of us smiling.

"This is good, very good, exactly what I hoped for. It's his job to be fair and unbiased, and it's so deeply ingrained in judges, I'm surprised he let it go this far. Thankfully, he's not interested in entertaining any more of her requests."

"No—he seems to be more interested in throwing her out of court. His wife is gonna be pissed."

We shared a quiet chuckle, turning for the exit without thought.

Momentarily, I'd forgotten that Maisie was right there, right in this very room with me. It had slipped my mind that I could not, under any circumstance, look directly at her for fear that everyone in the room would know every word in my heart, every moment, every kiss that had passed between us.

And that mistake nearly cost me when I found her standing before me.

She was close enough to smell the sweet gardenia soap she was so fond of, walking behind her mother and Thompson as they marched toward the door. But for a protracted moment, we laid eyes on each other with bald honesty, our defenses gone and the truth prone and exposed.

And the enemy pounced.

"Margaret," her mother said, sharp as a razor.

Evelyn stood in the aisle, her face a mask of impassivity but for her accusatory eyes, twin coals flaming in her skull.

She'd made no demand with words, but Maisie's name and Evelyn's tone directed her to get the fuck out of the room.

Maisie scuttled toward the exit without another look in my direction.

Evelyn dragged a long gaze up and down my body as if she were seeing me for the first time. It was not salacious but scrutinizing, that gaze, and I rose beneath it to meet her.

"What a show," she said blithely. "I didn't believe you'd put up a real fight, Mr. Bennet. Color me impressed. But I hope you don't get too comfortable. I'd hate for you to be disappointed."

"The look on your face when you lose will be enough payment to last me a lifetime."

A humorless laugh left her, and in her unpleasant joy, I caught a glimpse of Maisie as if in a fun house mirror, warped and stretched and distorted. "You seem to forget the repository of weapons I have at my disposal. I believe you're smart enough to know I'll use them."

Awareness climbed up my spine, raising every hair on its way up my neck. *Maisie*. But she couldn't mean Maisie. She couldn't possibly know.

Unless she'd really seen us just now.

I brushed the thought away. If she suspected, she wouldn't be covert. She'd have detonated on the spot.

But I reminded her of one thing that had everything to do with Maisie, whether she knew it or not.

"If you think I'll let you ruin one more good thing in the world, you're mistaken."

An indifferent shrug, a twisted smile. "I'll win either way. Shame you won't be able to save yourself." With that, she turned and strode out of the courtroom, and I let her go without another word.

Feeding that particular beast would only make it hungrier. And when I finally chose to battle her, I would end it once and for all.

Ben sighed. "She never quits, does she?"

"No. And I have a bad feeling things are about to get much worse."

He frowned, but I didn't elaborate as we exited the courtroom. Down the hall, Evelyn and Thompson had their heads together. Maisie sat on the bench next to them like a child told to be quiet and wait until the grown ups were finished. The second I caught her eye, she jerked her chin to the hallway under the restroom sign.

"I'll catch you later, Ben," I said.

His eyes narrowed, and when he sighed, it was clear that he knew. "Be careful," was all he said before turning and walking out, being sure to take the route that kept him away from the Bowers.

And I ducked into the hallway and out of sight.

It was the closest thing to privacy that we could have, and I leaned against the wall with my hands in my pockets as if I were waiting for someone to exit the restrooms, just in case her mother followed.

Maisie rounded the corner with a placid look on her face, but the second she was out of their sight, she rushed over, snagged my hand, and dragged me into the men's restroom.

I blinked, grateful it was empty.

"I'm sorry," she whispered. "I only have a second, but, oh God, Marcus ... I think she knows."

"No—I don't think she'd be able to keep it together if she knew. But she might suspect." I cupped her jaw in my hands, tilting her face up to search it. "What do you want to do?"

The wrinkle between her brows made me feel sick to my stomach. *You will ruin this girl, you selfish son of a bitch.*

"I ... I don't know."

"Do you still want to come over?"

"God, yes. I'll be over as soon as I can get away. She's going back to work, but I took the day. Shouldn't be too hard to get to you."

I brought my lips to hers, kissed her tenderly, ardently before letting her go. "I'll be waiting."

That wrinkle smoothed, her smile giving me the falsest of hopes that everything would work out.

With a swift kiss to her forehead, I made for the door, leaving first to make sure the coast was clear. She passed before I ducked back in to wait it out, looking back for the smallest moment of reassurance, which I both gave and took.

And then she was gone.

I stepped back into the restroom, catching a glimpse of myself in the mirror. I was the picture of sobriety—back straight, proud nose, lips flat, eyes stern.

No one would ever know that beneath that mask, I was a wildfire.

It was hours before she was in my arms, and I didn't calm down until that moment.

It had been an unbearable stretch of time, one consumed with imaginings of the worst. Her mother confronting her about me. A fight and disownment.

Maisie losing everything because I was too selfish to walk away.

The second she was through my door, I swept her into my arms, kissed her with reckless misery at the ways I'd hurt her simply for wanting her.

When the tension in her body dissolved, so did mine, and only then did I let her lips go.

The rest of her I held on to.

She smiled lazily up at me, sighing away the world beyond my door.

"Are you all right?" I asked, thumbing her cheek.

"I am now."

"Did she say anything? Does she know?"

"She didn't say a word about you, so she must."

I kissed her again and released her.

"They spent a long time talking about mediation," she said, leading me toward the stairs. "Their plan is to be as obstructive as they can without getting in any more trouble, and they're going to do whatever they can to bait you. And the carrot of choice is your mother."

I swore under my breath.

"It's going to be ugly, Marcus. I can feel it. I don't know what she'll do, how she'll hurt you, but she will. If she puts it together, she might bar me from legal meetings. Or worse. After today, I don't know how much good I'll be."

"Maisie, you'll always be good for me." *But I'm not good for you.*

She smiled over her shoulder. "I hope so. But ... well, where the lawsuit is concerned, I might be out of the game." Once in my room, she sat heavily on the end of my bed and kicked off her heels. "What are we going to do?"

"Something neither of us wants. We're going to have to be more careful."

This time, her sigh was resigned.

"Until the lawsuit is settled, we have to try not to see each other. Otherwise, we'll never throw your mother off the scent."

"Maybe I should change perfumes," she teased, stretching her feet. But her wan smile disappeared. "I don't want to stay away."

"Neither do I. But I've already put you in enough danger with her." I pulled off my jacket, then my tie. "It'll have to be lunches and extended work outings for the charity. Times when you're already out, things that can be easily explained."

Her frown was more of a pout, her chin flexed and eyes shiny. "It will never cease to amaze me how swiftly she can ruin everything good in my life."

I sat next to her on the end of the bed, pulling her legs into my lap. "There are many things she has control over, but not our hearts. She can't ruin *us*," I said to convince both myself and her. "This is temporary, Maisie—just a blip. I've made this hard enough for you, so let's do the smart thing instead of what we want. Just this once."

"Just this once? Promise?"

I chuckled, sliding her closer by the hook of her knees. "Promise. Because after we tell your mother, all bets are off. We're going to do whatever the fuck we want to do."

She giggled, the sound bringing a smile to my face. It was impossible to feel anything but pleased and easy joy at her happiness.

"So what'll it be?" I asked, unfastening the highest button of her tailored shirt, which she'd left blessedly low. "Whatever the fuck do you want to do after all this?"

"Well, let's see …" she started, smiling as I undid another button, rewarded with the view of her breasts, swathed in sheer nude lace. "I've thought about starting up another center, maybe like Harvest. But either way, I want to do something meaningful. Something that gives back."

"Maybe you could run the charity at Longbourne."

"You have a charity?" Her eyes widened in surprise. "Why haven't you told me?"

"We don't. Not yet at least." With a tug, her shirt was free of her skirt, and my unbuttoning continued.

"Oh, I would love to work for Longbourne. I've always imagined that's what a family business looks like, how it should be run."

"You mean into the ground?"

She swatted my chest, though her hand slid to my buttons having become aware that I'd nearly gotten her shirt off while mine was still unfairly on. "I mean that you would do anything to save each other, your mother, the business. Your priority is first and foremost to your family and everything else after. It's the exact opposite of what I know of family business and priorities—control, obligation, and duty. Walking away won't be hard—oh, don't make that face. I don't believe in miracles, Marcus, and deep down, you don't either. And short of a miracle, I can't find any reason to stay. But my point is that it feels like I'll be on to bigger and better things, if for no other reason than those things will be *mine*."

"But won't you miss it?"

"My mother? Does any criminal miss their jailer?" she joked.

"Not your mother, but don't you think you'll wish you'd stayed at Bower?"

She paused, considering. "Maybe it's naive, but I don't. Staying feels so much harder than going. Maybe it's just the allure of something new, a different life. I'd be sad if I were walking away from someone who loved me, but I'm not. I'm a possession to her, a pet, not a person. You should count yourself lucky—I'd give just about anything to have the kind of family you have."

"Maybe someday you will." My heart ached with longing for that day as I slipped her shirt off the curve of her shoulder, pressing a kiss to the revealed skin.

"Could you imagine," she said wistfully, "what it would be like for us to run Longbourne together?"

"I could. You taking what you've learned and employing it at

Longbourne. Taking the reins of the true business of it because my expertise is sadly lacking. I'm in finance and poorly versed in the inner workings of a flower shop."

"Oh, I think you know it better than you realize." Warm hands slid under my shirt and over my shoulders, removing the fabric to press a kiss to the curve, as I had hers. "I'd run the large-scale business operations and the charity department. You would run the finances. Your mother would be chairman of the board."

I chuckled, tracing her collarbone, her sternum, the swell of her breast. "You should really consider that before committing."

"Tess could run the shop's daily business, but I could help you expand, grow." Another sigh, this one longing. "Wouldn't that be lovely? I'd much prefer that dream than the dread of Bower."

"I think you would fit in perfectly," I mused. "I love this idea." *And I love you.*

My hand wandered up to her face to hold it like the precious thing it was.

*I love her,* I realized with a shock that split me open, exposed me. *When did it happen? Have I loved her from the start? Have I loved her my whole life?*

It felt as if she had been a part of me long before I knew her, and now that I'd found her, there was no choice to be made. I had never subscribed to the sentiment that one person could make another whole. But now I knew the concept had been born from the restriction of words.

There was no way to describe a feeling patently beyond description.

I had discovered a new sense, one tuned to her alone. When she wasn't with me, I could feel her far away. When she was here, nothing beyond us mattered. And I knew that one day, we would settle into a life, into each other, and things wouldn't be this intense, this overwhelming. But I also knew whatever thread connected us wouldn't fray or sever. Even if we should part, we were bound. And now that I knew the safety and peace that bond provided, being bound to her was the only thing I wanted.

I couldn't speak, my throat a pileup of words and feeling. So I leaned in to occupy my lips. They brushed hers, then captured them, pressing into a seam, and she opened to let me in.

I'd let her in long ago. Maybe it was that first day when we danced in the rain. Maybe it was the kiss, that first kiss in the dark boardroom full of goodbyes. Or the moment she stood up for the things I loved. Maybe it had been a mundane moment between now and then, some quiet glance, an honest kiss.

I didn't know when or how, but I knew without question that I couldn't have stopped it any easier than I could have stopped the sun from shining. When I looked into my future, she was there. When I looked back at my past, it was a colorless sketch of a life without her.

It was crazy. Reckless. Illogical.

And I didn't care. Because I loved her, and that truth became the only one in my life that mattered.

We wound together, chests flush and hands splayed, mouths wide and tongues seeking. With a twist, I laid her beneath me, sliding my thigh between hers, taking her pencil skirt with it. Her hands worked my belt, then my zipper, then my cock. Mine hitched her skirt, cupped her sex, tasted the heat of her with hungry fingertips.

I was very nearly on the verge of tasting her with my tongue when my front door opened.

We froze.

"Hallooooo?" my mother called from the entryway.

I hissed, flying off the bed as Maisie rolled the other direction, scrambling for her top and tugging at her skirt.

"One second, Mom!" I called too cheerfully, the two of us wild-eyed and speaking in gestures.

"What are you doing up there? You're not napping, are you? You haven't napped since you were an infant."

Her footfalls on the stairs sprang everything into a frenzy.

"No, I just had something to do," I said in a panic as Maisie ducked into my closet.

"In your room? At noon?" Her voice came closer, and I kicked Maisie's heels under my bed, adjusting my cock and buckling my pants. There was no time for a shirt.

I bolted into the hallway to find my mother at the top of the stairs. At the sight of me, her head cocked, brows drawn.

"Where's your shirt?"

"I was hot," I said, moving to put my arm over her shoulders and guide her back downstairs.

Her eyes narrowed, and she spun away from me faster than she should have been able to. "Is your furnace broken? Let me have a look, clunky, old thing."

"Furnace is fine, Mom." I tried to grab her, but she dodged me, beelining for my room. "I need a drink of water though—come on, and I'll make you some tea."

"Now, just a second," she said when I ran past her and put myself between her and the doorway. "I'd like to see why your room is so hot. Did you open a window? It's so nice outside," she said, trying to look around me.

"Mom. All right, all right," I said, hands out, brain a flurry of excuses, finally landing on one she'd never argue. "I'm gonna be honest."

One of her brows rose, but she quit trying to sneak a peek.

"There is so much porn in there."

She rolled her eyes with a laugh, but her cheeks flushed, and thankfully, she backed off. "I appreciate your trying to protect me, but after raising four boys through adolescence, I am immune to shock. There was a time when I was afraid to step foot in any of your rooms without knocking. God knows what I might have found. Or saw." She shuddered.

"Boys are disgusting creatures, Mom." She let me guide her toward the stairs. "Why don't you go down and have a seat while I put a shirt on."

"All right, darling. And you'll come tell me about the hearing."

"You bet. Just give me one second."

"And to think," she said, "I thought you had a secret girlfriend."

She smiled as I turned, and I thought I caught a shift of that smile into one of shrewd understanding as she cast a glance beyond me toward my room.

But there was zero time to wonder about that as I flew into my room and shut my door behind me, opening the closet. Maisie clutched her shirt to her chest, her lips pursed and eyes wide. She smiled when she saw me, stifling a laugh with her hand.

"Full of porn, huh?" she whispered.

I pulled her out of the closet and into my arms, pressing my lips to her ear. "Wait until she's gone, and I'll prove I wasn't lying."

She shook with silent laughter, pressing a kiss to my neck.

And I pulled on my shirt and buttoned it, leaving it untucked. As I left my room again, I closed the door behind me with a singular objective.

To get my mother the hell out of here so I could make good on that promise.

# Promises, Promises

## MAISIE

I didn't know how long I'd been waiting for Marcus—not too long, but far too long for my liking.

I hadn't wandered around his room like I'd wanted to, instead tiptoeing to the bed to ease in gently, worried I'd make a sound and alert his mother. I'd slid beneath his soft, fluffy comforter, not bothering with my shirt, ridding myself of my skirt to save us both the trouble. I would have taken it all off if I hadn't been afraid of her busting in like an amateur detective.

The last way I wanted Mrs. Bennet to meet me was with my nipples on display.

My phone was downstairs with my bag, and I hoped he'd hidden it somehow—his house was too tidy to lose things in a mess. As such, I had nothing to do except sit there in Marcus's big bed and think.

I thought about the hearing and the sheer terror that we'd been found out by my mother. I thought about what it would be like to dissociate from her, from my life, wondering if it'd feel like losing a limb or removing a tumor. I thought about how the only joys in my life were the ones my mother opposed to and how desperate I was to escape the misery she'd shackled me with.

But then I thought of Marcus, overshadowing every offense in my life with nothing more than his presence.

The suffering on his face when he'd asked me what I wanted to do, as if he expected me to call it off. The hours and hours I'd spent here in the haven of his arms. The longing to spend all of my time here. With him.

I thought about the way he'd looked at me in that moment when we were daydreaming of a future—*our* future. That look was a mirror of my heart, reflecting love back at me like a blinding streak of sunshine.

In the short time that I'd known him, I'd learned many very important things about the stoic Marcus Bennet. The first was that he wasn't as stoic as he seemed—when he let his guard down, he was anything but. My Marcus was playful and light in that quiet way of his. When he spoke, his words were exact. And you could take them to the bank.

He fulfilled his promises with a loyalty I'd never witnessed. And I realized with a desperate desire I wanted one of those promises for myself.

I'd meant what I'd said—my future was a shiny, terrifying thing, a glimmer of change on the horizon. When all this was over and I walked toward that future, I'd leave everything else behind. And though I hadn't realized just how deeply I felt it until I uttered the words, I found more peace in that future than the one my mother had planned for me.

I sighed, leaning back into the luxurious pillows. And with a smile on my face, I closed my eyes and daydreamed about that future with the wish burning hot in my chest.

The bed dipped, snapping me out of the *actual* dream and the unknowing sleep I'd slipped into.

Marcus chuckled when I bolted up, stretching out next to me. "Have a nice nap?"

"Good God, you scared the shit out of me." This was evidenced by the thud of my heart under my palm.

"I should have let you sleep, but I'm a selfish bastard—I had to kiss you." Leaning in, he did just that. "You were too beautiful, lying here asleep with a smile on your face like a Disney princess."

I laughed, lying back down on my side to face him. "How'd it go with your mother?"

"Fine, but she's definitely onto me. She knows there's someone, but she doesn't know who. Laney and Jett don't know yet, and I think Dad's still in the dark too. I can't believe Luke kept his mouth shut. Probably helps he's living with Tess and not at home. He's a worse gossip than Mom."

"We should tell her," I suggested.

He frowned. "You think?"

"I don't want her to find out some other way. Like with me naked in your bed."

He scooted closer, cupping my hip and eyeing my lips. "Remind me next time to bolt the door."

"I'm serious," I said on a laugh, which made me sound not very serious. "I also don't want her to find out from my mother."

At that, we sobered.

"I don't either." He paused. "Are you sure you're ready for that?"

"Absolutely not. But I'm absolutely certain about you."

I was rewarded for the admission with a searing kiss, one that went on until I was pinned beneath him and his fingers were tangled in my hair.

He looked down at me with smoldering eyes. "All right. We'll tell her, but we need a plan."

"*A* plan?" I teased.

"Fine, a few plans. But I'm not sure when we should do it. We're being careful, remember? If your mother finds out ..."

Neither of us needed to finish that thought. We all knew her finding out in the middle of the lawsuit would throw a block of C-4 in the dumpster fire that was this whole ordeal.

"I hate this," I muttered, fiddling with his buttons.

He pressed a kiss to my forehead, smoothing my hair. "I know. But it's just for a little while."

"A blip."

"A blip. And then it's you and me."

I sighed, angling so I could see his face. The strong line of his jaw, chiseled from stone. The angle and bow of his top lip, the lush swell of the bottom. The Roman nose and the blue of his eyes, the iris azure, shot in the center with silver and ringed in navy.

However did a man like him exist? He was the picture of dependability, the one you could always count on. He was truth speaker and protector—under his sleek exterior lived a lion, defending what he loved and what was his to the death.

And somehow I was his, and he was mine.

The thought was wiped away with a kiss and a shift of his hips, barred from close contact by the comforter. He realized it when I did and rose to draw it back, the cold air kissing my bare thighs and arms.

His eyes roamed my body as he unbuttoned his shirt, tossing it behind him. I lay there on display, unmoving as he admired me. The precise faithfulness of his gaze made me feel precious, like a delicate treasure, a prized painting, perfect and cherished. That look made me feel beautiful, desired, and gladly, I let him mark every inch of me with praise I didn't know I'd ever feel worthy of.

His long, square fingers unfastened his belt, lowered his zipper, but when he stretched out next to me, his hands abandoned his task to stroke the curve of my breast. On its bath, his thumb grazed my nipple—it tightened, reaching for his touch as it passed. His thigh slid between mine until that corded muscle rested firmly against the place that wanted him so acutely. The locking of our legs pressed the hard length of him against my hip, and God, how I wanted to slip my fingers into his pants and touch

STACI HART

him. But instead, I was still, knowing he wanted to pay some tribute, some homage to me that required nothing but my presence.

Every touch was slow, every moment drawn out. The slide of his hand into my bra that exposed my breast. The feathery feel of his fingertips skimming the tender skin, circling my nipple. The sight of him lowering his parted lips, the shock of pleasure at the heat of his mouth. A whimper from me, and his tenderness tightened with desire, a sharp intake of breath and a hard draw of my breast.

My fingers found their way into his dark hair as he spent a long, lovely moment where he was. With a snap of his fingers, my bra was undone and discarded, and when he returned to my body, it was with his chest spreading my thighs and his lips on a path toward my hips.

I propped myself up with a pillow, not wanting to lose the indulgent sight of him, his black lashes fanned on his cheeks, brows soft with desire, lips deft, tongue masterful. Big hands hooked the waist of my panties, backing away only to rid me of them, to leave me naked, unwrapped and waiting for his pleasure. First with fingertips, slicked with my heat, tracing the rippling flesh, circling the swollen tip of me. Then with his eyes, cataloging every stroke. Then with his blessed mouth, his divine tongue, the hallowed act of which stretched time out to minutes or hours.

Distantly, I felt his shoulders beneath my thighs, his hands splayed on my hips to hold me still. The chill in the room bit my skin, but I was hot despite it, the distinction sharp and sweet. But my awareness shrank, tightening, receding to the point where his lips latched him to me.

My body was his. The arch of my back, the roll of my hips, the press of my aching core to his mouth, it was all by his hand, by his lips and tongue.

Nothing about it was fast, even as heat rose within me, as my heart galloped painfully, as the orgasm he wanted from me began to heed the painfully slow call of his tongue. It bloomed through my chest, down my ribs, past my stomach to pool at his lips as they moved with deliberate resolve.

An unhurried flick of his tongue was the strike of a match.

A leisurely draw of my body into his mouth fanned the ember into flame.

A deep, rumbling moan, and I shattered.

Every shift of his mouth jolted my thighs, bucked my hips, set a cry on my lips. A groan and a hiss from him and from me, but he didn't relent. The sight of him buried between my legs sent another pulse of pleasure through me, and I scrabbled at his shoulders, shifting my legs, reaching for him.

He broke away, drunken and wild. Swollen lips met mine with relief and determination, and with me hanging on his neck, he laid us down, let me go, and backed away.

He rose before me, a god, not a man, his power over me absolute. I drank in the sheen of his skin glittering across his broad chest, the hard disks of his pecs, the ridges of his abs, down to his narrow waist. His pants hung open, his cock hard and long, his crown escaping the band of his boxer briefs.

My body clenched at the sight.

I watched him undress, watched every inch of skin as it was bared, mesmerized. Because it wasn't only his skin he revealed when he met my eyes. It was the bold and naked truth of his heart, the deep and unbound longing of his soul. And the sight wasn't an accident. It wasn't a slip of a mask or a moment of revelation.

It was a deliberate undressing of his very self, offered with the reverence of a sacrifice. It was a gift, one he'd never given before. One I'd never been given. One neither of us had received.

When I opened my arms, he occupied them. When he kissed me, I held that gift on tender lips. When he filled my body with his, I was given that promise I'd wished for. Without words, he promised me everything, swore his devotion. And I knew in my marrow that he would honor that vow.

We were a wave, a slow wave of pleasure, a long stroke of

love. We were racing pulses and shallow breaths. We were lost in the depths of each other's eyes, drowning in the bottomless fissures of our hearts. We poured ourselves in until each overflowed with the other, until neither could be distinguished. Together, our hearts stopped. Together, they kicked back to life. Together they raced, together, we came. And together, we came down, tangled in each other's arms with a single, infinite wish.

That we'd forever stay there.

# Hear Me Out

## MARCUS

**A** grueling and endless week ground me down like a stone mill.

I'd only seen Maisie once in the last seven days since neither of us was willing to tip her mother off. Since the hearing, Evelyn had been breathing fire down Maisie's neck, leaving zero room for error. So I buried myself in work, and Maisie divided her time between the charity and shadowing in the advertising department. I'd spent nights with my family, and she'd caught up on time with her dad, which I'd heard involved a John Hughes movie binge and repotting her collection of plants in her room.

There was no way for her to get away, not with her mother hot on our scent. And as such, we'd spent a miserable week apart.

But today, I whistled my way into Longbourne, light as could be.

Because tonight, Maisie was coming over.

She'd set up a cover with her friend Jess from work—they were having dinner and going for a drink as far as her mother knew. They'd even planned on leaving work together and sharing a cab over to my place.

All I had to do was survive a few more hours, and then I could fill up on Maisie.

Ivy was at the register with her baby strapped to her chest, the shop busy as usual. She gave me a shifty look when I walked in, and I gave her a look right back.

"What are you doing here today, Ivy? I thought you were still on maternity leave."

"I am. But they needed a hand, and I'm gonna be honest, Marcus—I'm bored out of my goddamn mind."

A laugh burst out of me.

"I mean, don't get me wrong. Motherhood is great and rewarding and all that. Look at my baby—she's cute as hell. Who wouldn't love holding that little thing all day?" She craned her neck to look at said baby, who was asleep and just as cute as she'd said. "But I really needed to put on a bra and brush my hair, and neither of those things were happening without a good reason."

"Well, I'm glad. Wendy's not quite ready to take your place, so Tess has been pulling a lot of double duty. So anytime you need an excuse to put on a pair of pants with a zipper, come on in."

"Psh, a zipper? These are maternity jeans, my blessing and my curse." She popped the elastic band, just in case I didn't believe her.

The baby wriggled, and Ivy bounced, patting the curve of the carrier. With a nod and a smile, I headed to the back.

I found Tess next, her face pinched and focus hard on the arrangement of zinnias in front of her.

"Watch out—you're gonna blow those flowers up if you think at them any harder."

She blinked, brightening up. But she still looked a little shifty too, and the sight set my hackles at attention.

"What's with everybody today?" I asked. "How come Ivy's

out front? Where's Jett? Kash asked me to come in, but I was under the impression we were talking about a missing shipment of succulents. Was I wrong?"

She squirmed. "Ah, they're in the greenhouse," she dodged. "You should go back there."

I stepped closer, smelling fish. "How come, Tess? What's going on?"

Her face was crimson, her lips pursed. "Nothing."

"Tess."

"I said, nothing!" she said with brusque finality, turning back to her bouquet. "I am not a Bennet, and this is a Bennet thing."

My eyes narrowed. "What's a—"

The look she cut in my direction stopped me, and I put up my hands.

"All right, all right. Don't shoot."

She pointed her shears at me and flicked them toward the door.

I decided then that someday Tess would make an excellent mother.

To the back I went, through the doors to the greenhouse and into the damp. But the only person I found was Kash, and he practically jumped out of his skin when I opened the swinging doors.

My brows stitched together. "Please tell me you've got something good to spill because everybody's acting like—"

"Mom's about to find out," he hissed, pointing me toward the basement.

My feet stopped, and I nearly fell over. When I'd caught myself, I picked up my pace.

Kash cranked up the radio before following, presumably for noise pollution to deter our mother should she come snooping.

The basement was dark but for the few lights in the center, one of which shone over a work table. And standing around it like the board of directors from hell were my siblings.

I came to a stop at the head of the table, and Kash took the other end. For a moment, we were silent. Luke scratched his neck. Jett cleared his throat. Laney looked at me like a traitor, and Kash mostly looked annoyed.

"I knew you couldn't keep your trap shut," I shot at Luke.

And that was all it took.

Everyone started talking at once. Kash went on about how he'd told me so. Luke promised it had been an accident. Jett was annoyed I hadn't told him myself, and Laney was just pissed.

"I mean, really, Marcus," she snapped. "A Bower. A freaking *Bower.* Mom is going to die. You are literally going to give her a heart attack, and I'm gonna put *Marcus Did This* on her headstone."

"I don't suppose Luke told you Maisie's helping us, did he?"

"Oh, he did." She folded her arms. "I just don't think that's enough reason to pretend like this is a good idea."

"Well, lucky for me, I don't need your permission."

Laney scowled, but her cheeks flushed, and I thought I caught a glimmer of angry tears in her eyes. "Marcus ... of all the women you could have chosen—"

"I chose her. Do you think I'd have chosen her if she wasn't worthy?"

Her mouth clicked closed, and she frowned furiously at me. "No," she fired, "but it's still fucking messed up."

Kash wore a magnificent frown of his own. "That's not why we're here, is it, Laney?"

"No, we're here because we have to figure out how to tell Mom without giving her a coronary," she said. "This girl had better be awesome, Marcus. She'd better be the best goddamn everything in the whole world."

"She is," I said simply.

Something in the way I'd said it softened her eyes, her jaw, but her arms remained locked across her chest in defiance.

Jett started, "I think you should sit Mom down. Break it to her easy."

"We definitely can't keep it a secret much longer," Kash said. "Look at Luke. He's gonna pop like a piñata, except instead of candy, he's spilling secrets."

Luke rolled his eyes. "I'm not that bad."

We all pinned a look on him.

"Hey, you try getting cornered by her. When she does that thing with her eyes," he said, making a pitiful face. "And she asks you with that voice?"

"You're the only one still a sucker for that," Laney answered. "It's the same trick you pull on her when you want something."

"Well, why wouldn't I use it if it works?" he asked.

"Exactly," Jett said on a laugh.

Kash shook his head and wrangled us in. "You could tell her yourself, or we could be there with you. Maybe if we're a unified front, she'll have a harder time arguing."

This time, we all pinned *him* with a look.

"I have a crazy idea," Luke said.

"No, you?" Laney answered on a laugh.

He made a face at her but continued, "What if you bring Maisie here?"

Once again, the room erupted in noise, me included.

Luke held up his hands. "Hear me out," he said over the din, waiting for us to simmer down.

Laney had the last word, and it was unrepeatable.

"Listen," Luke said, "if Maisie is right there in front of her, she's not going to sling all the hateful things about the Bowers around—"

Kash frowned. "You sure about that?"

"Think about it. Remember after that first deposition? Mom was singing Maisie's praises. Mom likes her, thinks she's nothing like her mother, right? Don't you think she'd have, I don't know … sympathy?"

Now Jett was frowning too, the expression identical to Kash's. "Just because Mom doesn't hate Maisie doesn't mean she wants Marcus dating her."

I scrubbed a hand over my mouth. "I've been thinking about this ever since you assholes found out, but I've *really* thinking about it since Mom nearly walked in on us last week."

They gaped at me like a quartet of trout.

I ignored them. "Telling Mom one-on-one would give her the freedom to completely lose her marbles. If we're all there, it'd be easier, but she'd still just call us all traitors and storm out in the end. But if Maisie's there to defend herself, to declare herself, don't you think Mom would understand?"

They were quiet.

"She's gonna be upset any way we look at it. At least this way, she can look Maisie in the eye and know the truth."

"And what's that?" Laney asked.

"That Maisie is on our side."

No one argued, which I took as a good sign.

"She has constantly put herself at risk for us. For me. She stuck up for us when it mattered, and she's been feeding us information on this lawsuit that has the power to sink us. Maisie nearly walked away from everything she's ever known because she's through with her mother. If that doesn't prove she's with us, I don't know how else to convince you aside from this—I trust her absolutely and without question."

The room went soft with understanding, even Laney, who perhaps wore the most emotional expression of us all. "Well, if you tell Mom like that, I don't know how she can argue," she said softly. "I certainly can't."

Jett snorted a laugh. "And that's saying something."

Kash nodded. "I think we should combine ideas—if we're all there *and* Maisie shows up, we should be able to manage Mom."

"And Dad," I added. "If he's got our back, she really won't fight it. We've just gotta make sure she doesn't feel ganged up on."

Luke smirked. "Leave that to me. I'll get her buttered up real good."

"So when should we do it?" Kash asked.

I considered for a beat. "I'll talk to Maisie tonight. If she's ready now, do you think we could pull something together last minute?"

Laney gave me a sidelong smile and said, "We're Bennets, aren't we?"

With a gentle laugh around the table, I felt the peace of their acceptance, not realizing I'd been carrying that burden around with me since the second I met Maisie. Because if they didn't approve, the things I loved in the world would divide. And I only wanted them to expand.

"Thank you," I said, swallowing down unexpected emotion. "Thank you for trusting me."

Laney took my hand, looking up at me with that smile still on her face. "Marcus, no matter what happens, no matter what's said, in the end, you will always have our trust."

And with a final look around the table, we began to plan the ultimate ambush—how to tell my mother I was in love with a Bower.

# Bring the Bottle

## MAISIE

"Think she bought it?" Jess asked as the cab took off, leaving my mother at work behind us.

"I hope so. We made a big enough show on our way out."

A laugh cracked out of her. "Going up there together to talk to your mother was a stroke of genius. I think she might have believed we were going to dinner, but I can never tell with her face like that."

"I'm sure she'll watch the security footage anyway, just to be sure."

She sighed, her smile fading. "How do you live like this?"

"Well, I'm not usually dating the son of her sworn enemy. I don't generally have to sneak around."

Jess gave me a look.

But I chuckled. "I don't know, Jess. It's always been like this, although I've never kept secrets from her. I've never done anything that required subterfuge."

"You sure picked a doozy for your opening act of defiance."

"And she accuses me of being unambitious." I scoffed.

"He must be something, Maisie. I've never known you to take such a stand."

"He's worth it. *I'm* worth it. It's all so stupid, Jess. I'm just ready for it to be over."

"What's stopping you?"

"Very little at this point. Only the well-being of the Bennets. But I can't say worrying about Harvest Center doesn't upset me. Because she'll end it, you know she will."

Jess nodded soberly. "Well, if she disowns you, then *she* initiates the end of it. Am I wrong in guessing you'll never stop feeling guilty if it's you who pulls the plug?"

With a pang in my chest, I said, "I don't think I would. I'd do something else, something on my own. But I'd always regret letting Harvest go. Does that make me a baby?"

"No. It makes you human, which is more than I can say for your mother."

All I could do was sigh.

"Do you think you'd feel like this if it wasn't for Marcus?"

I didn't even have to consider it, I'd spent so much time wondering the same thing. "I don't think I'd have gone this far, no. But I'm not doing it *for* Marcus. I'm doing it *because* of Marcus. Before him, all doors were closed but the one at the end of the hall, and at the doorknob is my mother, waiting to usher me across the threshold and into Bower. And now ... now, all the doors are open, and that gives me courage. He gives me courage."

Her face softened. "Sounds an awful lot like you might love him."

My heart sprang into my throat at the word, one I'd been thinking too often lately. "I feel an awful lot like I might too."

"You deserve this happiness," Jess said, covering my hand with hers. "Don't think for a minute you don't."

"I just wish it hadn't come with a price."

"Me too."

"And if it comes to that, I'll make sure everyone who needs the center finds another shelter to feed and support them. Everyone we've trained has the skills to be placed with jobs, and I'll volunteer on my own time to make sure no one's left behind."

The thought both broke and healed me. "And I'll help too, however I can."

"And who knows? Maybe someday we'll start our own center *together*. Take everything we've learned and strike out on our own."

"She'll fire you if she finds out you're working with me," I warned.

"Well, fuck her then," she answered, and we laughed at our shameless disrespect.

Though I reminded myself that one had to be respected before they could be *dis*respected.

The topic turned to happier things as we rode into the Village, and by the time we pulled up in front of Marcus's house, I was giddy with anticipation at seeing him. I slipped on my big glasses and tied a scarf around my head to cover my hair. My jacket hung on my arm—it was far too warm today for a wool coat—and with a glance toward Longbourne, I said goodbye to Jess and dashed out of the cab for Marcus's door.

I found myself inside in a flash, thankful again for my key. Standing on that stoop as I used to, waiting for him to answer, had been like standing under the sand streaming through an hourglass—I felt every second.

But then the door would close, stopping time. And it wouldn't start again until I left.

"Hello?" I called, tugging off the scarf to stuff it in my bag.

His footfalls rumbled on the steps too fast for a walk, and I smiled to myself as I hastily hung my coat, already leaning toward the stairs to greet him.

He rounded the corner, and the instant our eyes met, the

stiff, tense air about him melted away. That rare smile I loved so much touched the lips I'd wanted to kiss every minute since I'd seen him last.

Before I even knew it, I'd gotten what I wished for, swept into the safety of his arms. His kiss was a baptism, the washing away of everything sad and ugly, every worry and every regret. And when that kiss broke and he smiled down at me, I was as fresh and clean as new-fallen snow.

His forehead pressed to mine, his nose brushing the bridge of mine. "God, I missed you," he whispered.

"The blip doesn't feel like much of a blip, does it?"

"No, but I'm looking forward to the day when it does."

Marcus kissed me swiftly and set me all the way down—I hadn't quite realized he'd had nearly all my weight in his arms until I took it back on myself.

"Want a drink?" he asked, heading for the kitchen with my hand in his.

"Please. Rough day?"

"Not exactly."

I frowned, taking a seat at the island. "What happened?"

"First, a drink," he hedged to the clink of ice in crystal.

"If you insist," I answered with an enigmatic smile to match his behavior.

He handed me my gin, but before we drank, he raised his scotch. "To everything working out."

My brows quirked. "Hear, hear."

And we took a sip for luck.

"All right," I started once my glass was on the island surface, "what in the world is going on?"

Marcus started to take another sip but stopped, setting his drink down instead. "Everyone in my family knows about us, except my mother."

The sharp trail of gin halted somewhere behind my heart. "Oh no," I whispered.

"Oh, yes. I was ambushed by my siblings in order to plan an ambush for my mother."

"And what did you come up with?"

He moved around the island to get closer, looking down at me with his brows knit. "You don't have to do anything you don't want to. Whatever you're comfortable with, that's what we'll do."

"God, what is this plan? I don't have to take a public flogging or something, do I?"

He relaxed a little at the joke, the corners of his lips flickering with a smile. "No, no flogging or whipping—I mean, unless you're into that sort of thing."

"Not by your mother, thank you."

That earned me a single, lovely laugh.

"So tell me the plan," I urged, pressing down my anxiety.

"Well, we've got to tell her, that's for sure, and I don't know how much time we'll have. If I know Laney and Jett, they're currently talking about all of this, and if they're within a hundred feet of the house, Mom will hear them. So we discussed it, and we think the best chance of success is if you're there with me when I tell her."

The gin finally moved, but it went in the wrong direction. I swallowed hard to force it back down. "Okay. If that's our best chance, I'm ready."

"Ready enough to do it today?"

"Today?" I squeaked.

"Now, really."

I pursed my lips to stop myself from making that noise again.

"We don't have to," he assured. "I just thought that since you're here and it's so hard to get together right now—"

"I'll do it."

He paused, mouth still posed to finish what he'd been about to say.

"I want this to go as smoothly as possible. Whatever I have to do, Marcus. Even a flogging, if it'll help. Because if she doesn't approve ..."

Marcus slid toward me, framed my face with honest hands. "She'll approve."

"You don't know that. You can't possibly know that. And if she doesn't approve, it'll split your family in two."

He tilted my chin, so our gazes were level. "She will," was all he said, but the words held such conviction, I had no choice but to believe right along with him.

When I conceded with a nod, he leaned in, kissing me with tender assurance. And when he let me go and pulled his phone out of his pocket, I drained my drink.

Marcus fired off a text that was followed by a handful of buzzes as responses came back. And for that moment, I took stock of myself—shoes, dress, hair, lipstick—cataloging what I could improve before meeting Marcus's mother as his girlfriend.

She only knew me as the daughter of the woman currently trying to ruin his family's lives.

"So what's the game plan?" I asked, twisting clammy hands in my lap.

"Luke is gathering everyone up, even Dad—"

"Wait, they're *all* going to be there?"

"Only if it's okay," he soothed, his brows worried and eyes hopeful. "We just figured if we were all there to back you up, it'd serve as insurance."

"And they're all good with me?"

He hesitated just long enough to make me extraordinarily nervous. "They are. And they trust me. They know what you've done for us. Plus, you're impossible not to love." The word hung in the air for the longest heartbeat of my life before he smirked and carried on as if he hadn't said it, "Once they meet you, they'll see it for themselves."

"If you say so," I answered breathlessly.

"I say so."

And that was where the conversation ended because we spent the time it took us to get to the front door kissing.

Then we were too nervous to say anything, preoccupied with

the imaginings of what we'd say and what she'd do and how we'd all feel in a few crucial minutes.

The second I stepped onto their stoop, I became an intruder. A terrorist and traitor. Walking inside made me feel like a fraud, one who didn't belong in the grand entry, littered almost artfully with proof of life—shoes and shopping bags and mail. An umbrella propped on the banister, handle out but top closed, a balled-up coat and rolled-up socks, a cacophony of everyday things that whispered stories of family and home.

I heard the Bennets before I saw them, the lilting chatter, the occasional laughter, a playful groan.

My heart was a small, tight, galloping thing, my hands numb, unable to feel the warmth of Marcus's as he led me toward what I suspected was the kitchen and today, the guillotine.

He stepped through the casing and into the dining room, putting himself in front of me. The room fell silent.

Mrs. Bennet laughed. "Marcus, what are you hiding back there? Please tell me it's the girl you've been seeing." He must have made a face because she added, "Oh, don't look so surprised—I'm not as witless as you all think I am, and I know your brothers told you I'm onto you. Nothing happens in this house without my hearing whether I like it or not."

"But you always like it," Luke teased.

"And you don't know about this," Marcus said gravely before stepping away to reveal me to the room.

I stood in front of six Bennets, vulnerable and on display. The air in the room disappeared. The stillness was absolute—they could have been a painting, a shocked, modern version of the *Last Supper*. Hands stopped midair. No one blinked. Not a chest rose or fell with a breath, not a mouth formed a word.

Almost in unison, the Bennet family shifted their gaze to the matriarch.

"Margaret Bower," she muttered. "Is … if this is a prank, I do not find it amusing."

"It's not a prank," Marcus said with firm care.

One by one, his brothers and sister rose, filing forward to flank us as Mrs. Bennet watched on incredulously.

"You all knew?" she asked with watery eyes. "You all knew, and not one of you told me."

With an apologetic look on his face, Mr. Bennet reached for her hand. "Just hear them out."

"And *you*?" she whispered. "Paul Bennet, in all my life, I never—"

"Rosie," he urged, "listen before you say anything else."

The heave of her chest marked her breath as she looked into his eyes, and whatever she found there steadied her. "All right." She faced us. "Go ahead."

Marcus looked to me, asking silently if I wanted to do it or if he should. But I didn't want him to speak for me. I didn't want him to defend me to his mother.

I would defend myself.

So I took a shaky step forward, lifted my chin, and did just that.

"I know I'm the last person you want to be standing here. After what my mother has done to you—what she's doing to you—I won't ask for your kindness or forgiveness. But I want you to know two very important things. I am not aligned with my mother, and I'm in love with your son."

Something in Marcus sparked, some shift in the air that tugged me in his direction without moving an inch.

Mrs. Bennet's eyes shone, her gnarled hand covering her lips.

"It wasn't until meeting Marcus that I believed I had a future that my mother didn't dictate. And it wasn't until seeing you all stand up for each other, support and love each other, that I understood what family truly was. I've done what I can to protect you, to help you from inside Bower, because I couldn't live with myself if I didn't. I can't stand by and let her destroy you out of spite, not if I can help you fight." I swallowed, my gaze flicking to the ground and my heart thundering. "I only want you to know my intentions, and I understand if it's too much to accept—"

The creak of her chair called my attention as she hauled herself up on failing joints. Her face was bent, tears rolling down her cheeks, but I couldn't tell if she was distraught or elated. As she approached, I braced myself for a slap, a furious rejection, or the dressing-down of my life. Maybe all three and in that order. And terrified, I waited through a dozen racing heartbeats to learn my fate.

Because what Rosemary Bennet might say would hurt far worse than anything my mother could.

She stopped before me, her chest hitching. The room was otherwise breathless.

"Oh, you silly girl," she said with a quavering voice. "However could I turn away anyone who loves my son?"

"Even a Bower?" I asked as she took my hands.

"Well, maybe Marcus will do something about changing that name to something a little more palatable."

The room exhaled, the murmurings of laughter and relief floating around in a chorus of respite. But I stood in a small space with Mrs. Bennet, her hands soft and warm and twisted around mine.

"I believe you," she said. "And I forgive you, though you've done nothing to require my absolution. Thank you for your help, whatever it might be. Thank you for defending me in that room to your mother. I knew then that you were separate from them, different. And I believe Marcus would only bring you here if he loved you too."

I glanced at him over my shoulder, finding him watching me with such intensity, a flush of warmth passed through me.

Mrs. Bennet drew my attention again with a laugh. "You must have been terrified. Shame on you all for marching her in here like a lamb to slaughter. Julius," she called, and I didn't know who she was speaking to until Jett perked up. "I believe we could all use wine, if you'd be a dear."

"Whiskey for me," Luke noted.

One of Jett's brows rose. "Any other orders?"

"Just bring the bottle," Marcus said.

"Oh, stop pouting," Laney teased. "I'll help you."

"And when we've all had a drink"—Mrs. Bennet leaned toward me with a clever smile—"you can tell me all about how in the world this happened."

She still had my hands, and she used the preface to turn me toward Marcus, setting my hands in his when he extended them.

"I think I need to sit down," she said with that smile still on her lips, appraising us with a mixture of surprise, pride, and amusement.

Kash and Luke offered a smirk before turning to follow her back to the table, leaving Marcus and me where we were.

And though we weren't alone, it was just us.

The look he laid upon me was one of possession. Heavy with the arresting weight of command and surrender.

"You love me," he said. It was a statement of fact. A transparent truth.

"I do," I whispered.

His hand cupped my jaw, those blazing eyes searching my face. "Good, because I've loved you always. And it'd be a terrible shame if I were the only one."

There was no time for a breath before he kissed me.

And if I'd had one, he would have stolen it.

# Enough

## MAISIE

**T**he next day, I floated into work like a balloon.

Marcus and I'd had dinner with his family last night, and it was the rowdiest, funniest, loveliest meal I thought I'd ever enjoyed. And not just for the company or wit or their unexpected acceptance, but because of the sense of family that bonded them together, one they had unwittingly extended to me.

It was just the way they were, I gathered. It was impossible to be in their company and not feel a part of them.

The moment Marcus and I could get away, we'd said our goodbyes and hurried to his house where we spent the hours we had in each other's arms, whispering words of love and future.

*Love.* He loved me. And the world was full of possibility.

That love was armor against the world, against my mother, and I was instantly invincible. I could do anything. Even walk out on my mother and my duty without looking back. There was far too much happiness in front of me to bother with what was behind me.

I fantasized about leaving that final battle with the Bennets—mediation—to lay the full truth on her. To expose my betrayal. It was a fuse I'd been waiting to light for what felt like forever, striking match after metaphorical match in anticipation of burning the whole thing down.

I turned my mind back to the business proposal in front of me but found it almost impossible to concentrate. My thoughts were a million miles away, stuck on Marcus and all the things that were to come. Hoping to focus myself, I'd already reorganized my desk drawers and cleaned up the top. I'd wiped down my keyboard and buffed my screen until there wasn't a speck on it. The books on my small bookshelf had been haphazardly shoved in place when I claimed this office for my own, so I'd taken a minute to straighten them up and organize them by topic. With that, I was out of things to do.

In here, at least. A host of things could be addressed *out* of my office, like catching up with my staff, monitoring progress, heading to accounting to address the little inconsistencies I'd found. Jess had seemed just as surprised as I was when I showed her last week, but we'd chalked it up to a clerical error. What I'd discovered was too inconsistent—a little bit here, a miscalculation there—and I'd been meaning to go down to accounting for weeks. But between finalizing the proposal for the new center to present to city council and my preoccupation with shadowing in the advertising department, it'd been pushed down the priority list over and over again.

I couldn't pretend it didn't all feel pointless. In a few weeks, I would be gone, and though I hoped my mother wouldn't punish the charity division, I knew better.

But I cheered at the thought of getting up and moving around. As if doing something would give me control, even though it wouldn't. Nearly everything was up in the air, and I was no juggler.

With a sigh, I pushed back from my desk, snagging the

financial statements I'd gathered to take to accounting. But before I stood, a knock sounded, and the door opened without invitation.

Shelby's wide eyes met mine, her face pallid. She slipped into my office and closed the door behind her.

My brows quirked. "Shelby? What can I do for you?" I glanced at the clock. "Did I miss a meeting?"

"No." The word was grave. Ominous. "I didn't know what else to do."

"Didn't know what to do about what?"

She took a seat, her back ramrod straight and hands knotted in her lap. "I ... I just overheard something that you need to know."

She didn't continue, seeming to need a moment to compose herself.

"Are you all right?" I asked gently.

"I'm not. And I'm sorry to bring you into this, but I had to do something. You're the only one I could tell."

"Tell what?"

With a deep and heavy breath, she spoke, "Your mother was just in a meeting with Roland I was unaware of. She ... she'd sent me to pick up some files from billing, but when I realized she hadn't given me the codes I needed, I went back. I was about to knock when I heard them. I shouldn't have listened, Maisie. God, when she finds out, she's going to fire me and make sure I never get a job again. But you need to know." Her voice wavered, her throat working as she swallowed.

"Shelby, what did you hear?" I encouraged, dreading her answer.

"She ... she's been stealing from the company."

The temperature dropped ten degrees in a heartbeat.

Shelby rambled on, "Roland found out—apparently, they've been blackmailing each other, some kind of a standoff. She's been siphoning money out of Bower and into offshore accounts. And Maisie ... she's using the charity to do it."

Something in my brain imploded. "What?" I breathed.

"The charity is a front. Don't you see? This is why she shut you down from expanding in the first place, why she didn't want you to head it up. She's been keeping you out of it because she knows you'd figure it out. You'll blow her cover and Roland's too. The discussion was about what to do with *you*."

My vision dimmed, my hands and cheeks tingling painfully. *You're about to pass out. Breathe.*

I drew a long breath and exhaled. Then another.

"Your mother already has a plan to get rid of you, though the way she spoke …" She shook her head. "It sounded like she was just as happy to disown you as she would be to make you take the fall. And I couldn't—I *can't*—let her do that. Roland is trying to save you too, but by the way they were talking, it sounds like the jig is just about up."

I sat in that chair, detached and distant and unable to speak.

Because once again, everything I thought I knew about my mother had been demolished and reduced to rubble.

I knew my mother to be many things. Humorless and cold. Doggedly driven and immovable. She fought to the death for everything she had and many things she didn't regardless of whether she was right or wrong.

But never could I have fathomed that she had put her own company in danger.

What I'd believed to be an innocent mistake wasn't innocent at all. It had been calculated by the very last person I thought would do it. I'd imagined the firings she'd decree on finding out, the carving out of the hearts of anyone who dared steal from Bower, never fathoming that it could be her. Never believing it could be the one who held the fate and well-being of our company above all else, even me.

My mother.

And she'd been using my charity to do it.

"So I … I went down to billing and picked up some files, knowing full well they were wrong, and when I came back up,

Roland was gone. She was sitting at her desk as if nothing happened, and she ... she asked to see you."

A jolt, a thundering roll of reckoning.

*She's going to tell me. She's going to come clean, and then I'll have to go to the police or the Feds or whoever. How does one even get in touch with the FBI? Is there an eight hundred number for ratting out your mother?*

"What will you do?" she asked after a moment. "What should *we* do? Oh God, do you think I'll be charged if she's caught? Do you think you will? Should we go to the police?"

"I ... I don't know," I muttered, pausing to think. "Do you think you can keep this to yourself for just a day or two?"

Her face screwed up, but she said, "I'll do whatever you think will help."

"Let me see what she wants with me and take a second to think this through. In the end, we might not have a choice."

Shelby nodded, chewing on her bottom lip like a piece of gum.

"Should you go up first, or should I?" I asked.

"You go. She sent me back down to billing to get the right files. I'll try to make myself scarce as long as I can without raising suspicion."

"All right," I said numbly. "Thank you, Shelby. I ... I'm sorry. To involve you. That she involved either of us."

She stood, drying her palms on her skirt, her shoulders tight and lips flat. "Please, don't apologize. I'm just so sorry she's done this."

"So am I."

With a nod, she left.

When I moved my hands from the desk, hand-shaped condensation was left on the surface.

And I rose from my seat to face my mother.

With every step, my daze focused itself into a lightning rod of fury as the weight of her betrayal dawned on me. She'd jeopardized everything—the company, her place in it, my charity, even my own safety—all for her greed. That was all it could have been, because she had more money than God himself. But apparently, that wasn't enough.

As I waited in the elevator to reach her floor for what felt like hours, I wondered if perhaps she was stealing because she had to. Could the company be less profitable than it appeared? Had she been hiding that truth, skimming from the company to keep up appearances and her lifestyle? Had she been trying to save herself?

There had to be some reason, and I wanted to know what it was. I needed to know why she would betray the very foundation of her beliefs, beliefs she'd spent the length of my lifetime trying to shackle me with.

It was madness.

It was the final straw.

If she wanted to set herself on fire, that was her prerogative. But I'd be damned if I let her set me on fire too.

I marched through the bullpen of cubicles, vibrating with rage. Past Shelby's empty seat I stalked and into the office of the devil. But not to make a deal.

To rescind one.

I wasn't exactly sure what I'd find when I entered her office. Remorse was probably too much to ask for. Honesty, perhaps. An explanation about what had happened and how she was going to fix it. Even if it was indifferent, I expected the truth. And when she was finished with her excuses, I would explain to her exactly what I thought before quitting this job. Quitting her.

Quitting everything.

I imagined finding many versions of my mother behind that door as I walked through it, launching it shut behind me. Resignation. Indignation. Submission, in my wildest dreams.

Instead, she was ablaze with silent outrage.

The door slammed behind me, already in motion before I'd

gotten a full look at her. I screeched to a halt, disoriented from the raw and unexpected fury simmering in the room, licking at me like piping steam.

"Do you have something you'd like to tell me, Margaret?" Her voice was still. Calm. Coiled to strike.

"I'd ask you the same question."

Her eyes narrowed, the tension between us tightening painfully. "I gave you the chance to be honest. I told you to tell me the truth about your little secret or stop seeing him. But you didn't, did you?"

I watched in horror as she opened the folder on her desk, removed a large photograph, and held it up in display.

A sliver of Marcus, visible through the crack of his closing door. Me, was trotting down the stairs of his stoop with a blissful smile on my face and my coat slung over my forearm. It had been too warm for the coat, I recalled, and my scarf remained in my bag, right where I'd left it.

*It was a stupid disguise anyway*, I noted bitterly.

"Of all the betrayals," she seethed, her voice quivering with malignant rancor. "A Bennet. Marcus *Fucking* Bennet."

The fire in my belly for the fight I'd planned—for my accusations and refusals and rejections of her—was doused and left smoldering. In a split second, I tamped that knowledge down. If she wasn't going to come clean, my accusation might do more harm than good. Telling her might throw Shelby under the bus and could possibly incriminate us all. I didn't know what would happen, and until I did, there was only one matter to address.

The picture in her hand.

"You had me followed," I said. "Of course you did. We thought you would."

"*We?*" She nearly choked on the word, her eyes wild and ringed with white. "I knew that day in the courtroom, but I'd convinced myself you couldn't possibly be so stupid as to fuck Marcus Bennet."

"*Mother!*"

"You've told him everything, haven't you? You've sold out your family, your *mother*, your birthright for a *Bennet*? Of all the revolting rebellions you could have pulled, this is indisputably the worst." She stood, fueled by fury, walking so slowly, so raptorially around her desk and toward me, I instinctively moved backward to keep the space between us. "You have no idea what you've done, Margaret. You have no idea what I'll do to them. You showed your hand, so certain I was bluffing. But you've made your choice. And so I have made mine."

My mother came to a stop before me, judge, jury, and executioner.

"Get out. Get out of this building. Get out of my house. No daughter of mine would ever stoop so low as to fuck a Bennet just to get back at her mother. No daughter of mine would be so bovine and dense as to cross me in the most grievous of ways." Her lip curled back, exposing her teeth in a sneer of pure and unfiltered hatred. "I'd rather have no daughter than to be yoked to you."

I despised the pinch of tears at the corners of my eyes. The tear in my chest. The hot pain of rejection from the woman who was meant to love and protect me. Because even now, even after everything, I realized I still wanted her love and approval.

And I hated that most of all.

"I came here," I started, every molecule in my body trembling, "to tell you I was leaving. Because your mistrust is poison. Your greed is revolting. The bitterness that makes up the whole of who you are disgusts me. All of this pain, all of this suffering, and all because you weren't good enough for Paul Bennet."

Time stop-started with a gasp, a shift, the swing of her hand, the sound of flesh against flesh.

The slap cracked in the air, snapping my head toward the wall, leaving my ears ringing and my cheek blazing with pain. But I refused to react, refused to cry or flinch or press a hand to my stinging face. Instead, I turned my gaze on her again, thankful she'd made all this so easy for me to walk away from.

"You shut your fucking mouth, you ungrateful bitch." She gave me her back, saying stiffly, "Have your things out of my house by the time I return. And don't think to step foot in this building again."

With that, she sat, her attention wholly on whatever papers lay on her desk and whatever she wrote on them. Perhaps it was the contract for her soul. Though I suspected she gave that away long ago.

I took a final look at my mother and left her office for the last time.

The office bustled on from somewhere far away, everything distant, like looking through the wrong end of a telescope. I spoke to no one as I walked into my office and gathered my things. When I stepped into the packed elevator, I held my bag in front of me, taking up the smallest space I could. The revolving door dumped me onto the busy sidewalk, but no one saw me.

Into a waiting cab I slid, and off we went toward my mother's house. There were two men in the world I wanted to see, and one waited behind that grand old door of the only home I'd known.

James opened the door, directing me with worried eyes to the kitchen where my father sat, typing away on his computer. Dad's smile on hearing me enter instantly faded, and the second he wrapped his arms around me, I came unraveled. My numbness had been a levee, and when it broke, pain spilled out, filling every crack and space. He held me until my tears ebbed, then stopped, leaving me with nothing but a hitching breath and runny nose.

He sat me down and snagged a tissue box, tilting it in my direction. Gratefully, I took one. And while I mopped up my face, he took the stool at my side, hooking a heel on the foot rung, his face grave.

"Tell me what happened," he urged gently.

"She found out."

The breath he took was sharp and noisy. "I suppose we knew she would."

With my nod, a strange feeling settled over me. Not of sadness, not of fear. "Mother had me followed—I was with him last night, and now she knows, and she called me in and … and … it's over. It's all over."

Relief, I realized. The feeling was relief, tinged with shock and laced with disappointment. But that curious sensation was the weight of her control as it lifted, inch by precious inch. "I've been instructed to leave."

And then he listened at my side while I regaled her invasion of my privacy, the fight itself, my intent to quit and her beating me to the punch.

I did not, however, tell him about what she had done to Bower.

I couldn't tell anyone.

The knowledge of my mother's crime was a curse. Now that I knew, it was my responsibility to act, to decide. Because of that knowledge, I was faced with a choice that shouldn't have been mine to make. I didn't know what the consequences would be for her if I went to the authorities, but they would be dire. And to be the one to pull the trigger, fire the bullet that would put my mother in the ground … it was too much to decide in an hour or a day.

I hated my mother for putting me here. I only wished I hated her enough to pull that trigger without remorse.

For now, I couldn't tell anyone. The more people who knew, the more complicated things would get, and they were already labyrinthian. Not to mention my aversion to putting the responsibility I despised on someone I loved.

Once it was settled, they'd be the first people I called.

Until then, the burden was mine.

When I finished speaking, he spent a long moment watching

me. I didn't know if he'd be disappointed, if he'd scold or reprimand me. If he'd be upset or angry.

But to my surprise, he was none of those.

Instead, he smiled. "You're finally free."

"Free." I tested the word in my mouth, on my tongue. "I've forsaken everything, but somehow, I can't summon any regret."

"Then you know it was the right decision."

"Quitting?"

"I'm glad you told her you quit, but she fired you. It was a choice, but your fate had already been decided. What I meant was Marcus."

And that was the truth, the reason I couldn't seem to feel sorrow or loss. Because of all I'd gained.

"I approve of any man who inspires you to stand up to her. I'm sorry for the chance you've lost to make a difference in that company, but somehow, I think you're going to make a difference no matter where you go."

"I wonder where that will be. Where I'll go?" I asked myself as much as him. "I don't know what I'm going to do."

"Oh, yes you do." He leaned in, covering my hand with his. "You're going to live."

Tears nipped at my eyes, but before I could speak, he patted my hand and said, "Come on. Let's get you packed."

Companionable silence fell between us as I followed him up the stairs and to my room. While he retrieved my suitcases from the closet, I took a look around, uncertain if I'd ever see this place again. My plants and my flowers, all collected in the bay window. My books and my knickknacks, the documentation of my entire life. This room was my sanctuary in this house, the place where my happy memories lived. I wondered if it would be seized, liquidated, but wondering was all I could do. I knew too little of that world to do anything more than guess.

Dad opened up a suitcase and laid it on my bed, and I began to clean out drawers.

As he gathered my favorite books, he said, "What now? Where do you want to go? My apartment in SoHo? Take some time to regroup."

My cheeks flushed. "I thought I might stay with Marcus, if he'll have me."

He looked down his nose at me playfully. "I'm going to need to formally meet this boy."

"You will, don't you worry about that. I take it you're not staying here?"

A shadow passed behind his eyes. "Only long enough for a few parting words with your mother."

My hands paused mid-fold. "Because you're going to the apartment?"

"Because I'm going to file for divorce."

I blinked, a smile rising on my face. "Really? You're really going to do it?"

"Really. I've had enough. And I think that day I've been wishing for, the day when you were safe from her, is finally here," he said proudly. "I'll have the rest of your things brought over to my place, and your room will be waiting."

"Thank you, Dad."

"It's me who should be thanking you. You aren't the only one who's gained your freedom, and you're not the only one who gets to live. So let's make the most of it, shall we?"

And with a long embrace and a few tears, we would do just that.

# Emancipation Day

## MARCUS

I'd paced a nearly visible rut in the floor, I'd been at it so long.

From the second Maisie texted me with the briefest and broadest of explanations, I'd walked the stretch between my living room and the front door like a caged animal. Her message had been coupled with a request to stay with me, which I'd agreed to with more enthusiasm than I should have been allowed, given the circumstance.

I didn't know much, but what I did know was that it was bad. Catastrophic. Her mother had found us out and shredded Maisie's life to ribbons and bits, her future and security wiped away in a matter of minutes, by way of a few weighty words.

And it was all my fault.

We should have been more careful. I should have protected her. I could have stopped all of this had I not been so thoughtless, so self-serving. And now, she'd lost everything, just like we'd feared. Like we'd planned.

But now that it'd happened, the reality was far more grue-some than I'd imagined it would be.

And the timing couldn't have been worse. With mediation approaching, with the lawsuit still up in the air, my family could very well pay for the grievance—I had no doubt Evelyn Bower was loading her cannons with devious and dishonorable fodder now that a Bennet had stolen her daughter from her.

It was incredibly dangerous and potentially detrimental.

The only hope, the only brightness in the thick of this storm was that now, Maisie was mine, and I'd take care of her better than anyone could.

My hand slipped into my pocket, finding the velvet box where it'd been for a week, thumbing the curve, turning it around and around without purpose as I worried over her.

I didn't know why I'd been carrying it around with me ev-erywhere rather than leaving it at home. Perhaps it was the com-fort I felt when reminded it was there. The ring in that box was a promise. It was a future—our future. It was what I wanted, the thing I'd known since she first tumbled into me.

On paper, it was illogical. There was no reason to rush, no point in doing anything rash. We barely knew each other regard-less of how right it felt. It was ludicrous to even consider making this promise—*the* promise—until our hormones and infatuation simmered down. Until we had a chance to live together. To be to-gether openly, to see how we grew together when we had the real space to.

There were rules, rules I'd always believed were the only way.

But that was the thing about Maisie.

She defied all rules. All logic. All things I'd thought should be and would be and could be, she superseded.

I knew without a doubt that this was it. What she and I had together was undeniable. The alternative—living the rest of my life without her—was beyond my imagination. I could think of nothing she could say or do to change that. She had my trust, and she had my love, the words synonymous and definitive. And so, last week, before either of us had admitted our feelings, before I'd known how she felt, I'd walked into the jeweler knowing one thing for certain.

I loved her, and one day, I'd make her mine forever.

I'd wandered around the glass cases in the quiet shop, peering into the glowing displays until one winking diamond caught my attention, stopped my feet. Simple and beautiful, timeless and sparkling, it sat in that case, angled right at me as if to say, *Here I am.* The knowledge that this was the ring had struck me as fact, and that was that.

It'd been in my pocket ever since. Sometimes in my pants pocket—its preferred spot so I could fiddle with it—but more often in my inside coat pocket where she couldn't easily figure out what it was, should she notice it. The *when* was distant enough, because despite my eagerness, I knew a good time from a bad one. And this was not the right time. Once we were past the lawsuit, once her mother and the Bower mess was behind us and we had time to ease into a relationship free of constraint, then I'd ask. And God help me if she said no.

Because there would be no getting over her.

I sighed, turning the box around again in my hand. She'd be here any second, and the realization had me hurrying it into my coat pocket and removing said coat, hanging it on the back of one of the chairs at the island.

The instant I heard the key in the lock, I was off like a shot in her direction, whipping the door open to scoop her up. To hold her to my chest, to slip my fingers into her hair. To promise her it would be all right as she cried, to cradle her face in my hands and kiss her.

It was a long moment before we parted. She set down her bag and wiped her cheeks as I brought in her suitcase and closed the door.

"Drink?" I offered.

But she shook her head. "Bed."

With a kiss to the top of her head, I grabbed her suitcase and followed her up the stairs. The air around her was still and solemn, something about her resigned but not small. And it left me aching to know exactly what had happened so I could wash it away. So we could leave it behind us and start over.

We could see that dream of ours come true. I could bring her into my family, make her one of us. We could run Longbourne together, if there was anything left to run after this.

My stomach turned at the fear that there wouldn't be. *Future Marcus's problems,* I told myself.

She climbed into my bed, kicking her shoes off on the way, and I left her suitcase near my dresser before joining her.

Maisie lifted her chin, a silent request for a kiss. And so I wrapped her in my arms and obeyed.

For a long moment, that was all there was. A long and languid kiss, its purpose to be only that. A kiss with no intention, no directive, only a meeting of lips and tongues solely to be together, nothing more.

I held her until she broke away, until she'd gotten what she needed, and it left her slack and soft against me.

She settled into the pillow beneath her head, tracing the line of my jaw with her fingertips as I gazed down at her.

"It's done," she said simply.

"Are you all right?"

"It's strange, how I feel. The things she said to me ..." Through a beat, she recounted those things but didn't relay them. "It was awful. I should be torn apart, devastated, and in some ways, I am. But more about the death of one dream and the birth of another. I still thought that deep down, she loved me. But she doesn't. And now my dream is you."

I turned my face to kiss her fingertips, my heart aching with sadness and joy for her mother and me. "I'm sorry."

"I just ..." She paused. "I've been so worried I'd become my mother, but after today, I'm convinced I couldn't be. But I wonder. If I believed, *really* believed in something, could I forsake what's right? Because when I think about you and me ... I'd forsake anything."

"You are nothing like her," I promised again. I'd remind her forever.

The smallest of smiles touched her lips, but she didn't look convinced. "Well, at least it's done. At least it's over. And now that I'm here, it's hard to feel bad about much of anything."

"I can't pretend I'm mad about that."

"Me either," she said on a chuckle. "Dad is going to manage getting the rest of my things moved from Mom's house to his apartment, and then he's leaving too."

"For good?"

She nodded, her smile still in place. "He stayed back to talk to her before he left."

"Talk." I scoffed. "I'd love to hear that conversation firsthand."

"Oh God." She laughed. "I bet he's been saving up names to call her on this day for years. We should declare it a family holiday."

"Emancipation day."

"For all of us. Although I don't know what she'll do about you. She was so angry, Marcus. The things she said ..." A shudder trembled through her. "The things she's done for her own designs, for power. For money."

Something about the way she'd said it gave me pause. "What do you mean?"

But she shook her head, her brows ticking together and eyes drifting down. "Nothing."

"Maisie," I urged. "Did something else happen?"

"No, everything's fine."

And that was how I knew it was patently *not* fine. "You don't want to tell me."

"It's not that. I just—" Her guilty gaze snapped to mine.

I didn't speak for a moment, and neither did she. Instead, I smoothed her hair, cupped her jaw, tracing her lips with my gaze as I considered what to say.

"Tell me when you're ready," I finally answered.

"No, Marcus—I *do* want to tell you, but it's … I can't."

"You can't? Is she stopping you even now?"

"No, not exactly …" She huffed. "It's complicated, and … I don't know what it will mean if I tell you."

"For us?"

"Not for us. For you."

I scrambled to find some reasonable explanation, to try to guess what she could need to keep from me. "Nothing you could say could change how I feel and what I want. You can tell me anything."

"Even if it incriminated you?"

I stilled. "If it would incriminate me, I can only assume the knowledge incriminates you. And if that's the case, you absolutely have to tell me."

Her worry didn't ease, but her sigh was one of concession. "I … I don't even know where to start."

"It's all right," I soothed. "We'll figure it out together."

Her eyes tracked her hand as it fiddled with my collar, finally smoothing my shirt over my chest with a sigh. And then she lifted her gaze to mine.

"My mother is embezzling money from Bower."

My shock was total, marked by a tingling numbness that crawled down my spine like ants.

Maisie launched into her explanation, her eyes cast down as she spoke. She told me about the assistant and her mother's crime, about Evelyn using the charity as a front. About the exit speech Maisie had planned to give her mother before discovering confession wasn't what Evelyn had intended.

And Maisie told me the most pressing part of all—she didn't know what to do.

But I did.

Her eyes were so full of hurt and hope that I hesitated to say it plainly, but there was no other way.

"You have to go to the authorities."

Within a breath, her cheeks were smudged with color. "It's not that simple, Marcus. Think of all the people who rely on Bower and what will happen to them. Think of all the people at Harvest, all her employees … we don't know what will happen to them. Aside from the fact that she's my mother—she's evil and cruel, but she has been the strongest authority in my life, and betraying that is … it's …" Frustrated tears filled her eyes. "It's just not that simple."

"She's a criminal. I won't try to convince you with a recount of what she's done to you, because that doesn't matter. She has committed a crime, and now you know. And because you know, you're legally obligated to act."

Her chin quivered, her eyes searching mine.

"I know it seems impossible, but you have to. It's accomplice liability—you could be charged with aiding and abetting. Failure to report a crime."

"Could you be liable too?" she asked quietly. "Now that you know, have I put you in danger?"

I frowned. "Technically, it's possible. But if your mother is charged and they find out that you knew—her daughter and heir—there's a very good chance the prosecution will come after you. For me, it's a maybe. For you, it's almost certain."

Twin tears slid down her temples and into her hair. "She did this. She's responsible for this, but she's not going to make me choose everyone's fate. She's going to do that herself."

I frowned, not liking the idea of any plan that hinged on her mother doing the right thing.

"I'll go to her. Tell her I know what she did. Gather some proof so she can't deny it. And then I'll tell her if she doesn't go to the authorities, I will."

"I don't like it."

"Why not?"

"Because once she knows you know, she'll act. She could leave the country. Cover it up. Or worse—pin it on you. She's not to be trusted, especially not when her neck is on the block."

"I just don't understand." Her voice sharpened. "This is a real solution. She can't do anything but leave the country in that amount of time, and I don't think she'd ever run away—she'd rather it all go down in flames with her in the middle, holding a matchbook. I don't know if I can do this, not without giving her the chance to make it right."

"Even if she stabs you in the back the second you turn around?" I argued. "This isn't a petty crime or a minor violation—she *embezzled*. This is a federal offense, and it's not something to be taken lightly."

"Don't you think I know that?" She scooted out from under me and swung her legs over the edge of the bed, putting her back to me. Her head dropped to her hands. "I know what I'm supposed to do, but I ... I don't know if I can do it, Marcus. I don't know if I can." She broke into a string of silent sobs.

The sight broke my heart.

I moved to her side, and the moment my arm was around her shoulders, she curled into me. Her tears broke through in earnest, and there was nothing I could do but hold her close and curse Evelyn for doing this to Maisie. To herself. To her company.

"I know it's hard," I started. "But I promised myself I'd protect you, and I'd be betraying that promise if I didn't insist that you take matters into your own hands. But I've got your back. I'll always have your back, whatever you decide and come what may. Take a minute. And if you can't go to the authorities without giving her a chance, then that's what we'll do."

She lifted her head, looked up at me with dark eyes, her

lashes grouped together by tears. "Thank you," she whispered, and I wished I could make her mother pay for every single one.

"I love you, Maisie. No matter what."

When I kissed her, it was with hope that my fears would never come true, that it would all work out like it needed to—for our safety, our future. Or God help us all.

# The Seed

## MAISIE

The sun had been up for a little while, the city already awake and humming its good morning. But Marcus and I hadn't left the safety of his bed, preferring to stay tangled up in the nest of blankets as long as we could before facing what the day had in store.

Three days had passed since I'd come to stay, three days of joy and worry and the comfort of him. I smiled to myself, my head resting in the curve where his shoulder joined his chest and my body tucked into his side. Strange that I hadn't even considered whether staying together would be anything but easy. When I'd come here, I'd been in such a state that I hadn't really thought about much of *anything*. Only that I needed him.

Funny that I hadn't stressed about being together this much. To stand next to each other and brush our teeth. To chat idly while we changed for bed. To make breakfast and drink coffee in a sort of autonomous synchronicity, connected while remaining wholly independent.

But waking up with him was the best part.

After so much sneaking around and all the stolen moments and meetings, it was luxurious to spend nearly every moment together. An embarrassment of riches after rationing what meager time we had. Marcus still had work to do, but when he went to the greenhouse, I went with him. I'd met everyone, even Kash's girlfriend, the wedding planner. One afternoon, I'd helped Tess while she worked, comparing notes on not only flowers, but our Bennet men. And last night, after a rowdy and lovely dinner with the whole brood, Marcus had brought me to their greenhouse.

God, it was beautiful. Quaint and charming, warm and welcoming. The greenhouse *was* the Bennets—alive and a little messy, bursting with color and teeming with a feeling of home. And for the first time, I understood that feeling, that elemental sense of belonging, even though they weren't my home, even though the Bennets weren't mine.

More than anything—anything in the entire world—I wanted them to be. Currently, I was only an observer, someone invited to peer into their family and take a spare seat at the table. But I longed to have a permanent place, to etch my name on the family tree, to be a part of their lives.

To have a family. A mother. A sister and brothers. A place to belong, full of people who loved me. Where there was no cruelty and no betrayal. Only the deep and undeniable support and affection of those who cared most.

After Dad and I being so alone, with our guard always up and our discomfort ever present, the comfort of trust seemed a reprieve neither of us thought we'd ever get. But the Bennets hadn't only welcomed me—they'd welcomed Dad too. After Mrs. Bennet's reaction to her children's ambush regarding her having dated my father, I didn't know how it would go. I'd wondered if it'd be strange or tense, an awkward meeting after years on opposite sides. But within a few days, the Bennet children had turned the whole ordeal into a good-natured ribbing, and Mrs. Bennet let it go, though not without a little snark.

Dad and the elder Bennets dove in like only old friends do, with laughter and reminiscing and an unstoppable stream of conversation as they caught up on nearly thirty years of life. Dinner was rife with embarrassing stories about their children, the subject of my mother avoided at all costs. But afterward, we'd left the three of them in the living room and gathered in the kitchen to share stories of our own—five Bennet children and the three women they loved.

When I sighed, Marcus pulled me closer, shifting to press a kiss to my crown.

"Was that a happy sigh or a worried one?"

"Happy," I answered.

"Good."

The unspoken reason he'd asked materialized over us like a squall, dark and thundering and posed to soak our happiness with its haul. Because today, I would face the music.

I'd spent another large part of those three days digging around with Jess's help, looking for proof to lay upon my mother—my best chance at forcing her hand. Three days hoping I could find a way out of this without being the one to doom her, though Marcus impatiently supported the decision. *He* had spent those three days impressing—arguing—his points, and we'd discussed it endlessly. Though I knew what I needed to do, we seemed to have the same conversation over and over, agreeing but disagreeing. I'd come to hate the very mention of it, and if there was one thing I was glad to do today, it was to move forward, if for nothing more than to put the argument between Marcus and me to rest.

He believed with vehement conviction that I shouldn't inform my mother that I knew, nor did he believe her behavior warranted an opportunity at heroism. But I couldn't admit the truth—I was a coward for not readily condemning my mother. Beyond all choice or judgment, in the deepest and most instinctive way, I loved and wanted approval from her, a compulsion programmed into me from birth. The thought of being the instrument of her downfall felt wrong on all levels.

I would do it, if I had to. But I'd lay out my proof and let her make a choice in the hopes that if she had no other affection for me, she would at least do this to absolve me. It was a foolish and innocent hope. But it was the only way I could live with myself, my final extension of respect and care for my mother.

"Do you think there's any way to be ready for a thing like this?" I asked, memorizing the sight of my hand resting on the swell of his chest.

"No, I don't. There are too many variables, too many outcomes, especially when dealing with your mother. I can honestly say I have no idea what she'll do."

"Neither do I. I know she won't be happy, particularly with my giving her an ultimatum."

My hand rose and fell with his sigh.

"Maisie, I swear, if this somehow comes back on you, I'll never forgive myself."

"For what? Marcus, I love you, but this is not your decision to make."

"Where your happiness and safety are concerned, in many ways it *is*. There's more I could do to stop you, but I won't. I only hope I don't regret it."

"I've been controlled enough in my life," I said darkly. "Please, don't you start too."

Another sigh, the stroke of his hand on my bare arm. "I'd take a bullet for you. And right now, your mother feels like a round of twenty-twos."

"My mother says she wants to protect me too."

He shifted, leaning so he could look at me, disturbing my resting place so I had to meet his eyes. "I'd like to think this is a little different."

"It is," I conceded. "But every once in a while it doesn't feel like it."

Marcus didn't get angry, only sad. "I hope you know that's the last thing I want, for you to feel that way."

"I know." I stretched to give him a kiss. "Now, let's get out of bed so I can get this over with."

"I was thinking tonight we should stay in. Order Chinese. Watch movies, read—whatever you want."

"Bubble bath too?"

"Text me when you're on your way, and I'll draw one up for you."

"For *us*, if you please," I added with a smile.

He mirrored it. "Something we can both look forward to."

With a chuckle and another kiss, we peeled ourselves apart and rolled out of bed.

My happiness faded with every step that brought me closer to facing my mother. By the time I was brushing my teeth, I was unable to smile. By the time I stood in the entry with Marcus to say goodbye, I was pulled tight as a bowstring. But I drew myself up to do what needed to be done and walked out that door, hoping it would be over soon.

It was one of the longer half hours of my life. Traffic was a mess, the cab crawling toward Midtown at a speed that ratcheted my anxiety to unbearable heights. I should have taken the subway, given my brain and body something to do. Instead, I sat in that taxi and obsessed over what I was about to walk into.

The day was cheerful by appearance, the sun out and clouds absent. And when I finally made it to the building and stepped out of the cab, warmth greeted me, the promise of summer on its wings.

But all I could do was sweat.

In I went, past the front desk, ignoring the eyes tracking me. She'd know I was here—honestly, I was half surprised not to have been greeted by security to escort me right back out. But she let me pass, let me get onto the elevator. She allowed me to enter her space, a silent, sanctioned invitation to bring it on.

That challenge lit a fire in me. Because for once, I held the cards. And my guilt faded, replaced by sheer determination to force her hand.

Shelby was pallid behind her desk but unsurprised to see me. She rose, saying nothing as she opened my mother's office doors.

And there was the queen herself.

Mother sat behind her desk, the very picture of power and control. She wasn't tense, though she wasn't relaxed, only a shrewd and stately statue, somehow looking down at me even though she was seated.

Her eyes flicked to the door, and she nodded. The click as the doors closed was the only sound in the room.

"I believe I told you not to come back here, Margaret."

"And yet you so graciously granted me entrance."

"Only because I assume you're here to denounce *them* or beg. Both, if I'm fortunate."

"I hate to disappoint—"

"Do you?" The words were a lance.

I approached her desk but didn't sit. I didn't know why. Perhaps some instinct to prepare to escape should she put me in danger.

"Why are you here?" she asked.

"I wanted to give you a chance to do the right thing."

A merciless laugh burst out of her. "And what, accept your disloyalty?"

"No. To admit yours."

Her savage smile faded. "Regarding the Bennets? You must be joking."

"I know that you've been stealing."

I realized I'd never truly shocked her, not until that moment. "What?" The word was barely a whisper.

"You've been stealing from Bower. Through my charity."

Her mask slammed back in place. "I don't know what you're talking about. Is this some sort of grab to try to reclaim your place?"

"I don't want my place, not if it's under your command. And I think you know exactly what I'm talking about. Now that I know, I'm obligated to act. But before I go to the authorities, I wanted to give you a chance to turn yourself in."

The color drained from her face, her eyes so cool, they were nearly colorless. "Whatever you think you know—"

"Will you really deny it?" I shot. "Even now, even with me standing here with the truth, you would still lie?" I shook my head, pulling the financial papers out of my bag. "Maybe I should have listened to Marcus after all." I dropped the folder on her desk with a snick.

But she didn't see it for the blood red that overcame her.

A long, hot breath, and she detonated like a warhead. "You told him? You told a Bennet—*Marcus* Bennet—that I was an embezzler? You foolish child. If you think he hasn't already exposed us, you're an imbecile. Have you any idea what you've done?" She rose, trembling with fury and fear. "You are so sanctimonious, so quick to trust them. But they're liars and deceivers, and they will abandon you the moment they find a way to save their own necks. And you, my stupid, foolish child, have handed them the means to destroy us all."

A furious rush of denial ripped me open, tore me apart. "You'd villainize the Bennets, and for what? To make yourself the hero in your story? It's *you* who have stolen. It's *you* who have lied. And now it's you who will come clean, or I'll do it for you. I have no choice, Mother. You've taken enough from me. I won't go to jail for you too."

"You'll ruin us. You'll ruin everything," she snarled. "I have this under control. I'm *fixing* it. All of this is temporary, a means to an end. And when it's done, no one will ever know. So tell me, Margaret—what is your price? What will it take for you to bury this forever? Shall I invite the Bennet bastards over for dinner? Would you like a dozen of your stupid little charities to fawn over? Money? A title? Name it, and it's yours."

"The things I want, you've never been able to give me." My

throat jammed with emotion. "I want nothing from you right now but to be through with all of this. You have forty-eight hours to turn yourself in before I do it for you."

It was only a breath or two, but it felt like an eternity. She watched me with such hatred at my treachery, her hands flexed at her sides, her body sprung so tight, I braced myself for impact should she launch herself at me.

But the tension snapped when noise rose from beyond her office doors.

Voices boomed amid the scrambling sound of people moving. Footfalls and clinking metal murmured beneath commands that came closer. And we turned to face the noise just as those doors opened with such force, we stepped back.

It was chaos in a sea of black, of helmets and guns, of bulletproof vests stamped with the letters *F*, *B*, and *I*. Everyone spoke at once, but one faceless voice rose above the others with a command for my mother to put up her hands. That voice stated her crimes, read Mother her rights as officers handcuffed her. Someone moved me out of the way, ushering me toward the door where Roland and Shelby were being escorted out, tears staining her cheeks and her hands bound. The open office was a tangle of agents, some standing sentinel, guns in hand as they eyed the executives filing toward the boardroom. The rest swept the space with carts, confiscating computers. And I passed by, my elbow in the massive hand of an FBI agent as he guided me to another of the boardrooms, taking my things before he left me there alone.

I heard her approach as they led her out, her voice shrill with panic and thick with threat, the pitch rising when she saw me through the boardroom windows. Teeth bared, she thrashed in my direction, the agents at her sides subduing her quickly as they passed.

Quieter came her voice with every step.

And in the end, there was only silence.

I sat in that room, crazed and shaken, my thoughts coming in bursts and frenzies and circles.

I had done this.

I had done this to her.

Somehow, this was all my fault.

And my mother had put me here. My mother had been the architect of it all.

I hated her in that moment with the whole of me, with a boiling of blood and a trembling vent of steam in my lungs. I could feel that hatred sink into me with a sigh, with hooks that held fast, hungry after being kept out so long by the virtue I'd upheld with the tenacity of Atlas shouldering the world.

Rather than shrink from that feeling, I grew inside of it, expanded and consumed within its hot walls. I hated myself. I hated the entire fucking universe and every atom in it.

I hated everything except Marcus.

Tears rolled down stony cheeks that belonged to someone else, hot as the betrayal in my heart.

I needed Marcus. And I was lost. Something had to be done, but I didn't know what. I didn't know how to feel or what to think except for one undeniable truth: Marcus would understand. He would make sense of it all.

He would know exactly what to do.

He would make this somehow feel all right.

Somehow.

# Shadow self

## MARCUS

"**O**h my fucking God," Laney called as she ran into the kitchen.

"Elaine," Mom snapped. "Never utter that phrase."

Laney was ghostly pale, and I leaned in, instantly alert.

"What happened?" I asked, setting my newspaper down.

"This," she muttered, shoving her phone in my direction.

My hands went numb and clumsy as I took it, my eyes locking on the photograph, then the headline.

*"Evelyn Bower Arrested for Suspected Embezzlement."*

The photograph was as unflattering as expected—her face wrenched and mouth open as if arguing. I scrolled, skimming for details, looking for Maisie's name, but only cursory information was given regarding the arrest. There were a few more photos, one of her assistant and another of her accountant per the caption as they were all put into marked cars and driven away.

"What?" Mom asked. "What is it, Marcus?"

But I couldn't speak. I handed her Laney's phone and swept mine out of my pocket to call Maisie.

"Marcus," she answered on the first ring.

"Are you all right? What happened? I saw on the news—"

"I'm all right." Her voice quivered.

I couldn't tell what she felt, but it certainly didn't feel all right. "Where are you?"

"Nearly to your house. I need to talk to you."

"I'll meet you there."

She took a breath but said nothing. The line disconnected.

An alarm sounded in my heart.

I stood, my worry a fine point. "She's on her way."

My mother's hand was over her lips as she read. "Oh, that poor girl. Go, Marcus. Go take care of her."

Laney nodded, her brows knit and eyes sharp with concern. "I hope she's okay."

"Me too," I said as I passed, hurrying for my apartment.

I made it inside, poured myself a scotch, stood in the silence of my kitchen and sipped as I waited. Waited and worried and wondered until she walked through the door.

I moved to meet her, but she flew in before I could.

Broken. Everything about her was broken, from the curve of her shoulders from the weight of it all to the twist of her face when she burst into tears the moment our eyes met.

She was in my arms before I knew I'd moved to meet her, sagging against me, body shaking as the sound of her sorrow filled the room, filled my vengeful heart with wild fury at the witnessing of her pain.

I was glad Evelyn Bower had been arrested. God knew what I'd have done if she hadn't been.

It was a long time before the wave had subsided, and I held her until she pulled away.

I cupped her face, felt the fever of her cheek with my palm. "It's going to be all right," I promised.

But her brows drew together. "Nothing's going to be all right, Marcus." Her voice was rough, raw from crying. "Nothing."

She wasn't wrong. "I'm sorry, Maisie. Tell me what happened."

And with trembling words, she did. We moved to the couch as she recounted her mother's arrest, the army of FBI, the questioning she'd endured, the lack of information they'd given her. And then she quieted, her eyes on her hands as they twisted a tissue, wringing it and loosing it so she could wring it again.

My fury never abated. It only grew.

I wished I could wipe this away. I wished there was something I could do, something I could have done. Because I would have done anything to spare her this final, most heinous infliction of pain. And it was all by her mother's hand.

"They dragged her away," she said quietly, winding the tissue up. "Th-they had guns, and she was screaming at me ..." She watched the tissue open up, wrinkled and thin, but still whole. "They took her away. She's gone."

My hands squeezed into fists and released. "Good." It was a flat, furious word, a damning verdict.

She drew a sharp breath that jerked her away from me like she'd been hit. "Good? Nothing about this is *good*, Marcus."

"She did this," I said through my teeth. "She did this to you, and she deserves what she had coming."

For a handful of heartbeats, she watched me in confusion, still as a sculpture. And something dawned on her, something that etched betrayal into her very soul.

"Was it you?" she breathed. "I didn't believe her when she said it was you who made the call, but who else could it have been? Only five people knew. Three of them were just arrested. One is me. Which only leaves you. Did you do it? Did you do this?"

Cold disbelief settled over me, both quieting my senses and sharpening them. "Excuse me?"

"The media was there—someone told them too. Someone knew. Someone told the police, and someone told the press. And I don't know who it could have been but you."

"You ... you think that I would do this? That I'd betray you? That I'd go against your wishes?"

"You didn't think I'd make the call, so you did it yourself." Everything about her stiffened, her body winding tighter than the tissue that fell to the ground as she stood. "It was you."

"Maisie," I started as I rose, reaching for her in the hopes that I could soothe her, "please, come here. Take a breath—"

She jerked away before I could touch her. "Don't fucking tell me to calm down, Marcus. She said you were a liar, that you'd do this. I didn't want to believe it. But this solves all your problems, doesn't it?" A humorless laugh choked into a sob. "All this time, you were trying to convince me to tattle on her, but did you want to protect me or yourself?"

It was my turn to pull back from the sting. "Now, wait a goddamn minute, Maisie—"

"*No, I will not wait.*" The smallness she'd carried fell away like a shell as she expanded, bursting into flame like a phoenix. "If I wouldn't do it myself, and if my ultimatum had even the slightest chance to fail, you could head it off with a single phone call. Your family, your business would be saved." She drew a fiery breath. "I cannot believe you would do this. I cannot believe you would manipulate me like she would. Even if you did this for me, it wasn't your call to make. Protecting me wasn't your job, and neither was sending my mother to prison."

As I stood there facing her, something shattered, raining down on me like glittering glass. The girl in front of me with wild eyes and bared teeth was not the girl I knew.

The girl I'd thought I knew. The girl I'd thought I loved.

In that moment, the mirror broke, and I realized I didn't know her at all. She was a stranger, unrecognizable in her anger and accusation.

She'd already decided I was guilty.

And so I built a wall, brick by brick, word by word.

My hand fell to my side. I stepped back.

"That's not how this works," I said, cold and detached. "These cases take years to build—federal agents don't take over a building on a tip. Any number of people could have informed on her, and there's no way for you to know how far that knowledge stretched. But none of that matters. Because if this is what you think of me, you don't know me at all. You certainly don't love me."

She shook her head, grappling with herself. "That's not fair, Marcus."

"And this is?" I snapped.

*"Who else could it have been?"*

*"Anyone.* Her assistant. Her accountant. Someone else who knew. But you convinced yourself it was me when I've done nothing but prove my trust. I don't know how to love someone and believe without question they're capable of this level of mistrust."

"I suppose there's not," she answered shakily. "Because even now, you haven't even denied it."

The pain of the blow slashed a cut in my heart so deep, I knew it would never be mended. "I shouldn't have to." We watched each other across a chasm of space. "I never thought you were like your mother. Not until right here, right now."

Her rage cracked, shooting her face open. Her skin paled, her anger withering and fading, erasing every trace of her mother until only Maisie remained.

But the damage had been done.

I gave her my back, carrying myself on unfeeling legs to the kitchen where I'd left my drink.

She didn't follow. "Marcus—" The word cracked.

I didn't let her finish whatever thought she had. "I think you should go," I said to my scotch before draining it, unable to face her.

There was only stillness behind me for a long moment, and as she hesitated, the air shifted from accusation to understanding, then regret.

I listened to the sound of her walking away. Opening the door. Closing it again.

For the last time.

# Embers

## MAISIE

**W**hat have I done?

Through a sheet of tears, I navigated to the curb and into a cab.

My mind was chaos, a screaming maelstrom of truth and lies and doubt.

In the heat of his anger with my mother—had it only been a few precious minutes ago?—something in me had broken, tearing a tether, loosing a leash of shocking, white-hot fury. I'd become a churning storm, an unthinking and blind monster, and if I'd looked that monster in the eye, I'd have recognized her for the one who had raised me, who had bred and coaxed the creature in me to life.

Who had released it with accusations of Marcus's infidelity.

Pieces clicked together, flying into each other too fast, with too much force.

Every painful moment of opposition between my mother and I rose and fell in wave after wave of proof. Example after example of falsities and exploitations.

I'd been so stupid, so naive, just like she'd said.

I was a fool, unprepared to run a company. Unable to make the decisions she made, unable to face her choices, choices with consequences I'd shrink from in fear or disgust or both. I dug through the coals in my heart, looking for the one that had started the inferno. The image of my mother, teeth bared and eyes feral, when she discovered I'd told Marcus.

And the seed she'd planted burst open exactly when she wanted.

In that moment, in my grief and bellowing torment, there was no trust. I'd exploded with zealous certainty that he was the informer. Somehow, in my desperation to make sense of it all, to find someone to bear the hot brunt of my pain, I had convinced myself without question that it was him and only him.

Blind. I had been blinded, possessed by the ghost of my mother, come to ruin me from beyond the veil.

I pressed a hand over my lips, unable to hold back the wretchedness, the desolate tears, the anguished sobs as they seized me and didn't let go.

I hadn't waited for his answer before condemning him. And it wasn't until he'd turned his back on me that I realized just how deeply wrong I was.

How had I gotten here?

How had I, in my devastation, betrayed the one person I knew in my heart I could trust?

The realization split me open, snapped a wire, leaving a gnarled, twisted barb in my heart.

Perhaps it was years of manipulation that had driven me to assume something so egregious, the conditioning that even the woman who was supposed to protect me above all else was a liar and a thief. My mother had worn my ability to trust, worked it until a callus of suspicion stood between me and the world.

Between me and Marcus.

And I hadn't even known it was there. Not until now, when it was too late.

Trust. The commodity that he held above all, I'd defiled.

In this one most crucial place, we would always contrast. His entire construct for life was built around the unwavering love of his family, and that love was founded in trust. To Marcus, love and trust were synonymous. They didn't just go hand in hand—they were the sum and whole of each other.

My construct for life and love was a convoluted knot of opposites. Trust and betrayal. Truth and lies. Where my father showed me what it meant to love and trust, my mother ripped the ideal to ribbons through years of control and manipulation. I thought I knew what it meant to trust. I thought I had my relationship with my mother tidily boxed up and dealt with. But at the very first sign of disloyalty, I turned on Marcus like a wild animal.

I let my mother's programming override my father's influence. I let her persuasion negate every good thing he ever gave me.

And with that offense, I had forsaken Marcus in the gravest of ways.

I swiped at my face when the taxi came to a stop in front of Dad's apartment, paying with shaking hands before sliding out and slinking inside.

Dad was on his feet and rushing me before the door closed. When his arms were around me, I sank into him and let the storm inside of me loose.

I never stopped trembling, not even when I gained composure. Not with the help of a drink and certainly not as I told him what had happened. The guns and mayhem as my mother had been arrested. The sight of her fighting as they'd dragged her away. The accusations she'd laid on me, on Marcus. My fear I would somehow be indicted. That I'd have to testify against her.

And then I told him about Marcus.

His face was shadows and regret, understanding and sorrow as I recounted what I'd said and done. And by the time I was finished, I was as hollow as a jack-o'-lantern, deflated and rancid from being left outside too long.

For a moment, he said nothing. "Your mother put this into your head. She threw her last grenade, and look at what it did."

"Maybe," I said again, my voice as watery as my eyes. "Or maybe I am her. I became her without even realizing it, without knowing it until he noted it. Just before he asked me to leave."

"Maisie," he started, "don't—"

"But I did. Please, don't try to convince me I didn't behave exactly as she would have. We'd both know it was a lie."

He didn't.

His silence was almost worse.

I drew a shaky breath. "I can think of a dozen reasons for what I've done. But there's no excuse."

"I don't think I know a single person who would walk away from what you just witnessed without trauma."

"It doesn't matter, don't you see?" I stared at my fingers as if I'd never seen them before. "What's done is done. All that's left is to sort through the wreckage." I breathed for a moment. "What will happen to Mother? Do you know?"

"Well," he said on a sigh, "she'll be out of jail as soon as she's processed, questioned, and bail is paid."

"That's all? They don't keep her?"

"The rich have privilege enough to escape nearly anything. But we can debate the unjustness of the judicial system another time and preferably with more booze."

I wished I could laugh at the joke. "Will they ... I don't know ... put her under house arrest or something?"

"No, I don't think so. But she won't go anywhere."

"I'd feel a whole lot better knowing she was confined to one place."

He frowned. "Are you worried she'll confront you?"

"Aren't you?"

Another sigh. "I don't know. I hope she wouldn't, but your mother somehow manages to be both predictable and utterly shocking."

"And what happens to Bower? Will she keep it? She can't very well run it from jail."

"That I don't know, honey. And I don't know how to even find out. I suppose I'll hear from her lawyer, and if I don't, I should be able to figure something out. I'm still her husband after all. But until then, maybe we can focus on the things you can do something about. Like Marcus."

"I don't know if there's anything I *can* do. I have committed a cardinal sin. I'm afraid it's unforgivable."

"But you don't know that, not until you talk to him. Marcus doesn't strike me as an unreasonable man."

"He's not. But that's what makes the rejection so much more painful—he doesn't say anything he doesn't mean. And he said … he said …" I swallowed a dry stone. "He said he doesn't know me at all. He looked at me like a stranger and told me that there's no way to love someone and believe them to be capable of something this damaging."

"That's not fair—we're human, and we make mistakes. Love is also about forgiveness."

"In his world, love is founded first in trust," I explained.

"But not *only* in trust."

"I'm sure he'd agree, but to him, it's paramount."

"Then talk to him and plead your case."

I shook my head, unable to meet Dad's eyes. "He doesn't want to see me."

"He does even if he thinks he doesn't," Dad answered without hesitation. "Because he loves you even though you hurt him. I don't care what your ideals are—you can't just walk away from love without looking back. Without wondering *what if*. Because love is another important thing—it's hope. Love hopes that things will get better. It looks for the best in those it loves and believes it can bring those best parts out for the world to see. In a lot of ways, love *can* change you. Take a look in the mirror. The girl you are now is not the girl you were just a few short months ago, and Marcus's love nudged you on, gave you courage. Not only should you fight for that, but you should hope. Because if he loves you, he won't give up as easily as he might have made it seem."

Every time I brushed tears from my cheeks, more came. So I gave up and let them roll in warm streams down my face, gathering at my chin, dropping to my hands.

Hope. I found a spark of it somewhere deep in my chest and fanned it until it was embers, then a flame, slight and wan as it was. Because one undeniable truth in my heart rose above the rest, cupping that flame in its hands.

I couldn't imagine a future without Marcus.

With all of my hope and all of my wishes, I shouldered the herculean task of earning back his trust.

And I wouldn't give up until I did.

# No Questions. No lies.

## MARCUS

I didn't know how to erase her.

Her clothes mingled with mine in the laundry basket. Her heels sat in wait under the window on her side of the bed. Her toothbrush leaned opposite mine. The scent of gardenias hung in the air of my bathroom.

Her ring sat on my dresser, watching me.

I could pack her things, put them away. But she wouldn't be gone. Not from my home. Not from my thoughts. And never from my heart. Her name was etched in the muscle, and though it might someday heal, there would always be a scar to shape the letters once shaped by my lips.

Yesterday had been gruesome, a timeless stretch of suffering. Telling my family what happened had been unbearable. Home had been painfully, tangibly empty.

And the night had been unending.

I gave up the fight for sleep sometime around five in the morning, my eyes stinging and bleary. I made coffee because that was what I was supposed to do. I took the cup to my room, sat in the chair in the dark. Stared at those heels where they stood, innocuous and empty, as the sun rose. And when my coffee cooled, full and forgotten, I stood and dressed for the day.

All the while, my thoughts blurred together, indistinct and without purpose. There was nothing to decide. No action to take. There was nothing to piece together, no question to answer. Only the echoes of what had been said and the companionship of my heartbreak.

I'd tried to distinguish what hurt the worst. Her shocking fury. Her certainty—absolute and irrefutable. Her instinct not to trust me even though I'd given her no reason to doubt. Her unwillingness to listen to me.

She blamed and condemned without question, unshakable in her rightness.

That. That was the most painful of all.

She hadn't even given me a chance.

And I wasn't willing to fight her faithlessness to change her mind.

If this was what she thought of me, our troubles ran deeper than this fight. I'd known the second I saw her hysteria. I knew what she'd seen, what she'd lost, the magnitude of which had torn her in two. I even knew she didn't mean what she'd said, not really. When she calmed down, she'd realize she was wrong.

But the damage had been done. The rosy haze we'd floated through since we met cleared in the span of just a few moments, moments that could never be taken back or redrawn. Words that couldn't be reeled in or erased. And in those moments, I saw another woman, one I didn't recognize. One who reminded me very much of her mother, a bond I hadn't believed existed until right then.

Maybe her mother had done this to her, conditioned her. Perhaps that likeness had been there all along, and I was too blinded by my feelings for her and her rejection of her mother to acknowledge it. But in the end, she'd turned on me at the very first opportunity and in such a savage way that I instantly doubted every emotion I'd felt, questioned every minute with her.

Our trust had been shattered, and there wasn't enough glue in the world to put it back together.

If she mistrusted me so immediately, so deeply, then I didn't know what we were doing together. I didn't know how to go on, and I didn't know what she could say.

I did know that I missed her. I knew that I loved her even though I no longer trusted her. I wished wishes came true so I could take us back in time, so I could recapture that magic when we were still pure and untainted.

But we couldn't go back, and the path before us was a soupy wall of fog so thick, it had become an impasse. The only thing that could break it up was sunshine, and I had a feeling we wouldn't see that for a long, long time.

I walked to the window, stood for a long moment with my eyes on those empty shoes. And then I picked them up and placed them in the bottom of my closet, right next to her suitcase.

As I closed the door, I knew this was the only way to erase her. One little thing at a time until she was gone.

I shoved my mind in the direction of my day, listing the things I would do to occupy myself. My only hope was to exhaust myself enough to fall into bed when I finally came home. Though somehow I knew that no amount of exhaustion would stop me from spending the sleepless night thinking about her.

When the doorbell rang, I stopped, my heart staggering, her name on my lips.

As I walked to the door and pulled it open, I knew without question I would find her standing there.

She was too small, too colorless. Pale hair and skin, dark eyes smudged with shadows from a sleepless night of her own.

A flare of pink rose in her cheeks when our eyes met.

The instinct to reach for her sent a blazing streak of pain through my chest.

Neither of us spoke.

"I ..." she started, instantly fumbling. "May I come in?"

I moved out of the way, watching her as she passed.

We didn't make a move beyond the entryway. I didn't invite her in further.

She watched me with those starless, sad eyes. "Would you believe me if I said I was sorry?"

"Yes. But I don't know what it would change."

Her throat worked. "It doesn't seem like enough, those words. They can't explain the depth of what it means to be sorry, too common and shallow for how I regret what I said yesterday, what I did. I could tell you all the reasons, but I think you know them already. Mostly, I wasn't myself."

"No, you weren't. Or maybe you were. I'm not sure I know anymore."

"Please, don't say that. On some fundamental level, you and I *know* one another. You said so yourself."

"I remember," I said softly.

"I don't know what possessed me yesterday. It was all so much, and I just ... it made sense. In my mind, in that moment, it made sense—your pushing me to come clean, the math of it all, even the possibility of you getting her out of the way. But I was wrong. I know you'd never have betrayed my trust. Instead, I betrayed yours."

"It wasn't just a betrayal of trust. You defaulted to accusations. You defaulted to blaming me. Without thought, without reason, you put my head on the block and swung the ax."

"I know," she said to her shoes.

We were silent for a beat.

"Why did you come here today?"

Her gaze lifted to meet mine. "Because I love you. Because I was wrong, and I want to make it right. How can I earn your trust again? How can I beg your forgiveness? How can I say that I'm sorry when words aren't enough?" A shake of her head, a glance at the floor. "Of all the things I've walked away from, of all the things I've lost, you're the one I will never forgive myself for. So I had to try."

The fissure in my heart cracked wider, drove deeper.

"Is there anything I can say?" she asked. "Is there anything I can do? Tell me, and I'll do it. Just don't say it's over. Please, don't say that." Her voice broke, her eyes shining with tears.

Emotion gripped my throat, my heart whispering acceptance and my mind screaming defense. But when her tears spilled over, my heart won.

Slowly, I pulled her into my arms, held her to my chest, warred with myself. Because this felt right—she felt right. But what she'd done was wrong, and my mind held fast to that violation, wielding it like a mace.

"You asked me what you could do," I said.

"Anything, just ask."

"Give me time." I rested my chin on her crown, unable to look at her. "I believe you, every word. But somewhere deep down, you don't trust me. And after yesterday, I've lost trust in you. If we don't have trust, the whole thing falls apart."

I felt every shallow rise and fall of her breath.

"Is it over?" she asked.

*No*, my heart answered. But it was all too fresh, too soon to know what to do without question. Until I had an irrefutable answer, I had no answer at all.

"I don't know."

She broke from my arms, taking a step back. Hurt etched her face, edged with a new sort of betrayal. "I don't think I realized you'd be willing to walk away because I made a mistake. Because I overreacted."

"That's not what I said."

"But it's a possibility?"

I said nothing.

Now her tears were proud and pained, and she swiped hastily

at her cheeks to dash them away. "My father said love isn't just about trust—it's about forgiveness and hope. It's true, if we don't have trust, the whole thing falls apart. But if you can't forgive, then what we have won't last anyway. So while you take your time, consider that too."

I should have stopped her. I should have argued. I should have told her what she wanted to hear in the hopes I'd come around to that forgiveness.

Instead, I watched her back as she opened the door. A sliver of golden sunlight spilled in for the briefest of moments before it was cut off again.

And once more, I was left in the dark.

# Queen of Ashes

## MAISIE

It took the entire cab ride to Midtown to compose myself.

My life had become defined by treachery. Mother's I'd expected. Mine had cut me off at the knees.

But what I'd done to Marcus might be the one to drag me under once and for all.

Stupidly, I'd convinced myself that he'd forgive me. That he'd understand. That together, we'd find a way for me to regain that trust I'd broken. But of course it wouldn't be so easy. Of course he would need time. Of course he would need to consider it all. Marcus did nothing until he was absolutely certain. He wouldn't tell me it was all right if there were even the slightest chance that it wasn't.

I reached into my bag for my phone, opening my messages. Touching his name.

*I'm sorry. And I understand. Take whatever time you need. I'll be waiting.*

And then I turned off my phone, shoving it to the depths of the bag where I wouldn't be tempted to wait for word.

As the cab pulled up to the curb, I did my best to shove my feelings in too, because I was about to walk into Bower for a legal meeting.

With every step away from the taxi and into the building, my blood pressure rose.

Roland had been released late yesterday, as had Shelby, and this morning I'd woken to a call requesting a meeting with Roland and the head of the company's legal department. Even if I'd wanted to refuse or postpone, I wanted to know what they had to say, how bad things were. I had *not* expected the meeting to be at Bower, assuming the floors we occupied would be a crime scene or something.

When I exited the elevator of the executive floor, it didn't look like a crime scene.

It looked like a robbery.

The floor had been gutted of everything but furniture and harmless electronics. The carpet was littered with scraps of paper and a flotsam and jetsam of everything from loose staples to pens, sticky notes and paperclips. Drawers of every desk and cabinet hung open like gaping mouths, emptied of anything that could have held even a trace of evidence.

All that was left was trash and unused office supplies.

The sight was reminiscent of the remains of my life.

There wasn't a single soul in the bullpen, the space so quiet, I could hear the hum of the fluorescent lights. The sound of my footsteps on the industrial carpet almost echoed in the wreckage of my family's company.

It was so quiet, in fact, that when I opened the boardroom door and found Roland and the lawyer there, it very nearly startled me.

They stood when I entered, their faces grim and seemingly sleepless. And after cursory greetings, we sat across from each other.

Roland pulled his baffling handkerchief out of his pocket and swiped at his glistening forehead.

"I'm sorry to disturb you after yesterday, but I'm glad you're here," he said. "I'm sure you can imagine that we need to get Bower back up and running as quickly as possible, and we could use your help."

"Thank you for the consideration, but I would just really like to know what is going on and what happened. I'd like to help, if I can. But I'm not sure if you're aware that my mother fired me a few days ago."

Roland paled, sharing a look with the lawyer before speaking. "Yes. Well, in light of your mother's arrest, I think it's safe to say whatever she might have said is moot." He squirmed through a pause.

The lawyer, whom I didn't know, gave him a look. "Start with the charges."

"Yes, yes. Of course," Roland started, relieved to have a thread to pull. "You see, I first discovered the misappropriation of funds a few years ago, shortly after you opened Harvest Center." He handed me the folder on the top of the stack in front of him. I opened it as he continued, "At first I thought it was a clerical error, but when I went to Evelyn with it, she explained it away. But I don't deal in excuses, I deal in math. Math doesn't lie. Your mother does."

My mouth went dry. I reached for the water pitcher and poured a glass with shaking hands.

"I watched the accounts over the course of a few months—you had left for England by that time—and when the missing money accumulated, I went to her again. But that time, she was ready for me. Her counter was the threat to make sure I took some, if not all, of the blame. She had orchestrated a setup, one designed to implicate me. And so she left me with no choice." He straightened up, lifting his chin though his eyes were heavy with apology. "I approached the FBI that afternoon."

Blank. I was as blank as a fresh sheet of paper.

"For the last eighteen months, we have been building a case against her. There was so much data to process, so many patterns to find. Too much research for anything to move quickly. So I let her believe she had the upper hand while they gathered what they needed to arrest and indict her. I'm sorry, Margaret. I'm sorry to have done this to you and your family. But there was nothing I could do or say to change her mind."

"Maisie," I heard myself say. "Please, call me Maisie."

A small fatherly smile touched his lips. "When you came back, our new worry was *you*. I don't know why she lured you here with the charity—I told her not to put you in charge of the front for her theft, but she thought she knew better. I really did try to turn it around, which likely only made the case against her stronger. If she had only restructured, closed ranks, *saved* money instead of stealing it, everything would have been fine, or at least better than this. But to Evelyn Bower, that would be admitting defeat, publicly and openly. Convincing her—I'm sure you'd agree—is a fool's errand."

I couldn't answer, so I nodded.

"I told her not to involve you—the chance of you looking like an accomplice was too high—but when you asked for the charity as a contingency for returning ... well, there was no talking her out of it. She tried to tell me—her accountant, for Pete's sake—that she would fix it all." He scoffed. "But I thought you should know that her attempts to keep you away from the charity wasn't strictly for her purposes. It was to protect you. Even firing you, I believe, was to try to separate you from the company and her mess. The pressure had mounted, and we all knew it was coming. Only difference is, she didn't know *what* was coming, nor did she know how bad it would be."

*Protect me. She was trying to protect me.* The words were unbelievable, even in thought. Unfathomable.

But they didn't shock me in that disbelief. Because if ever my mother did protect me, it would be through abuse.

The lawyer slid another folder in Roland's direction, perhaps to get him on track.

"Oh, yes." He opened it up and rifled through the papers

inside. "And so the state of the company. As of this morning, your mother has given you the entirety of her shares of Bower Bouquets, fifty-one percent."

Shock bolted me to the chair. "What?"

"Had she not, the board would have insisted. They might have bought her out, broken up the shares, taken the control from a Bower, and your mother would never allow that. So she has gifted them to you. Franklin here is drawing up the paperwork."

At his introduction, Franklin spoke, though his words came from what felt like a very great distance, "Miss Bower, the shares are yours to do with as you wish. The board has already requested a meeting, and if you'd like, I can accompany you. I suspect there will be quite a lot of talk on what's going to be sold and how the company will be turned around ..."

I heard nothing else, my horizon shifting, weighted on one end by surprise as the dogma of my upbringing shot into the air and away. Everything I knew. Everything this company was.

Everything it could someday be.

I could not parse it. The information tumbled and jumbled around in my brain like laundry in a dryer set too hot.

"... I'm sure you can imagine everyone is anxious to get things moving again," Franklin was saying. "This company needs a head, a leader. We can limp along while it's sorted out, but the sooner we get you into that boardroom, the better."

"And what about Mother?" My voice was rough, unrecognizable. "How will she survive?"

"Well," Franklin said, "she's home now, and she'll stay there for some time. Your mother isn't without investments. She'll have to call those in—her houses, her retirement funds and stocks, anything we can liquidate—to pay back what she embezzled from the shareholders."

"What's the total?"

A pause. "Just shy of twenty million."

My lungs filled, my gasp audible. But I was suffocating.

"Try not to worry yourself with that," Roland attempted to comfort me. "This was her choice. She had many, *so* many opportunities to set things right, but she didn't. She put herself here. And now you have a chance to save the company."

But I didn't know how. I didn't know how to speak, let alone save our crippled and overextended company. But I sat and listened as they rolled through lingering details. When it was all done, we stood and shook hands, and I left that boardroom a shell.

I stepped into the silent remains of the company. It was our kingdom in ruin, laid to waste by my mother.

And I was queen of the ashes.

# Legacy

## MAISIE

I didn't know how long I had been standing on the stoop of my mother's house.

When I'd left Bower, I'd walked, so lost in thought that I looked up and found myself on the subway, nearly at Christopher Street. In a haze, I exited when the doors opened and wandered up Hudson and toward her house. And I hadn't stopped, not until I was standing here, in front of her door, without a plan or a purpose or a thought.

James didn't open the door on my approach, which struck me as odd in itself until I realized he'd likely quit or been let go. I wondered if I should knock or ring the bell, having never come to the house when I didn't reside here. The key was in my purse, but it somehow felt criminal to enter a house where I wasn't welcome with a key I shouldn't have.

Without expecting a result, I reached for the doorknob and turned, shocked when met with no resistance. Instead, the door creaked open, casting a long rectangle of light in the otherwise dark room.

I stepped in, confused and on alert.

It was too dark for daytime, unnaturally dim for a cloudless day.

It was too quiet, and my mind ran away with thoughts of finding her hurt, finding she'd hurt herself. Or worse.

But I closed the door, the sound of my heels echoing too loud.

"Mother?" I called, moving through the entryway and toward her office.

Things were untidy—a pair of toppled-over shoes next to the writing desk, which was littered with letters. Her designer bag lay on the floor on its side, the contents spilling onto the parquet.

"Hello?" My pulse picked up as I approached her office doors, which were cracked only a sliver.

I laid my damp palm on the unlatched doors and pushed.

The curtains were drawn, so heavy that only splinters of light came through. But the small, round window in the pointed eave cast a column of light into the room, just enough to see the visage of my mother, sitting in a chair in front of her grand desk, glass of scotch hanging delicately from her hand and the bottle at her bare feet.

"So you've come to gloat." Her voice cut through the silence like an arrow.

I would have been hurt had I not been so relieved to find her alive. Though on inspection, I couldn't imagine Evelyn Bower's ego ever consenting to take her own life.

"No. I've come to ask why."

She brought the crystal glass to her lips, tipping it until it was empty. And then she stood, moving to the stand where more glasses waited. "Why what, exactly?"

When she turned, a second glass was in her hand. And she made her way to sit once more before pouring a finger of scotch into both, extending one to me.

Dumbfounded, I accepted it. She nodded to the chair next to her, and I sat.

For a moment, we sat in silence, facing that opulent desk and the history of our family on the wall and mantel behind it.

The grand Victorian mantel held a dozen gilded picture frames marking Bowers through the generations. Faded wedding pictures in black-and-white vignette. My great-grandmother and her sister at a farm in the forties, cheeks high and smiling. A formal portrait of my grandmother, grandfather, and my mother and aunt as babies. A wedding photo of my parents. A baby picture of me.

But on the wall hung a massive painting of my grandmother, the portrait grand and stern and commanding. She sat in a stately chair surrounded by bouquets in shocks of color—every color in the world, I'd thought when I was a little girl. But the thing that always struck me was the ghost of a smile she wore like a crack in her mask. It was the only warmth, the only humanity in the imposing painting, and I always wondered where the rest of that smile was. Who had seen it and who had wiped it away.

"She was a terrible old bitch," my mother said from my side. "For twenty years, I've sat at this desk under that look on her face. Under her shadow. Funny that I didn't want to be her since I became her."

I took a sip of my drink, which was all the answer I had to give.

"You want to know why? A vague question with too many possible answers. If you want to know why I stole from my own company, it was because I believed I could put it all back. The reason I needed it was my own vanity—to keep this house and all the others we own. To keep up appearances as our profits waned. To pretend it was fine so as not to be strong-armed by the board into retreat. I didn't want to face humiliation." She laughed humorlessly. "I was too sure of myself to even consider this a real consequence. And look at me now." She held up a hand in display.

Still, I had nothing to say, and she seemed to require no response as she continued, "I think you've sorted out why I didn't want you to have the charity and even why I fired you—had I not, it was very likely I'd have taken you down with me. And despite popular belief, I do want you to succeed. I do want you to thrive. I just didn't think you were capable on your own. Although I will say that your sleeping with a Bennet is the deepest wound you could have inflicted. I should be thanking you. You made it very easy to fire you. I didn't have to act at all. And I meant it when I said they would ruin us. They always would have, if given the opportunity."

We stared up at Grandmother. I tried to ignore the flicker of warmth from her admission—she wanted what was best for me and had tried to give it to me in her own twisted way.

She took a sip of her drink as if to fortify herself.

"And if you want to know why I gave you the shares, it's because I can't keep them. If Bower is to go on, it has to be with you. I've tainted it, and even had I not, it cannot be seized. It will not be dissolved. And somehow, you are the only one who can save it from that fate."

"I'm surprised."

Her face turned to me, but I kept my eyes on Grandmother. "By what part?"

"All of it. I was convinced you'd gladly disinherit me if I didn't do what you asked."

"This company has been passed down through generations. It was going to be yours regardless of what I threatened. I had to protect you, or the company would go to God knows who. It was the only way."

The warmth I'd felt for my mother's shocking display of maternal protection cooled. "So it was about the legacy."

"Everything is about the legacy, Margaret," she said as if I were tedious and exhausting.

"Yes, I suppose it is." I took a long pull of my drink, and when it was gone, I extended a hand for the bottle.

"Oh, don't sound so disappointed. The reason doesn't make

it any less true." She handed it over. "You've got it all. Everything. The company lies in your capable hands. I no longer have a say. So congratulations. You got what you wanted."

"It's not what I wanted. It's what you wanted."

"And it seems neither of us had a choice in how it happened, no matter how we thought we did. The keys to my kingdom are yours. Do try not to waste the opportunity."

"Silver linings and all that." I poured two fingers and set the bottle on the ground between us.

Silence fell. We drank.

"What will you do?" I finally asked.

"Go to jail," she said on a dry laugh. "Sell the house. Pay my debts so they don't get any worse. Move to Paris. Join a garden club. And for the sake of Bower's future, stay away." She paused, then sighed. "For decades, we have shaped this company with biblical Bower law. My grandmother always fell second to the Bennets—sometimes by fortune, sometimes by perception. My mother didn't fare much better. I built an empire under their doctrine and set fire to my spoils. The most I can hope for is that you'll better than we did."

It was almost a compliment, *almost* an admission, but she'd said it with a snide sort of arrogance, as if she knew I wouldn't.

I was a Hail Mary. A long shot.

But she'd underestimated me my whole life. It would be silly to believe anything should change now, even though, for the briefest moment, I naively had.

I kicked back my drink and set the glass next to the bottle. When I stood, my gaze shifted from my grandmother to my ruined mother.

"I'll do my best," I said.

Pride and pain flashed behind her eyes. "I wouldn't expect anything less."

When she looked away, it was a dismissal. Whatever thread we'd been holding fell.

So I turned. I walked out of that room. Out of that house.

And I stepped into a brand new world, closing the door on my past.

A curious feeling settled over me, a quiet and calm sense of … I didn't know what. It was all the things left over when the tsunami receded. Bits of proof nestled in wet sand, touched with sunlight for the first time. There was acceptance, smooth from years of wear. The broken shell of the life I'd known, jagged and sharp.

But there, amid it all, was a glimmer of gold, a burst of color. A treasure lay, visible only in glimpses, waiting for me to dig up each jewel, uncover every gem. Bower was mine. My father was free. My mother would be gone. And as I brushed the sand from each beautiful thing I discovered, I came to the greatest treasure of them all.

Marcus was a diamond, faceted and transparent, unbreakable and rare. He was blinding. Dazzling. Breathtakingly brilliant, his strength forged in the fire of the earth.

He was, without question, the most valuable of all the riches in the world.

As I appraised all that I'd discovered, I saw for the first time how they all fit together. I understood what I wanted to do, what I was meant to do.

And filled with purpose and hope and love, I set about doing just that.

# A Family Affair

## MARCUS

"**I**t's not that simple," I huffed.

Luke gave me a look from where he sat in the study, draped in one of Mom's armchairs like a king. "It seems pretty simple to me," he said.

"That's because *you're* simple."

"And you make everything more complicated than it has to be. The way I see it? You love her, and she loves you. So she was an asshole. It's been three days, and I'd like to note that you weren't much better—"

"Why, because I didn't lie to her?"

"No, ding-dong. Because you didn't stop her."

"She stormed out."

"And there wasn't even one tiny little opportunity to stop her?"

I said nothing.

"Exactly. But listen—if you think you're going to get through any relationship without *both* of you occasionally being an asshole, you're delusional."

"That's true," Kash said from behind me as he entered the room, flopping into the chair next to Luke. "Everybody's an unintentional asshole from time to time. What matters is how you handle what comes after."

"Not you too." I laid my own look on the two of them. "It's not like she did something trivial or small. She accused me of ratting her mother out to the FBI, for God's sake. She didn't even consider my side for a single, solitary second. She *decided* I did it. What I don't understand is how the hell none of *you* understand."

"Understand what?" Jett asked, dropping onto Mom's chaise and crossing his ankles.

"How right he is about Maisie's wrongness," Luke said.

"Ah," Jett answered with a smirk.

"Look," Kash started, "I get it. I really do. I'd be mad as all hell, but after everything Maisie has done? After all she's given up, I don't see how you couldn't just accept her apology outright."

"Because," Luke clarified dramatically, "*someone* has very high moral standards."

Jett folded his hands behind his head. "She apologized. Do you really think she didn't mean it?"

"Of course I believe she meant it. That's not the point."

"Then what *is* the point?" Kash asked.

"The point is, she threw me under the bus the second the wind changed."

"And immediately apologized," Jett added.

"Yes, but—"

"What are we talking about?" Laney asked as she entered the study.

"About how Marcus is being a brat," Kash answered.

"What's new?" Laney snorted a laugh, stretching out on the floor in front of the fireplace. "Somebody hand me a pillow."

I handed her one as hard as I could fling it, and it hit her in the face with enough force to knock her back.

"Spoilsport," she said on a laugh, propping herself up on the pillow.

"Know-it-all," I shot back.

She stuck her tongue out at me.

"You love Maisie," Kash said, reeling us back in. "How many woman have you loved in your life?"

"Besides Mom," Luke added.

A collective groan sounded, and Jett flung another pillow, this time in Luke's direction.

"None," Laney answered for me. "He's never even brought a girl home for dinner, but he brought *Margaret Bower* home to meet Mom. If that doesn't say commitment, I don't know what does."

My siblings turned their gazes on me and, for once, said nothing.

I swallowed hard, wishing they would. "I do love her."

"Enough to forgive her?" Kash asked somberly.

"Little enough to let her go?" Laney added.

"And here I thought you were violently opposed to the idea," I said, raising a brow in her direction.

She sighed. Shrugged. "But I'm even more violent opposed to your unhappiness. Maisie makes you happy. Happy enough to *whistle*." A chuckle rolled through them at my expense. "She messed up, but I think you know her well enough to know her character, her heart. Don't make her pay for her mistake too long. And don't deprive yourself of happiness because of your pride."

I looked around the room, assessing them. "Not one of you thinks I should be upset?"

"No," they answered nearly in unison, along with another voice from my shoulder.

Mom walked around the couch and sat next to me. "Did you ever know," she began, adjusting the pillows to her comfort, "I always worried you would be the child to miss love?"

I frowned.

"Oh, not because you're unlovable or that you're incapable—you, Marcus, are capable of more love than perhaps all of them." A couple of potshots were mumbled, but she continued on, "But because I feared that somehow, it would find you, and you wouldn't recognize it. Or worse—you'd reject it on the grounds of some defied principle. You're hurt, and you should be. What she did was unfair and unjust, and she broke your faith. So there's only one question to answer—can you look beyond that hurt to forgive her?"

"Can you imagine your life without her?" Luke added.

"Or will you spend the rest of your life wishing you had?" Kash tacked on.

"Well then, three," Mom said. "Three questions with your happiness on the line."

"And your grandchildren," Laney popped.

"Yes, and that," Mom noted. "If I'm not swimming in grandchildren within the next five years, I'm arranging marriages for the lot of you."

Jett groaned. "Garden club babies."

But Laney laughed. "Thank God there are no men in garden club."

"Oh, but there are plenty of sons," Mom snarked, and Laney put on a spectacular grimace.

I, however, was lost in thought.

It wasn't so much that I had to consider what they'd said—they were right, and I knew it. I'd known it all before I sat down on this stupid couch. I'd known it for three long and silent days. I'd known it since the second I last saw her.

None of this was news.

As hurt as I was and as unsure as I thought my feelings were regarding forgiveness, there had never been a future without Maisie. Was it just my pride as they'd said? Or was I afraid? Afraid of being hurt again. Afraid of being heartbroken by the only person I'd ever let see that heart, the only one who'd ever held it in their hands.

Was it my vulnerability that scared me most of all?

She had shaken my belief that she'd protect my heart as I would hers. That she would sacrifice anything to protect mine. Because I would.

Except I hadn't.

The realization struck me like an arrow. She *had* protected mine. She had sacrificed more than I ever could. She'd given up everything simply because she loved me.

And I'd rejected her first fault just as devoutly as she had accused me without grounds.

But I didn't realized *my* mistake.

I didn't apologize.

I didn't beg her forgiveness.

"I'm an asshole," I breathed, leaning into my hands until my face was covered.

"Like I said," Luke mentioned.

Kash punched him in the arm.

Mom laid her hand on my back, shifting it in slow, familiar circles that made me feel safe and loved. "We all are. What matters is how you make it right."

"Like *I* said," Kash said, and Luke returned the favor with a sock to his arm.

They rubbed their biceps, scowling at each other.

"So, how are you going to make it right?" Laney asked.

"An apology would probably be a good place to start," Jett noted.

"Not just for making her wait so you could lick your wounds, but for not accepting her apology on the spot," Kash added.

"Probably wouldn't hurt to grovel a little," Luke said. "Always works for me."

"Just talk to her." Mom smiled, lips together and eyes soft. "If you're ever going to marry her, she'd better know you're good at apologizing. So the grander the better, I say."

Laney rolled her eyes. "Don't you ever think about anything other than us getting married?"

"Of course I do."

"Or grandchildren?" Laney's brow climbed.

"Oh. Then, no. That's the bulk of it."

They laughed, but I didn't.

I was wrong, and I had to tell her.

I had to show her.

I bolted off the couch so fast, they leaned back as if I'd blown them that direction.

"Whoa, I don't think anyone meant to go *now*," Laney said.

"I think I've waited long enough."

With a smirk on my face and the wind at my back, I flew out of the house too fast for anyone to question me.

Because I knew of one undeniable way to swear my fealty to Maisie.

And it ended with forever.

# Pocket Change

## MARCUS

Forty-eight of the longest hours of my life ticked by.

The second I'd left my family, I'd texted her asking to meet, and for the rest of that day, that message went unanswered, my voicemail box painfully empty, my screen black as pitch, disturbed only by my siblings. Every time they texted the group chat, my heart stop-started with hope enough times that I nearly turned my phone off. But I didn't. I couldn't.

I'd spent a long night wishing I'd shown my cards, laid it all on the table when I'd seen her last. I could have begged. Pleaded. Told her that I loved her and apologized. I considered a telling her right there in a message. But for all I needed to say, a text would never do. A voice message could never suffice.

The only way was face to face.

At six the next morning, she answered.

She agreed to meet the following afternoon to talk. And I'd practiced my speech every minute since, all the way to right now, waiting impatiently for the message that she was free.

I only hoped I wasn't too late.

Enough had happened in the last few days to keep me occupied. Yesterday, a long meeting with Ben informed me of the most shocking revelation of all—Evelyn Bower had given Maisie full control of the company. It was a deduction made when the call came in from Thompson that the lawsuit had been dropped. But not by Evelyn.

By Maisie.

There was much to do in the wake of that disclosure. Paperwork to sign, meetings to attend.

But she wasn't at any of them.

Last night, we had a proper Bennet brouhaha, complete with enough booze to put down a rhinoceros and one of the more lavish meals Jett had ever made—beef Wellington and trimmings, the whole of which had taken him nearly eight hours to complete. Everyone was there, including Tess and Lila on the arms of my brothers, and we had such a night that it ended well after midnight when the slow dancing in the dimly lit living room turned to canoodling.

Jett, Laney, and I hurried away and didn't look back.

The night was a success for them. For me, it only served as a reminder of what I'd lost. And I started to wonder if I'd ever get it back.

Late last night, I sat in the armchair in my room, lit by a solitary lamp at my elbow, writing a letter I didn't know would ever be read. But the words were too much to live only in my heart, too painful to hold in those four chambers. So I let them go, poured them onto a page by way of my hand. And once I released them, I was left empty, exhausted. Rumpled and worn, I'd turned off that light, casting the world in darkness again.

I stood in the kitchen, hip resting on the island, staring at nothing as I turned the velvet box around in my pocket where it had been since I escaped the Bennet ambush. And I waited.

There was nothing else to do.

When my phone buzzed in the other pocket, my heart gave its familiar lurch of hope. My expectation was my siblings. My wish was Maisie. But instead, it was a text from Ben.

*Have some papers to sign for the lawsuit. Meet me at your mom's.*

I frowned at my screen as I texted him back.

*Shouldn't we meet at the office?*

*I was in the neighborhood, so I'm already here*, he answered. *See you in a few.*

With the dismissal, that was that.

I hauled myself off my couch, feeling older than my years. Creaky in the bones, worn to weariness. I wondered as I slipped on my suit coat if it was the result of fading hope, draining joy. But I brushed the thought away. Because I wasn't ready to give up, not yet. I'd give her time. But I'd find a way.

I had to find a way.

The day was warm and cheerful, a cloudless spring afternoon that whispered summer's beginnings. Leaves had sprung from their buds, rustling in the breeze and dappling the sidewalk as the Village bustled around me. And I walked toward Longbourne with my hand cupping that little black box, wondering why Ben hadn't just come over. Maybe there was something for Mom to sign or go over, by which I meant for me to go over on her behalf. Of course, nothing about us was conventional, so it didn't strike me as too odd. Just enough to question.

Until I walked in the front door.

A host of whispers and shuffling around floated toward me from the dining room, followed by an extremely loud *Shh* from, if I had to guess, my sister.

I closed the door, knowing I'd just walked into some sort of trap. I just had to figure out what it was and how to get out of it.

Mom appeared in the hallway, her face flushed and smiling. "Ah! You're here. Ben is just this way. How are you?" she rambled, shuffling over. "Here, let me take your coat. It's warm outside, isn't it? Oh, I'm just so glad winter is over. Felt like it would never end."

I eyed her as she hung up my suit coat, still babbling.

"Mom, what's going on?"

She scoffed and tittered, but her cheeks flushed another four degrees of red. "Why would you think something was going on? You're so suspicious. Don't you trust your mother?" she asked, taking my arm.

"No."

But she laughed, pulling me toward the dining room and hissed whispers. "Silly. Ben just has some papers for you to sign. They're very important papers, so you see, we had to do it right away. Why go to the office?" Another nervous laugh.

I stopped. "Have you taken your medicine today? Do you feel feverish? You haven't come in contact with anyone carrying malaria, have you?"

"A mother can't ask her son over?"

"Ben asked me over."

"Marcus Bennet," she chided, cheeks pink and brows furrowed in consternation, "stop questioning me and get in that dining room right now."

"For the papers."

"Yes, for the *papers*," she said, tugging me into the dining room.

But I froze in the threshold, dragging Mom to a stop with me.

Because sitting at the long table next to Ben was Maisie.

It was strange, how memory worked, how it could never quite recall the glory of the real thing. How a face I thought I knew better than my own could surprise me so desperately in its beauty. And not the beauty of her form, of her small chin or soft eyes, of her shining hair or the gentle curve of her lips. But in the expression of her love and devotion, so true and real that in a heartbeat, I knew. I knew every thought and feeling of her heart with nothing more than a breath and a glimpse into her eyes.

But still, I paused, not understanding what she was doing here, why she hadn't called me but inexplicably sat in my family's dining room, looking at me like she was. Was I supposed to sit? Speak? Sweep her out of that chair and into my arms? I didn't know.

She didn't seem to either.

The crowded room watched us silently.

When it had been too long, Ben stood, gesturing to the chair across from him as he said, "Marcus, have a seat."

I strode to the chair, my gaze locked with Maisie's, questions and affirmations flying between us, though neither of us spoke. As bidden, I sat.

My family hovered around us like specters.

Ben wore a mysterious smile, as did all of them with the exception of Maisie. She looked as nervous and hopeful as I felt.

He laid a hand on the folder in front of him. "We've received an offer from Bower that you should see."

I frowned, taking the folder as he pushed it toward me. "A settlement? I thought the lawsuit was over."

"It is," Maisie said, her voice like a bell in the night. "This is another offer altogether. A partnership, if it pleases you."

"A partnership," I mused, flipping open the folder to view the document inside.

"This is a preliminary offer, just a jumping-off point," Ben explained as I skimmed frantically, looking for answers. "But I think you'll get the idea," he said on a laugh.

Words jumped off the page at me. *Merge. Joining. Shares. Longbourne* and *Bower. Trademarking* and a staggering dollar amount. I looked up from the pages to meet her gaze.

"What is this?" I asked her.

"A merger of sorts," she answered, suddenly shy. "My ... my mother turned over her shares to me. Bower is mine."

"I heard." I smiled. We could have been alone in that room.

"We're faced with quite a problem. I have inherited a company in shambles and ruin, and to save it, I have to burn it all down. Our brand is in tatters, and our finances are in a desolate state, especially once I pay back what my mother took so she can leave us without me worrying for her welfare. But I have a plan to save it, one that will wipe the slate clean, and the board agrees. And I'd like your help to do it."

"How? How could we possibly help you? We can't invest, can't afford to buy in."

"Oh, but you can." Hope radiated from her like sunshine. "Bower Bouquets would like to acquire your business and your brand to adopt as our own, and in exchange, you will receive twenty-five-point-five percent of my shares. We'll acquire branding rights to Longbourne, and you'll acquire an equal share of the company. And you and I would own it together."

My lips parted, my brain lagging, unsure I'd heard what I thought. I glanced at my expectant family, landing on my mother last, who wore the most optimistic look of them all.

"You knew about this." I didn't ask.

Mom nodded emphatically. "Oh, Marcus. She came here after you rushed off a few days ago, asked for our blessing. How could we say no?"

Luke laughed. "You should have seen her trying to keep that one from you. If you hadn't locked yourself in your house to lick your wounds, I don't know if we could have kept her quiet."

Mom swatted at him, and he flinched dramatically.

Laney beamed. "You said yourself we could be allies. If this isn't a golden opportunity, I don't know what is."

My siblings and father nodded as if to say, *Go on, dummy. Do it!*

"Bower was founded on family," Maisie started, "but it was a foundation only in name. Longbourne is—"

"Failing," I noted. "Broke."

"*Family*," she corrected. "Do you remember our dream?"

My heart ached at the remembrance of the dream we'd had, a dream I'd thought we'd lost. "I do."

"We could do this together. We could make the dream come

true with you and me at the helm. Even if ... even if you and I aren't to be, we can save our family businesses together. The board agrees, especially after the strides you've made with Longbourne in the short time that you've been in charge. Longbourne is everywhere—magazines, celebrity weddings, newspapers. And in order for Bower to survive, we have to strip it down to the bolts. We have to restructure, gather the troops. We have to start over. And if I'm going to rebuild, I want to rebuild with you. Because despite what I've said, what I've done, I trust you more than anyone. With the business. With my heart." Her eyes fell to her hands. "I hope one day I can earn your trust again. But in the meantime, I'd like to ask if you'd be my partner. All I've wanted—all I've ever wanted—is to be enough. To be equal. To hold a place of my own next to someone I love. Will you help me save Bower? Will you be my equal?"

Wordlessly, I rose, never breaking our gaze as I walked around the table. My family faded away, the room a shade with Maisie crisp and clear in the center, brows clicking together in curiosity. She turned in her seat as I approached and dropped to one knee.

Her hand flew to her mouth, and gasps sounded from behind me.

"Be your equal," I mused, taking her hand. "How could I be equal when I fall so short? I should have told you then what I knew in my heart, what I've always known. That I love you. That I betrayed that love by not forgiving you the moment you spoke. That there is nothing you could do or say that is unforgivable. You don't have to earn my trust again because you've always had it. I was just too shocked, too scared, too hurt to fight for us. I should have. Forgive me. I swear I will always fight for us, if you'll give me the chance."

"Of course, Marcus," she whispered and smiled and cried all at once. "I'll always forgive you."

"Then I'd like to make a proposal of my own. A proposal of

partnership and equality. One of love and forgiveness. A proposal of forever."

Releasing her hand, I reached into my pocket and retrieved the box, opening it in display. "Longbourne has always been run by a Bennet woman, and I'd hate to break tradition now. Marry me, Maisie."

She stared at the ring, wide eyes full of tears, hands pressed to her lips. When they fell, she said, "I ... this is not what I expected."

Fear struck me like lightning, but a smile brushed my lips to cover it. "Well, I tried to call."

A laugh caught in her throat, dissolving into a hitch of her breath. "I'm so sorry, Marcus." She reached for my face, hers etched with regret.

"So am I. I was wrong, Maisie. Forgive me."

"I'll always forgive you. Will you promise the same?"

"I do promise." I glanced down at the proffered ring. "I'd hate to put this back in my pocket, it's been there so long."

She laughed. "You'll make me a Bennet?"

"There's not a single thing in the world that would make me happier."

"Only forever with you," she said with a smile that split me open. "Yes, Marcus."

"Oh, thank God," I breathed in relief, rising swiftly to punctuate the words with a kiss that washed every worry and fear away, replacing them with this. With us.

It took a moment to become aware of the clapping and laughing and whooping around us. We seemed to notice it together, breaking the kiss to laugh and smile while I slid the ring on her finger, both of our hands trembling. And then she threw her arms around my neck and kissed me again, deep enough that it had me wishing desperately that we were alone.

When we finally parted, it was to stand and greet the reception line of my family. It was a flurry of laughter and tears and slaps on the back. Of hugging and oohs and aahs over Maisie's ring. It was a chorus of happy welcome, of love and approval, so perfectly chaotic that I didn't see Jett leave or return, but champagne popped in his hand and flowed into glasses, then another bottle to accommodate us all.

We raised our glasses, and their eyes turned to me.

But mine were on Maisie, my heart too big for my chest, straining my ribs. "If love were a commodity, we would all be filthy rich. To family and future. To faith and forgiveness." I pulled Maisie into my side, where she fit with perfect precision. "To the Bennets, every last one."

*Hear, hear!* rang out, but she and I didn't drink.

We occupied our lips otherwise instead.

# Can Do

## MAISIE

**A**bsolute and utter joy.

It zinged around the room, riding every laugh, clinging to every hug. It sparkled in tears, lingered on fingertips, hung on every word.

After the tumult of the last few days, I rode that high like a bird on the breeze.

Marcus and I didn't separate by more than a foot through it all, and the minute the champagne flutes were empty and the conversation slowed, he swept me away like I'd been dreaming of since the whole ordeal began.

I truly was swept—he towed me out the door, the two of us rushing toward his house without speaking even though there was so much to say. But I sensed there would be plenty of time for that. Forever in fact.

Now wasn't the time for words.

And moments later, the world was locked away outside his door, and it was only us.

A breath, and I was in his arms, his lips against mine, my back against the wall, his hips pinning me, holding me still. As if there were anywhere else in the world I'd rather be. Hands roamed, tasting what we'd missed, cataloging what had been absent, promising never to leave again. Never to doubt.

Only to trust. Only to forgive.

Only to love.

Rough and possessive was the unending kiss, wild were his hands. With a shift and a purposeful press of his body, my thighs hooked around his waist, skirt hiked to my hips and a gasp on my lips. He was demand and request, assertion and submission. He was a living declaration of relief and adoration.

It was a claiming of my lips, of my body. Of my heart and of my soul.

Marcus broke the kiss to bury his face in my neck, his lips slowing as he tugged the reins of his composure. Breathless, I mewled.

He chuckled, pressing a final kiss to the bend of my neck before leaning back to look at me. To catalog my features, recording and registering them, smiling at them with the admiration of a collector.

"I missed you," he said simply, tenderly.

"I'm sorry I didn't answer you sooner."

"I should have been more clear regarding my intentions, but I didn't quite know how to ask you to marry me in a text."

With the flip of my heart, I laughed. Until he chased that laughter away with a kiss, swallowing it until it was his.

It took little more than a hitch for him to lift all my weight, holding me in place with a hand on my ass, my legs still locked around his waist as he carried me up the stairs. I kicked off my shoes with twin thumps on the stairs behind us.

"You asked me to marry you," I mused.

"And you said yes."

"I told you I wanted to be a Bennet. Did you really think I'd say no?"

"Well, I hoped you wouldn't, but there was always a chance."

"No, there wasn't."

He stopped near the top of the stairs to kiss me again, breaking only to trot up the rest in a gallop that had me giggling and bouncing around his waist. And in a few breaths, I found myself in his bed, looking into the eyes I'd love my whole life.

For a moment, we just watched each other with quiet smiles.

"Your mother gave you the company," he said in wonder. "I cannot believe she gave it up."

"I can't even imagine how deeply she'll regret that when we rebrand as Longbourne."

I laughed it off, but Marcus's brows gathered.

"Are you sure that's what you want? The business is Bower. It's always been Bower. That is your legacy."

"But that's the thing. I don't want Bower for what it is. I want it for what it could be. I don't want *her* legacy. I want to make one of my own. For me. For us. For *our* children." The word lingered between us, thick with hope and promise.

"Bower will not survive, not as it is. The board and I came up with a plan, a way not only to survive, but to rebuild. We'll close the offices and the magazine. Trim down our staff and tighten the business. Our distribution is strong, but the flash my mother so loved has to go. We'll focus on our storefronts. Take a boutique approach. Use what we already have in the way of marketing and management to shift us in a new direction. And what better direction than a rebrand? What better way to rebrand than to separate ourselves from what we were? I am the face of my company—a fresh, new face with new ideas. If there was any time to rebrand, it's now. And if there's one thing I want to invest in, it's the Bennets."

He opened his mouth to speak but kissed me instead, his hand holding my face and his lips slow. And after, he watched me again.

"Why Longbourne though? Why not rebrand both of us as something entirely new?"

"Why strip your legacy simply because I've forsaken mine? Longbourne is iconic in the boutique world. Think of it, Marcus—all my mother ran were impersonal, big-box flower shops. No one would trust a Bower *boutique*, especially not after what she's done and the press that's come along with it. And no one would know what to make of something entirely new. But if someone walked past a Longbourne shop with one of Tess's displays in the window, they would be charmed and enchanted, just like everyone is. What you have, what your family has built, is spellbinding. Your story is alluring in its honesty, in its truth. Your family is inspiring, and I ... I still can't quite believe I'll get to be a part of it."

"Believe it." He took my left hand and pressed a kiss to my knuckles.

"And now you and I can save *both* of our legacies. We can save them together. I don't think I'd be brave enough to do it without you."

"I don't believe that for a second. You can do anything, Maisie."

"If you're by my side, I know I can."

"I'll be by your side forever." A pause. "I should have forgiven you."

"And I never should have doubted you. I didn't blame you for being hurt, not when I betrayed you like I did. I'm just so thankful you took me back. Even if you hadn't, the only way I'd keep my Bower shares was if you were running it with me."

"What would you have done?" he asked quietly.

"I'd have bought the charity from the board and sold the rest of my shares off. Thrown myself into that. Probably would have adopted a handful of cats while I was at it, really kick off my spinster life."

Marcus chuckled. "No way you wouldn't get snapped up."

"It wouldn't have been fair to them, seeing as how I'll love you until I die."

"From the first time I ever saw you until the last breath I take."

"I knew it even then. Even when we were apart, I think I knew we would find a way back to each other."

"I wouldn't have given up," he said.

"I think I knew that too. And now, all of my wishes have come true. You love me. Enough to be my partner. Enough to give me your name. Enough to bring me into your family."

"And your dad too." He thumbed my bottom lip when my mouth opened in surprise. "My mother has been looking for someone to take the Bennet mantle, to run Longbourne like the women of my family have for generations."

"What about Laney?"

He shrugged one shoulder. "She never wanted it, maybe just because Mom wanted it so much for her. Laney never did do what was expected of her."

I frowned. "You don't think Laney will be … I don't know. Upset?"

At that, Marcus laughed. "Please, trust me when I say you're doing her a favor."

"I do. Trust you. Tell me the sky is purple. Convince me two and two is five."

He made a face that told me exactly how disturbed he was at the math.

"Tell me you love me," I said.

With a slow smile, he leaned in and whispered, "Now that I can do."

# epilogue

## MAISIE

*Three months later*

**M**arcus stood in front of my desk in our office, making *hang up the phone* gestures, one dark brow arched and his lips tilted in a smile.

*One sec*, I mouthed, holding up a finger.

"Uh-huh," I said into the phone, closing my laptop and packing it up. "We'll see you tomorrow then. Thanks, John."

I ended the call and stuffed my phone in my bag.

"We were supposed to leave a half hour ago," he scolded as I stood.

"I know—I had to confirm that meeting with the distributors. I'm sorry."

His hand slipped into the curve of my waist, and he pressed a kiss to my temple. "You never have to apologize to me. My mother, on the other hand …"

On a laugh, I said, "Think I can woo her into forgiveness by telling her how happy said distributors are?"

"Probably not, but you can try."

Smiling, we headed out of our office.

Shelby stood and smoothed her skirt. "Do you need anything else before I go?"

"No, thank you, Shelby," Marcus answered. "Do us a favor and try not to work this weekend, would you?"

"There's just so much to do," she argued.

"You might be the best assistant in all of Manhattan, but even you can't work for two months straight without burning out," he insisted. "I mean it. If I see that you worked over the weekend, you're in trouble."

She pouted. "What am I supposed to do?"

"Go to a bar. Read a book. Sleep for forty-eight hours. Doesn't matter, just don't work, all right?" he asked with such authority that all she could do was sigh.

"All right. Have a good one, and let me know if you need anything."

"We won't," he snarked over his shoulder as we walked away.

I nudged him in the ribs. "You told her to go to a bar."

"Desperate times. If she burns out, we're all in trouble."

"We could always get your mom to take her place."

That earned me a solid, boisterous *Ha*. "I thought we were trying to *save* the company, not push it off a cliff."

"Oh, somehow I think we'd be able to keep it all together, don't you?"

He smiled down at me. "Without a doubt."

We walked through the new office space, wishing those who were still left a good weekend. Marcus had found the space—two cozy floors in the Village with plenty of room for our pared-down staff and close enough to home to walk.

The last three months had been a whirl of paperwork and proceedings. I'd been subpoenaed for my mother's mounting trial, issuing depositions and statements on behalf of the company. At her request, I'd agreed to visit her monthly to answer questions about Bower, but at that very first meeting, when I'd outlined our plan to merge with Longbourne, she had flown into the most vicious rage, one that didn't end until my father—who had insisted on accompanying me—pulled her off of me.

I hadn't been back since. And I hated that I wished things were different. I hated that I still mourned her. But I did.

I always would.

The high-profile rebrand was in motion, covered in various magazines and newspapers as well as garnering a few televisions spots that had gone by in a blur and a blackout, though watching them back, I'd been charming and eloquent in my fugue state. The process of our merger would be lengthy and expensive. But we had already closed every superfluous division of Bower, sending three-quarters of our staff home with a healthy severance, and half of what was left had received an invitation to work from home. Distribution was still in motion, as it had been, the process largely uninterrupted by the drama and changeover. We'd lost some accounts after my mother's arrest, but what was left had been *very* pleased with Marcus's presentation, which we'd spent a few weeks flying around the country to give.

We'd liquidated everything we could, using the money we made to pay back our board members, who were also pleased. The turnover had been encouraged from the start, two of the four ready to sell their shares and get out until I presented my plan and bought us all time to renew their faith and trust. We'd kept one and lost one, the hit to buy the shares an expense we couldn't really shoulder, even under the market rate. But Marcus and I had taken it on together, splitting the shares down the middle.

Equal in all ways.

I sighed happily, leaning into him as we stepped outside and turned for home.

"That good?" he asked.

"That good."

"Lila told you she'd be at dinner tonight, right? Something about invitation paper ... I can't remember."

"She told me." I paused. "Are you really sure you want to tackle a wedding on top of our merger?"

"Hundred percent. The only merger I'm eager for is *ours*."

"I told you we should just go to the courthouse, but you wouldn't listen."

"Do you really think my mother would let us get away with a courthouse wedding?"

"Well, she doesn't have to know," I noted as we turned onto Bleecker.

We were silent for a long second before busting out laughing.

"At least we have Lila to plan it all," I said. "And while she's busy with her own wedding. She's superhuman. I can't imagine Kash helps all that much."

"I honestly think he would, if she'd let him."

Longbourne was all closed up when we passed, the window display cheerful and welcoming. On either side of the door hung gorgeous monochromatic walls of flowers, all shapes and sizes, in shades of yellow. Hanging in the center of each were vertical planters bursting with succulents to form the words *Sun* and *Shine*.

"Tess is a genius," I said.

"If it wasn't for her and Luke, who knows where we'd be?"

"If we ever start up a magazine again, I'm making her the editor in chief."

With a chuckle, we walked up the steps to the Bennet house.

As always, we heard their voices through the door, the din rising as it opened. When we made it into the kitchen, we found everyone.

And I meant *everyone*.

It was a ruckus, as always, an eruption of chatter and laughter. Tess sat on Luke's lap at the table in the nook, laughing at something Lila was saying. Kash sat behind her with that sideways

Bennet smile on his face, his eyes on her like she was the most interesting creature on the planet. Laney was perched on the counter next to Jett as he cooked, the two of them a sight for sore eyes.

With our marketing department up and running, Laney had passed off everything she'd been working on with social, staying on part-time as an advisor after getting a big offer from Wasted Words—the bookstore where Jett worked. The twins had moved to the Upper West near Columbia so they'd be closer to work, and we'd seen precious little of them. But they looked revived and fresh, and I figured it was due to putting a little space between them and their mother, who had been on a matchmaker's streak from hell.

They were her last two to pair off, and she clearly didn't take the job lightly. I was honestly surprised there weren't a couple of strangers she'd brought to spring on Jett and Laney, although I hoped she'd learned her lesson after the last ones. Laney had nearly argued hers into the floor when he made a crack about women and PMS. It sounded worse than it had been—I suspected Laney had been looking for a reason to hate him from the minute Mrs. Bennet presented the poor guy like a dead bird.

At the other end of the table sat Mr. and Mrs. Bennet, chattering with my father.

Dad smiled up at me when we entered, and the conversation broke in order to take turns greeting and scolding us for holding up dinner.

I headed over to him, sliding an arm around his shoulders and kissing the top of his head. "What are you three conspiring about over here?"

"Who has the best milkshakes in Manhattan," he answered with a smile that told me that was a lie.

"Uh-huh. Sure."

"I believe," Mr. Bennet started, "Rosie has a pool going as to who will give her a grandchild first."

"Oh? Who's in the lead?" I asked.

"Well"—Mrs. Bennet perked up, her gossip face sliding into place—"Tess is a planner—she won't have a baby until some timeline has been met. Lila's just too busy … I think she'll wait until she and Kash are settled, what with all the business she's got. So I'm betting on you two. Didn't think I'd ever see the day that I bet on *Marcus* being spontaneous."

My cheeks warmed as I laughed. "Well, I don't know if you've noticed, but we have plenty to keep us busy for a minute."

"Oh, I know," she said, a wily look in her eyes. "But I'm still betting on you."

"She's not an incubator, Mom," Marcus said from my side. "How come Laney and Jett aren't on your list?"

"Because *somebody* keeps insulting all the nice boys I bring home for them."

"Mom, Blane is a ballet dancer who couldn't stop talking about himself through an entire hour-and-a-half dinner. I can't believe you thought *anyone* would go out with him, let alone me."

"It's true—that guy was a douchebag, Mom," Luke added. "I don't know if I could have made it through a second dinner with him without giving him a black eye."

But Mrs. Bennet waved a hand. "You're all too stubborn, that's all. Don't you worry, I'll find someone for you yet," she said in the general vicinity of her twins.

They shared a look, and Jett changed the subject. "Dinner's ready. If it's overcooked, blame Marcus."

With a laugh, we filed into the dining room, but Marcus pulled me to a stop behind everyone else, ducking me into the butler's pantry, holding me close.

My heart fluttered from the surprise and the proximity of his smiling lips. "Your mother's going to walk in here and crack another baby joke."

"Funny that you think she's joking."

I gazed up at him, cocking my head. "What do you think? Will we win the pool? Beat the rest of them to the nursery?"

He pressed me against the cabinets with his long, lean body. "Why? Want to?"

Another flutter, this one lower. "Yes, please."

But he didn't laugh, just watched me.

"You're not kidding," I said breathlessly.

"Not even a little." He traced my jaw, thumbed my lip. "I don't want to wait, Maisie. Not when I've waited my whole life for you."

I sighed into him, and he swallowed the sound with a kiss. Deep in my chest, I felt him there, taking up all the space. Someday, we would make room for one more. Then another, if we were lucky. And it would all be built from love.

His love for me.

My love for him.

And for the rest of my days, I'd have everything I'd ever wished for, everything I wanted.

More than I could have imagined.

# thank you

Jeff Brillhart—Thank you for always supporting my dreams. For holding me up when I crumble. For rolling with the punches, which we've endured in plenty and have the fat lips to prove it. I love you.

Kandi Steiner—Every goddamn day. Every single one. Thank you. Particularly for putting on your ass kicking boots and helping me shape this story.

Kerrigan Byrne—Thank God we're both like this so it's not weird. I love you forever.

Abbey Byers—I have notebooks full of our conversations and musings over stories and characters. People who we created together. And it's been the most fun I've ever had, even when it sucks and I want to die. Because I've had you by my side.

Kyla Linde—Hours and hours you've spent hashing out the details of this beast, and without you, I wouldn't have figured out how to fix any of it.

BB Easton—Thank you for eighty kabillion gigabytes of gifs we've communicated through. They say life is all about balance, and you are one of those people who always keeps my scales even.

Tina Lynne—I just cannot even function without you, and I love you so, so much. Thank you every single day.

Alex Garrett—thank you for the hours you spent advising me, the time you donated (since a retainer wasn't in the budget for this book) building a fictional case between good and evil flower shops. Thank you for all your advice regarding corporate structures and all the ways we could take that she-devil Evelyn Bower down to the ground. You were instrumental in the creation of this story, and I just cannot thank you enough.

To my betas, new and old—you are MAGIC. You made this process so much less stressful, and I haven't felt so good about the end result in ages. Thank you, thank you, thank you!!

To my team, you are forever the motor that keeps me running. Thank you for all of your time and energy and love.

And to my bloggers, my SweetHarts, my readers, to every one of you—thank you for letting me into your heart for a few hours. I can't wait until the next time <3

# also by
## STACI HART

### CONTEMPORARY STANDALONES

**Bad Habits**
With a Twist (Bad Habits 1)
*A ballerina living out her fantasies about her high school crush realizes real love is right in front of her in this slow-burn friends-to-lovers romantic comedy.*

Chaser (Bad Habits 2)
*He'd trade his entire fortune for a real chance with his best friend's little sister.*

Last Call (Bad Habits 3)
*All he's ever wanted was a second chance, but she'll resist him at every turn, no matter how much she misses him.*

The Austens
Wasted Words (Inspired by Emma)
*She's just an adorable, matchmaking book nerd who could never have a shot with her gorgeous best friend and roommate.*

A Thousand Letters (Inspired by Persuasion)
*Fate brings them together after seven years for a second chance they never thought they'd have in this lyrical story about love, loss, and moving on.*

Love, Hannah (a spinoff of A Thousand Letters)
*A story of finding love when all seems lost and finding home when you're far away from everything you've known.*

Love Notes (Inspired by *Sense & Sensibility*)
*Annie wants to live while she can, as fully as she can, not knowing how deeply her heart could break.*

## The Tonic Series

Tonic (Book 1)
*The reality show she's filming in his tattoo parlor is the last thing he wants, but if he can have* her, *he'll be satisfied in this enemies-to-lovers-comedy.*

Bad Penny (Book 2)
*She knows she's boy crazy, which is why she follows strict rules, but this hot nerd will do his best to convince her to break every single one.*

## The Red Lipstick Coalition

Piece of Work
*Her cocky boss is out to ruin her internship, and maybe her heart, too.*

Player
*He's just a player, so who better to teach her how to date? All she has to do is not fall in love with him.*

Work in Progress
*She never thought her first kiss would be on her wedding day. Rule number one: Don't fall in love with her fake husband.*

Well Suited
*She's convinced love is nothing more than brain chemicals, and her baby daddy's determined to prove her wrong.*

**The Bennet Brothers:**
A spin on Pride & Prejudice

Coming Up Roses
*Everyone hates something about their job, and she hates Luke Bennet. Because if she doesn't,
she'll fall in love with him.*

Gilded Lily
*This pristine wedding planner meets her match in an opposites attract, enemies to lovers comedy.*

Mum's the Word
*A Bower's not allowed to fall in love with a Bennet, but these forbidden lovers might not have a choice.*

The Hardcore Serials
*A parkour thief gets herself into trouble when she falls for the man who forces her to choose between
right and wrong.*

HEARTS AND ARROWS
*Greek mythology meets Gossip Girl in a contemporary paranormal series where love is the ultimate game and Aphrodite never loses.*

*Paper Fools (Book 1)
Shift (Book 2)
From Darkness (Book 3)*

# meet staci

Staci has been a lot of things up to this point in her life: a graphic designer, an entrepreneur, a seamstress, a clothing and handbag designer, a waitress. Can't forget that. She's also been a mom to three little girls who are sure to grow up to break a number of hearts. She's been a wife, even though she's certainly not the cleanest, or the best cook. She's also super, duper fun at a party, especially if she's been drinking whiskey, and her favorite word starts with f, ends with k.

From roots in Houston, to a seven year stint in Southern California, Staci and her family ended up settling somewhere in between and equally north in Denver, until they grew a wild hair and moved to Holland. It's the perfect place to overdose on cheese and ride bicycles, especially along the canals, and especially in summertime. When she's not writing, she's reading, gaming, or designing graphics.

www.stacihartnovels.com

CPSIA information can be obtained
at www.ICGtesting.com
Printed in the USA
LVHW111047060422
715481LV00007B/70